All the Trimmings

By the same author:

Always the Bridegroom
Country Matters
Heat of the Moment
Masque of Passion
Earthy Delights
The Ties That Bind

All the Trimmings
Tesni Morgan

BL

This book is a work of fiction.
In real life, make sure you practise safe, sane and
consensual sex.

First Published by Black Lace 2001

2 4 6 8 10 9 7 5 3 1

This edition first published in Great Britain in 2009 by
Black Lace
Virgin Books
Random House, 20 Vauxhall Bridge Road,
London SW1V 2SA

www.blacklace.co.uk
www.virginbooks.com
www.rbooks.co.uk

Addresses for companies within The Random House Group Limited can be found
at: www.randomhouse.co.uk/offices.htm

The Random House Group Limited Reg. No. 954009

A CIP catalogue record for this book
is available from the British Library

ISBN 9780352345325

The Random House Group Limited supports The Forest Stewardship Council [FSC],
the leading international forest certification organisation. All our titles that are
printed on Greenpeace-approved FSC-certified paper carry the FSC logo. Our paper
procurement policy can be found at www.rbooks.co.uk/environment

Printed in the USA

Chapter One

*T*he young man in the filling station is definitely worth a second glance, she thought, making a totally unnecessary check on tyre pressure. She could see him through the kiosk window. He was standing behind the counter, just like when she went in to pay for petrol. Normally she was too preoccupied with domestic trivia to notice men, old or young. Maybe it was because she'd spent the weekend in the company of nineteen-year-olds. Mostly male. Tim's house-share mates.

For the first time in ages she had felt young. A bit self-conscious when she went to the pub with them, hoping she didn't look like mutton dressed as lamb, but Tim had been reassuring. 'You look great, Ma. All the guys say so.'

Their girlfriends had been nice, too. No one seemed to bother that she was the same age as their mothers, give or take a year or two. It had made her realise just how much she missed Tim, and Daisy as well, scatty, gorgeous, talented Daisy, who was taking a fashion design course in London.

But now it was back to boring routine, though nothing could stop that upsurge of desire as she surreptitiously scrutinised the young man's neat, denim-covered buttocks. He had come outside, arranging the bunches of flowers on sale, but he looked directly at her and smiled. Had he made the flowers an excuse, hoping to see her again before she drove off?

Don't be an idiot, Cheryl, she told herself sternly, then she got in the car, adjusted her sunglasses and switched on the ignition. He stood there, hands on hips, grinning as he watched her.

Cheeky little sod, she thought. I've a good mind to tell him off! Who the hell does he think he is?

But, catching a glimpse of herself in the driving mirror, she could see that she was smiling in response, a pleased, cat-that's-been-at-the-cream smile. How daft! Just because some lad had taken the trouble to pay her attention. Get a grip, she told herself, but she could feel a sudden ache in her groin and, as she pressed her bottom into the squashy leather seat, she became aware of a dampness in her knickers unnoticed till then.

'Bugger me!' she exclaimed, and wriggled slightly as she slipped into gear and drove the sleek, black BMW across the forecourt. 'I must be on the change, or something. Getting wet because of a boy. You should be ashamed of yourself.'

But she wasn't, turning into the road with that smile still plastered on her face.

Cheryl had plenty of time. Ashley wasn't expecting her back till the evening, but she'd left earlier than planned, Tim busy on a project that would occupy him for hours. She reached Westcombe and drove through the streets thronged with holidaymakers, then along the promenade, wide and straight, flanked by solid Edwardian hotels on one side and the wide curve of golden sand and blue, white-crested sea on the other.

She drew in a deep breath. The air was like wine. After stuffy Bristol in a heatwave, she was glad to be back. I'm spoiled, she decided. Living by the sea, maintaining a healthy tan, able to dabble my toes in the briny any time I feel so inclined. Which isn't often these days. I'm afraid I've lost my spark. The sunshine seemed to dim suddenly, and she noticed the elderly people in wheelchairs, and others hobbling along with the aid of walking sticks.

WESTCOMBE BY THE SEA. YOUR BRIGHTEST AND BEST HOLIDAY RESORT, declared a hoarding.

I don't want to get old, Cheryl thought with a shudder. I don't feel I've lived yet, let alone settling down to await the Grim Reaper. Stuff that!

Ruffled, the good feeling engendered by the garage assistant faded and gone, she turned into a side street and along a tree-lined avenue. The house stood just as she'd left it: solid, mock Tudor frontage, detached and surrounded by a secluded garden. A double garage, a swimming pool and a conservatory. They had lived there for years. It was in the best area of Westcombe, naturally, away from the guest houses and B&B establishments, even far removed from the Atlantic Hotel, the Fisherman's Inn, the King George's Arms, all five-star and fiercely expensive.

If she and Ashley went away, it was usually somewhere abroad, the Canary Islands or Malta. But in reality he preferred to take breaks alone, entering his boat in regattas up and down the country, open seas, lakes, reservoirs, anywhere the sailing fraternity could meet, talk jaunty nautical talk and spend hours carousing in the clubhouse.

Cheryl had stopped going with him long ago. It wasn't easy when the children were small, far too much hassle, and unnecessary when they had the sand and sea on their doorstep.

This was probably the beginning of the split. Now we hardly speak to one another, she thought, leaving the car in the drive and walking round to the back. She liked going in through the kitchen. Ashley couldn't understand it. The front entrance was rather grand and he was always first to answer the doorbell if any visitors arrived. He liked impressing people. Cheryl was finding him increasingly boring. Now she kept seeing the jeans-clad youth in his clinging white T-shirt. His pectorals were well developed, arm muscles too, and she had made a note of the fullness behind his fly buttons. He'd be bursting with testosterone. Probably go on all night, orgasm after orgasm. But would he know how to give one to her?

A cup of tea, she thought, and switched on the kettle. It was lovely to be back, though it had only been three days. She embraced the atmosphere, shrugging it round her like a warm blanket. Her house, her home – the nest she had built for rearing her young. Once she had had a promising career as a lawyer, but she had given it all up when she met and fell in love with Ashley. They married and she became pregnant right away. His doing, for he didn't want her to go on working. No pill for her, and a year after Tim, Daisy arrived on the scene.

Cheryl hadn't resented them, but they had been a lot of hard work. 'Two children are enough,' Ashley had decided when, after Daisy had started infant school, Cheryl had got all broody and wanted another.

'I'd like to get a job,' she had suggested, the house empty daily; too tidy, too quiet.

'There's no need, darling. The business is doing really well. I've jumped on the computer wagon just in time. Everyone will have one soon. We'll be rich. I'd prefer you to be here. You never know when one of the kids is going to go down with something. I don't think mothers should work.'

End of conversation and very nearly the end of story. Certainly the end of romance. Cheryl went through the motions, but sex for her became dull and meaningless. He never had been much of a lover and she no longer cared, having given up trying to indicate what she needed to bring her to orgasm, and masturbating when she was alone. She couldn't be bothered with him any more and if he chose to stick his cock in her and seek his own selfish pleasure then she would while away the time till he finished by taking a mental shopping tour round Sainsbury's. With any luck, by the time she reached the checkout, he would have come. Then she knew she'd be left in peace and could turn over and go to sleep.

4

She peered in the mirror and pushed up her nonde-script hair. Her face was what she called 'experienced', though others might have unkindly dubbed it 'weath-ered'. Her bone structure was striking. She had greenish-grey eyes and a wide, generous mouth. Having reached the age when the double chin tends to take over, she was glad to see that her jawline was taut. Going lower, she was critical about her body; the neck wasn't bad, the breasts could have been better. I really must buy a new bra, she thought. Her waist was slim, her hips too, and her legs were long, hairless and suntanned. She wore shorts and vest tops most of the time.

'God, can't you find any suitable dresses? What is all this? A nudist colony?' Ashley would comment cuttingly whenever he saw her casually clad, or caught her naked in the pool.

She tried to avoid this, because seeing her nude gave him a hard-on, and there were many things she'd much rather do than have sex with him. The kettle boiled and she poured the scalding water over a tea bag in her horoscope mug, a deep, heavenly blue, with LIBRA writ-ten in gold lettering.

'It's a lot of tosh. You don't believe in all that rubbish, do you, Cheryl?' Ashley scoffed.

She wasn't sure, but at least kept an open mind on the subject, which was more than he was prepared to do. Daisy was into it – astrology, the Runes, the Tarot cards, communicating with the spirit world. She's like my mother, Cheryl ruminated, stirring sugar into her tea. Mummy's a pagan and believes in everything from flying saucers to fairies at the bottom of the garden. It seems natural to call her Mummy, though she agitates for me to address her as Joanna. I keep her away from Ashley. He's always rude to her. I sometimes think the only reason I married him was as a kind of revolt against her artistic, bohemian lifestyle.

'She's not an artist; she's a nutter. The landing light's on but there's no one in. Have you seen her paintings? I wouldn't give them houseroom! I wouldn't hang them in the bog! People pay good money for them. Sometimes thousands. They must be as cracked as she is.'

Needless to say, Joanna Newman hated him too. 'I'll never see much of you, Cheryl, while you stay married to that pompous prick,' she said every time she phoned.

'I know, I know, but what can I do?' Cheryl would ask.

'Leave the bastard! You know there's always a bed for you at Fell Tor.'

'Thanks. That's kind, but I'm not ready to do it yet.'

'Why not? The kids are off your hands now.'

Cheryl always muttered an excuse. She wasn't willing to admit defeat. Besides, Fell Tor was run on the lines of a commune, and she didn't feel able to cope with so many different temperaments under one roof. The work was supposed to be divided among them, but there was always a nucleus who were put upon, performing all the chores. She knew it would scramble her head. She needed order in her life to function properly.

I've lived with Ashley too long, she thought wryly. His fussy Virgo perfection has rubbed off on me.

Bollocks! her other self retorted rudely. That's just a bloody excuse. You don't want to get up off your fat arse and do anything about it.

Cheryl started as she heard a thump overhead. She had been convinced the house was empty. There was no sign of Ashley's Mercedes. They had no animals, not even a cat – so who or what had made the noise? Had she disturbed a burglar? A quick vision of *Crime Watch* flashed across her brain: 'Housewife disturbs robbers in her house in Westcombe. An identikit has been complied after her description of the men. The police have commended her for her bravery. Please ring this number if you have any information.'

Would it be one or two, or maybe more? She didn't feel in the least brave. We should have got a dog, she thought. Ashley wanted one but I don't like them. I'm surprised he didn't put his foot down and insist that I took on puppy training and mopping up puddles and

6

getting everything chewed, to say nothing of fleas and threadworms. Ugh! But just for now she wished she had something big, mean looking and hairy to protect her, and she wasn't thinking of a man.

She held her breath when another thud shook the kitchen. Quietly opening a drawer, she took out a carving knife and, holding it close to her chest, crept into the hall and up the stairs.

They curved gracefully. The banisters were railed. A floor-to-ceiling stained-glass window lit the upper landing. It depicted an Alphonse Mucha-type lady with a swanlike neck, a mass of dark hair and a seductive expression. Tulips and acanthus leaves twined round her, merging with her flowing, diaphanous robes. This window, above all else, had sold the house to Cheryl. She was a pushover for art nouveau. Couldn't get enough of interiors from that period; opulent, overblown, sensual – the kind of sexy decor used in late nineteenth-century high-class brothels. She would sometimes fantasise about being the madam of one of these establishments, seeing herself in a tight corset and a bustle, made up to the nines, the toast of Paris, perhaps, graciously welcoming her clients and introducing them to the bevy of beauties who graced her establishment.

She was so drawn into this scenario that she reached her bedroom without being really aware. The noises were issuing from behind the closed door and it was almost as if she was checking up on one of her whores, for they were definitely sexual in origin. Unmistakable, animal noises straight from the jungle, or the barnyard. Moans, panting, grunts. Puzzled, she let herself in.

She halted, framed in the doorway, unable to believe the evidence of her own eyes.

The first thing she saw was the extraordinary spectacle of her husband, naked and spreadeagled on the bed, his wrists bound by silk scarves – *her* silk scarves – and attached to the pillars of the brass headboard. His ankles were tethered to those at the foot, and his cock pointed to the ceiling from which white lace drapes were sus-

7

pended. Cheryl could not remember seeing it so thick and long. Had he ever sported such an impressive erection for her? Ashley into bondage? It was beyond belief.

He wasn't alone, of course. A woman was poised over him, about to lower herself on to that stiff appendage. She was wearing a black suspender belt and fishnet stockings. She had platinum blonde hair, ample breasts and wide hips. It was Yvonne Harper, wife of Allan, commodore of the Westcombe Sailing Club. The last time Cheryl had seen her, she was officiating at the regatta, dispensing sandwiches and cups of tea, congratulating the winners and presenting silver trophies.

For a fraction of a second Cheryl wondered if she should be dignified, back out and close the door behind her, then she screeched, 'You bitch!' and launched herself at Yvonne.

All her frustrations poured out through her clawing nails, flaying feet and the abuse that cannoned from between her lips. She used words she hardly knew she possessed, dirty, derogatory, insulting words. When Yvonne finally succeeded in escaping, she was bloodied and bruised and weeping.

'Cheryl! Stop it!' Ashley shouted from the bed, alarmed by the glinting kitchen knife.

She laughed in his face. He was helpless and she could do and say whatever she liked. Now she was the dominant one. 'You despicable worm,' she hissed. 'What would your buddies at the sailing club say if they could see you now? And with Mrs Commodore too. Well, well. Who'd have thought it?'

She slapped him across the cheek, the chest, the cock. It didn't shrink under her blows. It became even stiffer. I should have done this years ago, she thought. He's a powerful man in business, always in control. He wants the reverse in sex. I didn't know. Why didn't he say?

'Untie me. Let me explain,' he begged, struggling to maintain a semblance of command.

'I don't want to hear it.' Her voice was steady, though she was breaking up inside. She used the knife to slice through his bonds. He looked frightened. Scared she was going to hack off his cock, maybe? He sat up, rubbing his wrists.

'Cheryl, be reasonable,' he began.

'Reasonable? You've got to be joking,' she snarled. 'Now dress and get out. You, too, Yvonne. You'll leave the house at once, Ashley. Do you hear? I shall be seeking advice from my solicitor.'

'He's mine too,' Ashley said, looking stupefied, as if this was the last thing he expected to happen.

'I shall change.'

'Can't we talk about this?'

'No,' Cheryl said, thinking, how ridiculous he looks in his socks and nothing else. How pathetic. I can't even summon the energy to hate him. Hate is akin to love, a strong emotion, and he rouses neither in me. I just want him gone, and his floosie as well. I always knew she was as common as muck. Blonde indeed. Her dark bush gives the game away. She's no more blonde than I am.

Yvonne turned watery blue eyes to Cheryl. Her mascara formed black runnels down her cheeks. 'You won't tell Allan, will you?' she pleaded, struggling into her skirt and blouse. 'It was only a bit of fun. You could have joined in. Allan's always fancied you, and I wouldn't have minded.'

'Get out of my sight,' Cheryl repeated wearily, running her hands up and down her cold arms.

Jesus Christ! Did she know any of these people? She'd been associated with them for years – sailing club dinners and dances, Christmas and New Year's Eve parties, even the millennium celebrations, events galore, but it had all been a sham. Behind that façade of bonhomie, of supporting charities and doing good works, they were as much into scheming, conniving, lying and fornicating as those whom they considered their inferiors. Ever so nicely, of course. What, us? We don't worry about class. Anybody can get membership of the club, as long as they are proposed by one of us.

And now the commodore's lady was on her knees,

retrieving her panties from under a bed that certainly wasn't her marital one. Her large pink buttocks quivered as her skirt rode up. The black suspenders strained across her thighs, clipped to the tops of those tarty stockings. Her crack was visible from that angle. It glistened with moisture. Whatever she and Ashley had been doing, it had excited her, making those plump lips swell.

I wish I had a camera, Cheryl thought, or better still a camcorder.

Ashley, dressed now, came towards her, saying, 'Look here, Cheryl. Let's talk about this.'

'Out,' she repeated doggedly, flourishing the knife.

'But –'

'If you don't sod off, I'll go and see Allan. I'm sure he'll be interested in what I have to tell him. So will his workforce. You'd better believe that I'll shout it across his office.'

'You wouldn't.'

'Try me.'

He didn't put it to the test. One glance at her face and he hustled Yvonne from the bedroom. Cheryl stood there, as if turned to stone, listening to their hurried retreat. The back door banged. He wasn't risking using the front way. He must have left the car further down the avenue. Unless they'd taken a taxi. How long had this been going on? she wondered. Anger had turned into a dull throb. She felt numb.

Then indignation swept up. She dropped the knife on the dressing table, then ran across and stripped off the valance sheet, duvet cover and pillowcases, bundling them up and rushing down to the utility room. It wasn't until the washing machine was pounding away at them that her disgust abated. How could Ashley have brought another woman to their bed?

She kept seeing him lying there like a landed fish, his cock dribbling pre-come. Strangely, another figure was superimposed over him. It was that of the youth who had served her in the garage. Her fingers itched to tie him up and subject him to her lust. There was no doubt about it, she had not felt so horny for a long while. The sight of Yvonne's big breasts, her broad thighs and naked crack had caused an ache in her clit that needed release.

'You're a bastard, Ashley! A bastard!' she muttered, and phoned a solictor; not the family one, but a friend from university days.

He had an office in Taunton, in partnership with two others, and he listened to her story in silence for a while, then said, 'My advice is stay put. Don't leave the house. Come and see me and file for a divorce. That is what you want, I take it?'

'Yes. As quickly as possible, Mark.'

She felt steadied by the sound of his cool, impartial voice and wondered if he had changed much since she last saw him when they graduated. They'd celebrated by getting drunk together and then fucking. He'd been handsome, a distinguished-looking man, an intellectual and philosopher. I should have married him, not Ashley, she thought bitterly. Tears stung her eyes and she wanted to break down and cry.

'I can see you at eleven tomorrow morning,' he said, and his calmness brought hope.

'Thank you. I'll be there,' she said.

'We're in River Street. Bartlett, Bingley and Warfield.'

'That's you.'

'Dead right,' he answered, and she caught a hint of laughter. Memory flashed. He had been fun to be with, sharp-witted and sarcastic.

After she had replaced the receiver, she dialled her closest woman friend.

It had happened by chance when Laura was cruising the net. She hadn't intended to spy on Stuart, far from it. She had only recently mastered the computer and had been practising on the one at home. First she had found the search engine, then logged on to several websites – one that had a huge amount of books, records and videos, another dealing with history, a further that held information about gardening.

11

This was wonderful and she glowed with pride inside, having mastered technology to some extent. James had said she might use his PC, but she intended to buy one of her own. Now that Harry was backpacking in India and Vicky married, she ran her house like clockwork, which left her with time on her hands. She could have done voluntary work but had decided to fulfil a dream, that of becoming a writer.

She had dabbled before, using an ancient portable typewriter bequeathed to her by her father. But Stuart and the children had been demanding. Now there was only him, and he could be childish too, although heavily into the firm, which he had inherited. Tilford's Haulage was a byword in the area. Not that his education had been allowed to lapse. He had done his stint at college with the best of them.

Laura had fallen in love with computers. They were a gateway to her literary ambitions. She realised that they couldn't write the books for her, but she revelled in the joy of spell- and grammar-checking and the ease with which one could edit. No more Tipp-Ex and carbon paper. Now it was all down to her, stripped to the bone in search of talent.

She had set up a page and was dallying around, putting off opening a file she'd tentatively named Chapter One. She didn't know what to call the novel but had roughed out a plot, courtesy of several informative manuals with titles like *How to Write a Romance and Get it Published*.

It was romance that filled her creative vision – historical romance, and she'd already decided on the period and begun research. It was while she was idling on the net that she accidentally went into a chat room. A sexy one, by the look of it. But far from the nude and busty girls she expected to see, the photographs were of men in various stages of undress, and the messages were undoubtedly male oriented. She had stumbled across the Gay Chatline. She was trying to stumble out again when suddenly a name came up. It was Jimboy. And following in quick succession was a picture of her own, handsome, dark-haired and well-built husband.

She sat there with her hand poised on the mouse. She wanted to get out; she wanted to delve deeper. She was excited, her nipples crimping under her cotton sundress. What on earth was Stuart doing there? His message to an unknown, called Big Jock, soon made everything clear. It was a dirty e-mail, explicit in the extreme, as Stuart discussed in detail what he would like to do with Big Jock.

Laura felt physically sick and terribly aroused. Fascination kept her there, a peeping Tom kind of compulsion that forced her to read on, to click and review, to repeat and find other sites that offered Stuart a choice of partners. He had already met some and arranged to meet others. Those with whom he had rendezvoused had kept in touch. Most of them he had ignored. But there was one name that came up repeatedly – Terry. She logged on to his photo. He was lithe and long-haired and girlish, a beautiful person indeed, and Laura could have fancied him herself, had he not been so blatantly gay. The correspondence between Terry and Stuart revealed that they had met several times and the relationship was becoming serious.

This is how a woman must feel when she finds out that her husband has a mistress, she thought bleakly. But this is far worse, for how can I compete with Terry? He can give Stuart something I never can. What shall I do?

Making a note of how she got into the chat room in the first place, she logged off.

'Is that you, Laura?' Cheryl said, when she put down the phone on Mark and rang her.

'Yes, it's me,' Laura answered, and Cheryl smiled, picturing her seated at the computer or scribbling in a notebook. But there was something in Laura's voice that arrested her attention – she sounded agitated.

'What's up?' Cheryl asked.

'Nothing. How are you?'

13

'Could be better. I came home this afternoon from Tim's and found Ashley in bed with Yvonne Harper, the commodore's wife.'

'Good grief! What did you do?'

'Told him to get out.'

'Has he gone?'

'Yes, and I've been in touch with Mark Warfield, a friend of mine from uni. He's a solicitor. I'm seeing him tomorrow.'

'You're going to divorce Ashley?'

'Yep!'

'Then maybe I should see him too, and divorce Stuart.'

Cheryl almost dropped the phone with shock. 'You what?' she exclaimed.

'Divorce Stuart,' Laura repeated.

'Why? What is it? Another woman?'

'Worse than that. Another man, maybe even other men.'

'You're having me on.'

'No. It's true.'

'How do you know?' Cheryl could not believe it. Stuart was so big and burly and macho, in charge of a fleet of long-distance lorries and their drivers.

'I've been taking this course ... Computers for the Terrified.'

'So you told me.'

'Well, I've just been on the PC at home ... and I came across this site where gay men can talk to one another and send photos and arrange meetings. Stuart was on it.'

'Jesus wept! Is this true? You weren't mistaken, were you? You're new to networking.'

'No mistake. It was him all right, and a guy called Terry. I should think they've known each other some time.'

Laura sounded calm, but with that dead calm that Cheryl was also feeling. Phrases sprang to mind, including 'the calm before the storm'. Poor, unworldly Laura, she thought. At least I'm a bit more sophisticated, whereas she always sees the good in everyone. They had met when their children were in the toddler group and had been friends ever since. They were neighbours. They shopped together and visited each other's houses. They had shared problems as the children grew up and consoled their loneliness when they were no longer living at home. Cheryl trusted her implicitly and hoped she felt the same.

'Have you tackled Stuart about it?'

'No. I've only just found out.'

'Are you going to?'

'I want out,' Laura said, a brittle edge to her voice unknown till then. 'I haven't been happy with him for ages, not truly happy, and he must have been discontented with me. I never dreamed . . . never thought for a moment that he was a . . .'

'Closet gay.' Cheryl supplied the words. 'Well, neither did I. It's quite funny really. There are he and Ashley, friends of the bosom, as it were, and Ashley would have run a mile if he'd known. He's homophobic.'

'I don't find it funny. I feel soiled.'

'So do I, love. Man or woman, it's the deceit and betrayal that hurts. I'd come over but I don't want to leave the house. It will be bad enough driving off tomorrow, but I think I'll ring Mother and get her to hold the fort. What do you want to do? Come with me?'

'Yes. I need to know where I stand legally. Till then, I'll say nothing to Stuart. He won't think I'm computer literate enough to have called up the gayline.'

'Mind you download the material before he finds out. You'll need that as proof.'

'Don't worry. I've already done it. I'll bring it with me.'

What a team, Cheryl thought. We should go far once we're freed from these tiresome husbands. She was in an optimistic mood when she said goodbye to Laura and poured herself a glass of wine before tackling her mother.

Though far too hip to say it, Joanna was bound to think, I told you so.

She wouldn't tell Tim, not yet. He was fond of his

father and even crewed for him occasionally. There was no need to disillusion him for the time being. That meant she'd have to keep it from Daisy too, who never could be trusted with a secret. Cheryl sipped her drink and reached for the phone, thinking, after I've done this, I'll move into the spare room. There I'll take a shower and possibly play with myself, thinking of a bright future filled with handsome men.

Chapter Two

M ark was everything a competent solicitor should be: thorough, efficient, firm but kind. He took on Laura's case as well as Cheryl's and, after not too long, had finalised their divorces and arranged settlements.

Cheryl went to see him to sign the last of the papers. Ashley had not put up much of a fight, too afraid that she might name Yvonne as co-respondent. Though Cheryl was sure this was nothing more than a casual affair, he didn't want to lose face with the sailing club. He had bought her silence by agreeing to her demands. Through the proceeds of the sale of the house and a share of his assets, she was coming out of it with a very large sum indeed.

I'm a woman of substance, she thought as she parked her car outside the eighteenth-century house in River Street, off Taunton's market square. The brass plaque on the door gleamed, so did the lion-headed knocker and letterbox. Cheryl pushed the door open and went in. I might shag Mark brainless today, she thought. It's brewing, I can tell. Throughout these months of solicitors' letters flying back and forth, of Ashley coming in to collect his clothes, of the inventories pertaining to the contents and wrangles about what belonged to whom, I've been aware of the chemistry bubbling away between Mark and me.

It was more than an exhilarating sense of freedom that had made her go on a diet, visit a beauty parlour, have her hair restyled and indulge in a shopping spree second to none. Laura had been persuaded to do the same, transformed from dull brown to tawny blonde. There was no doubt about it, they had both concluded, having money helped cushion the blow, that insecure feeling of failure that haunted female divorcees and made them easy game for prowling wolves.

Not Mark, however. He was the perfect gentleman. He stood when Cheryl came into the gracious, high-ceilinged room. He held out his hand and she took it. His palm, tight against hers, generated heat and tranquillity. There was peace in that gentle clasp. 'My word,' he said with a smile. 'You're looking fabulous.'

She blushed under her cover-all base. It was a glad-to-be-complimented blush, and she knew she deserved admiration. Mario at Corner Cutters had worked a miracle on her hair. No longer nondescript, she was now a deep chestnut, curled and backcombed and twirled into an amazing style, dashing, almost brazen, making her feel thirty again. A reckless thirty at that, a 'come on, boys, let's get to it' kind of thirty. She'd read somewhere that women came into their own as they got older, and it was ideal for them to have young lovers, seventeen-plus, for youths were at their peak, wanting to bang away all round the clock.

Mark wasn't particularly young, but she felt horny just thinking about him. He was so well groomed, whiplash lean, with wide shoulders and long legs. His hair was thick and dark, with only a sprinkling of grey at the temples. Best of all, he wasn't married. No one had snapped him up. He had said, the first day they'd met again, that he had been waiting for her. A joke, of course. Or was it? Laura seemed to think he was smitten, but then Laura was incurably romantic. She was trying to channel this into authorship, but not doing too well to date. She contemplated taking a course for would-be writers, but had not been able to concentrate on it yet.

Cheryl agreed with her that getting divorced was time-consuming and exhausting. She wasn't sure that she'd ever recover from it.

Mark kissed her hand with old-world gallantry before letting it go, then pulled out a chair for her opposite his. He sat down and steepled his fingers together, looking at her across them. Her heart skipped a beat. God, but he's a good-looking creature, she thought. I wouldn't mind those slim, strong hands on my body and his mouth between my legs. Spring is in the air again, when a mature woman's thoughts lightly turn to love. She had come here with another purpose than simply scrawling her name on stuffy, lawyer-speak documents. She was dressed to kill, in a mulberry silk dress and stack-heeled mules. Her perfume was French and had cost a bomb. Her underwear was nothing short of scandalous. It made her cream her panties just to feel them caressing her mound and bottom, so red, so brief, so naughty, and the underwired bra matched them.

After the startling revelation concerning Ashley's liking for being restrained, she had looked at Mark and other men in a different light. What secret desires did they hide behind their bland exteriors? Was she missing out on her vocation? Could she become a dominatrix?

'Here we are. The last batch of papers,' Mark said, pushing them towards her across the desk's green leather top. She signed and returned them, with hardly a glance at their contents.

'What a relief,' she said. 'I can't believe it's all over. I'm no longer Mrs Barden. It feels empty somehow and I'm as drained as a long-distance runner reaching the finishing post.'

'Others have said just the same,' he replied, and considered her with twinkling brown eyes. 'The break-up of a relationship is in the nature of a bereavement, no matter how much it was wanted. Old habits die hard, and you were married for a long while.'

She listened to him with half her attention. The other, livelier half was imagining him in a courtroom, defending

19

a client. The black robe would suit him, so would the white wig. He'd seem even more authoritarian and, just for an instant, she wanted to be the prisoner in the dock. She thrilled as she thought of him grilling her, his cool, crisp voice causing mayhem in her body, sending shivers down her spine and making her nipples peak.

With an effort, she dragged herself back to the present, saying, 'That's right, Mark. I've heard this too, and I know Laura feels the same.'

'Why don't I take you out to dinner tonight?' he said suddenly, leaning forward, his elbows on the desk.

'I really should get going,' she faltered, unsure of herself despite the hot scenarios played out in her head, thinking, when you've only ever slept with one man for years, shared his life and borne him children, the reality of having sex with a stranger is formidable. You need a lot of faith in yourself to take that leap into the void.

'You could always stay in my house,' he offered, and she read in his eyes the hope that she would agree. He wasn't pushing anything, content to let matters develop, or not, as the case might be.

'I haven't brought an overnight bag. I wasn't intending to be more than a few hours.'

'Then let's have lunch. I know a place on the outskirts of town that does a very decent meal.'

'All right,' she said, awash with uncertainty. She wanted him, lubricious at the thought of bedding him, yet what problems might this bring? Did she really want to hurtle into another relationship?

Hey! Don't project. Like you, he's probably out for a quick one, that's all. Long-term doesn't come into it, reminded the little demon who sat on her shoulder and whispered comments in her ear.

She followed Mark in her car, leaving the shopping centre, reaching the bypass and taking a meandering secondary road. They were soon in the country, the trees and hedgerows burgeoning, primroses studding the green banks like yellow stars, real warmth to the sun, and a blue sky dotted with fluffy white clouds. Cheryl tingled from toes to cortex. Spring was here and she, too, felt reborn. She had come out of the darkness of winter, the months of disruption, all the unpleasant aspects of divorce – breaking the news to Tim and Daisy and enduring the coldness of mutual acquaintances. The sailing club folk ostracised her. She had heard that they failed to understand how she could possibly kick out such a charming, helpful, wonderful man.

She could have retaliated and implicated Yvonne. But, as she said to her mother, 'I can't be bothered.'

'You're right. Let it go. He's an arsehole. But no, even arseholes have a use,' Joanna had replied acerbically.

And here I am, about to have lunch with a man who obviously thinks I'm the bee's knees. I'm living at Fell Tor, and I can endure its eccentric inhabitants short-term. Laura and I are going house-hunting this week. That can't be bad.

The houses became cottages. Some were thatched. No longer farmworkers' humble homes, these had been upgraded, modernised, extended – two into one, maybe three in a rank – now expensive, trendy, within-reach-of-the-motorway retreats for executives. The Yew Tree Inn echoed their ambience. Cheryl pulled up in the orchard-surrounded car park at the rear. AD 1400 was carved into the weathered stone above the inn's main entrance.

'The original building is from then,' Mark said, standing with her and looking up. His shoulder brushed hers. She lost interest in ancient monuments, a frisson coursing down her arm, through her body and into her sex. 'Recent restoration unearthed murals painted by itinerant artists who couldn't pay for bed and board and worked the bill out that way,' he continued. 'There were also timbers which, when carbon dated, proved that the trees were felled at the start of the fifteenth century.'

'You're still keen on all this?' Cheryl asked, recalling an aspect of his personality from student days. They'd often trudged round ruins in the rain.

His hand cupped her elbow, and goose bumps raised

the fine down on her limbs. 'Oh, yes. You really must let me show you my house.'

The Yew Tree had retained most of its early features. The stone-flagged floors sloped. There were arches and rooms leading off the reception area, up one step and down the next, worn in the middle by generations of innkeepers and clientele. It had that smell Cheryl associated with old buildings, a combination of must, dust and the essences left by hundreds of years of weary travellers seeking stabling for their horses, a pint of ale, a roast capon and a bed for the night. Even the necessary modernisation of kitchens and bathrooms had failed to mask it. She could almost see figures in costume occupying the taproom and lounge bar, the winding stairs and courtyards.

Lord! Hang on there! She chided herself. You're getting like Laura. Leave the historical imaginings to her.

But she couldn't help saying to Mark, 'Laura would go mad over this. I must bring her.'

'There's plenty of history in the area,' he said, drawing her down on a bench in a corner of the dining room and settling himself next to her. 'Much of it is to do with the Monmouth Rebellion of 1685, the Bridgwater Assizes and Judge Jeffreys, known as the Hanging Judge.'

Ferreting back in time, Cheryl vaguely recalled learning something about this at school. But she never had been much good at dates and kings and battles. The atmosphere was relaxing and Mark fitted into it perfectly, so charming that women at other tables were ignoring their escorts and staring across at him. He seemed unaware of this adulation, his attention focused on her.

He ordered, familiar with the menu and able to recommend this dish or that. The waiter addressed him as Mr Warfield. Mark came there regularly then, but did he usually bring a female companion? She wanted to pin this delectable young man against the wall and ask him, after she'd given in to the impulse to fasten her hands round his taut bottom cheeks.

Their corner was small, arranged so that they were not

22

overlooked. But when Mark's hand came to rest halfway up her thigh, she nearly dropped her fork with surprise. I'm not used to this, totally rusty, she thought in blind panic. Do I move away? Do I ask him to stop, even feign indignation? She did neither, sitting quite still while electric sparks darted along her nerves. The rapport between them seemed to have gone askew. More than friends, then, but not yet lovers.

He looked her straight in the eyes and moved his hand to one side, saying, 'Pull up your dress.'

His tone was masterful, no doubt the one he used against recalcitrant criminals and unreliable witnesses. It was not to be gainsaid. She slid her left hand down to her lap and raised the hem slowly, first her knees, then her bare thighs exposed. The tablecloth hid her from view. She felt incredibly wicked, and her nipples stiffened under her bra. Was he stiffening too? A glance down showed a promising distortion at the front of his black trousers.

He couldn't see her but was going by feel alone. 'No tights or stockings?' he murmured.

'It's too warm today,' she replied, amazed at her ability to speak. She hadn't been so aroused since the early days of her courtship with Ashley. Oh, she might have thought about it – played with the notion, adding to her excitement when she brought herself to orgasm – but this was real.

Despite a wave of bourgeois panic lest someone see, her excitement mounted as Mark moved higher up her thigh. She couldn't stop opening a little, so that his fingers found the tiny strip of scarlet lycra that covered her mons. Her pulse was racing madly. He eased round the edge of her tanga and combed through her dark bush, then, so skilfully that she gasped, he arrived at his destination – that delicious spot where her cleft unfolded over the swelling clit. There he rested, simply subjecting it to gentle pressure.

I could come, she thought. If he just rubs it from side to side, as I like it, I could bloody well come, right here

23

in the dining room. She closed her eyes, that hot surge beating upwards, filling her loins, her lower belly, and making her nipples ache. Then, I mustn't sit here with this soppy expression on my face, she lectured herself. I know my mouth is open. I'm almost drooling, but oh, God! That's feel so good . . . brilliant . . . better than when I do it myself.

'Now will you let me take you to my house?' he whispered, and gave her clit a quick flick that almost, but not quite, tipped her over the edge.

'Yes,' she gasped, ruled by lust but unable to do anything about it.

He took his hand away, lifted it to his nostrils and said, 'Ah, yes. Your inimitable smell. I'd recognise it anywhere.'

She wondered how he was going to cope with his erection, but when he rose, his suit jacket hid it. He seemed cool and controlled and they only remained in the inn long enough for him to pay the bill. She was swollen and wet between the legs, aware of this as she got into her car and followed his Jaguar. Not far: it seemed as if the Yew Tree was his local.

He lived in a converted barn, a long structure where an upper floor had been added under the arched timber roofing. The grounds were set out to lawn and a water meadow. He took her round to the back where he had constructed a Zen garden. It was a harmonious place. The gravel was raked into swirling patterns set round a large boulder representing a mountain, a statue of Buddha, a water-feature constructed of bamboo, and several dwarf trees.

'You're interested in bonsai?' she asked. This was enlightening, and at any other time she would have lingered, but she wanted to get down to the real reason for her visit – fucking.

'Very. It means "tree in a pot". Some of these are two hundred years old. I'm starting to incorporate feng shui in my garden and house. So calming, and helpful in business and love.'

'And you're on your own? No girlfriend?'

'No. Just the inestimable Mrs Harvey who "does" for me.'

'And no boyfriends?' She said it teasingly, but wondered. Weren't all men looking for an orifice to house their pricks? Man or woman. Did it really matter?

'I'm almost boringly straight,' he said with a smile.

He pulled her close so they were chest to chest, their hands meeting at their sides, fingers linked. She could feel the hardness of his cock prodding into her belly through his trousers and her dress. There was something else she had to say before this went further.

'I haven't screwed anyone else since I met Ashley,' she confessed, looking up at him.

'I believe you. But I also remember how it was between us once, years ago, when we'd graduated. Do you remember too? I wanted our relationship to carry on. Why didn't it? Can you tell me?'

'I don't know. It wasn't the time or the place. I thought you were superior to me in every way. I couldn't keep up with you.'

'Funny, I thought that about you. Seems we had our wires crossed. And then you married Ashley.'

'Mistake number one.'

'And had children.'

'No mistake. I love them.'

'I'm sure you're a wonderful mother.'

He slung an arm round her shoulders and they strolled into the house, both taking it easy, though she felt as if she were about to explode with the sexual tension building between them

They stopped in the vestibule and kissed, small, nibbling kisses that began with the merging of lips, then Mark's mouth moved, finding the fragrant nape of her neck and lipping her ear lobes. From somewhere near the hollow of her throat he murmured, 'I want you naked.'

'I know you do.' She chuckled, daring to close her

hand on the upright thickness of him, hot through the fly fastening.

It felt familiar, a male appendage, after all, yet oh so different to her ex-husband's. Ashley had never wanted to prolong foreplay. After the honeymoon period was over, lovemaking had become a boring ritual, and yet – he'd been keen enough to experiment with Yvonne. Anger blazed up from the smouldering ember of pain that still endured within her. She gripped Mark's cock tightly.

'You stripped when we were fledgling lawyers, and went back to my poky little flat after the graduation ceremony,' he said, his voice unsteady. The spot above his flies became damp. 'We'd had too much champagne, and this got rid of our inhibitions. We'd just been mates, till then. My room was squalid; dirty washing lying around, mouldy cups and plates with food scrapings welded on them kicked under the bed. Heaps of books, a battered typewriter. But to me it was heaven. You, on my bed, naked. I buried my face in your cunt. It was over too soon, even the alcohol couldn't slow me down. My orgasm was brusque. I came as soon as I entered you.'

'I was disappointed, but I hardly knew what to expect. I'd only had one boy before you and he was inept. He didn't make me come either,' she said, rubbing her hand up and down that irresistible cock.

'I want to make it up to you,' he insisted. 'No premature ejaculation this time.' Seizing her hand, he almost dragged her into the sitting room. It was huge, lofty, with antique Persian rugs hanging on the whitewashed walls and deep window recesses. 'Sit there,' he ordered, and pushed her down on a chesterfield drawn close to a large, black, wood-burning stove standing in the chimney breast.

She sank into the feather cushions, each covered in William Morris fabric in greens and orange, printed with those fantasy flowers she loved so much. Mark's taste coincided with hers. Glorious sound filled the room. She remembered his passion for classical music. He had played it often on a cranky old hi-fi system. Now it swelled from the very lastest equipment.

'Tchaikovsky,' she said, as the sweeping strings vibrated on her eardrums, trickled down her spine and filled every nook and cranny of her being.

'Yes. Ah, you *do* remember. The *Romeo and Juliet Overture*. Full of lush harmonies and vigorous panache. I've tried the moderns, but I always return to the Romantics.'

'I love it. Glorious stuff.'

'Take off your clothes,' he said, and stood before her, stripping rapidly, his skin red as a fiend's in the glow seeping through the burner's glass door.

Cheryl was smitten with shyness. Her fingers shook as she undid the buttons that fastened her shirt-waister. The silk slithered to the floor, lying there like spilled claret. She braced herself and turned to him, sensing that he was inspecting her. For what? The devastation that the passing years can bring? She was confident that he'd not find many flaws – a stretch mark or two, perhaps.

'Beautiful,' he breathed at last, and his cock danced, bumping against his navel. 'You haven't changed a bit. Still beautiful. Put this on for me,' and he handed her a condom.

She fumbled with it. She had been on the pill, so she and Ashley had never used them. Maybe I should have done, she thought with a stab of fear. How often has he been dipping his wick or digging someone else's potatoes? Has he been careful?

Ashley. Why couldn't she forget him? Maybe I'm not built for fornication? she thought. Too old and set in my ways. Mark's cock is that of a stranger. I'm half-afraid to go any further. OK, Ashley wasn't much in bed, but I was used to him. We did it with the light out, and I never felt aware of my body as less than perfect. It didn't much matter anyway. But it does now, too intimate an act to perform with any old Tom, Dick or Harry.

But Mark isn't just anyone, her demon pointed out smugly. You've had him before. You know and trust him. Don't be such a wimp.

27

Mark leaned over her, and Ashley was relegated to the back of her mind. Serves him right, she decided with childish venom.

Against that sensuous background music she focused on Mark's kisses. The air vibrated with the pure energy of rich-hued colour as the overture wound up and up, the 'star-crossed lovers' theme moving and lyrical. It was as if Cheryl lingered between reality and fantasy, where sex was the only thing that mattered. Mark lay beside her, toyed with her and sucked her nipples. She held his rod, rubbing her fingers up the stem and wetting the tips with its own pre-come, familiarising herself with every vein and ridge. He felt velvety smooth.

He kissed her neck and her breasts, then licked her nipples till she squirmed; he went lower, dipping the tip of his tongue in her navel, then he parted her swollen lips and massaged the engorged clit till she was riding a huge wave bearing her to euphoria. She was awash with sensation, the intensity of it wringing a cry from her.

'Good girl,' he whispered. 'You came for me. I told you I'd make sure you did.'

She lay in his arms, handling his cock as she recovered from the sharp climax. She drew him over and into her, raising her legs and resting her ankles on his shoulders. It was only then that she realised the CD had ended. The only noises in the room were their own hurried breathing and soft, wet sounds as he drove into her body and out again, then in once more.

She was drowning in sensation; his passion, the painful grip of his hand in her hair, the pressure of his pubis against hers. He slid in and out easily. She was so wet. It seemed as if she was swallowing him whole. The harder he pushed, the more she opened, striving to come again but unable to do so. The base of his cock was only an inch or two from her clit. It might as well have been a mile. She put her hand down and rubbed it with her thumb, and heard him gasp, then waited for his final surge as her own climax faded away.

She lay, panting and trembling, a shining beacon blazing bright against the darkness of her eyelids. She'd done it! She'd screwed another man. This had severed the ties between her and Ashley more effectively than signatures on a dozen divorce papers.

Laura quite liked the solitude of the flat she had rented as a stopgap between the sale of the family house and her purchase of another. It was odd to be living alone. No husband.. No children. Not even the need to keep a spare bed made up in case one of her brood dropped in. They wrote, phoned or e-mailed her, but they had definitely flown the coop. She missed them, but this was her time. Now, responsibilities shucked off, she could read, get tickets for musicals, watch soaps on TV and catch the latest movies. Above all, it was a haven of peace and quiet in which to log on to her computer and write.

This might be short-lived, however, and she stopped tapping the keyboard, pressed Save and sat back, twirling slowly in her operator's chair. She still wanted to do it, of course, she still liked the notion of buying a hotel with Cheryl and, once the place was up and running, then both of them would be able to follow their own pursuits, hopefully.

Cheryl had a strong personality, and Laura was usually prepared to go along with her suggestions. She glanced in the mirror, seeing herself from where she sat. She still wasn't quite used to the sight of the streaked blonde shag cut. It made her look ten years younger, much more like her daughter than her once matronly self. She had dared to indulge her secret desire to dress retro 1970s: trouser suits with wide-lapelled jackets; geometric print A-line skirts and colourful leather ankle boots. Stuart had been stunned into silence when he saw this newly emerged woman whom he had once taken for granted. That moment had been intensely satisfying, and she felt she had triumphed.

Men. They haunted her thoughts, yet she really didn't have time to get involved, even if someone offered. Relationships were time-consuming and emotionally

29

wearing. Yet she didn't fancy growing old alone. Well, she wouldn't be. Cheryl would probably be with her, and Harry, when back from fresh fields and pastures new. As for Vicky? Last year Laura had been The Mother Of The Bride. She'd even worn a huge organza hat, and felt a right twit. Vicky was in America with her lecturer husband. One day, perhaps, in the not too distant future, she would make Laura a grandmother.

Will you shut the fuck up! she screamed to herself. I shall be on the first steamboat up the Amazon if that happens. I've a lot of living to do on my own account before settling down to bounce her babies on my knee.

The Amazon. South America. Buenos Aires and the Argentinian tango that had started among the low-life in the bordellos, the whores who sold themselves and the crooks who'd been their customers. She allowed herself to drift away, thinking, dreaming, deliberately encouraging that ache inside her, the one that made her wet. She got up, walked into the living room and turned on the television, then searched the shelves for a particular video recording. She found it and slipped it into the machine. Even before she had curled up on the couch, the evocative music began, the imagery startling – clips from an old black and white movie where a male heartthrob of the silent screen danced in a smoky bar. Then the film proper began, Laura's favourite – *The Naked Tango*.

It was an odd, quirky, erotic and violent movie, set in the 1920s. Laura had watched it many times and it never failed to excite her. The lighting, the sets, the dark, bloodred decor. A bordello – decadent and magnificent. The staircase supported by two enormous statues of female legs in the garters, stockings and shoes of the period. The heroine, running away from her elderly husband. And the gangster who is obsessed with tango. She falls for him but he refuses to admit that he loves her. It was near-the-knuckle, brutal and filled with world-weary whores and bad guys.

How strange that I could function as a housewife,

shopping and doing the daily chores, yet inside I'd be living in the Argentina of the film, acting like a harlot, doing the tango with a dark-haired, slinky-hipped brute wearing a black striped suit and a black fedora cocked at an angle and white spats and dancing shoes.

Laura's lips parted and her hand wandered down to her crotch. It was only lately that she had been experimenting with pleasuring herself. Cheryl had recommended the books and videos of several American writers, adding, 'They're the doyens of the clit. The mothers of masturbation.'

Inspired by the story unfolding on the screen, Laura opened her legs and pushed aside her panties. She was slim and her pubis lacked plumpness, covered with a sprinkling of sparse fair hair. The slit was sharply defined. Greatly daring, she fetched a hand mirror then, according to instructions in one of the sex books, sat on the floor with her thighs apart and the mirror positioned so that it reflected her sex. She stroked over her slit with her free hand and the lips swelled, her clit poking from its folds. It was a wonderful feeling and Laura was rather afraid she might become addicted to it. She reached down and dabbled her finger in the juice seeping from her sex. It was of just the right consistency, her lips responding to the slick wetness, her clit throbbing as she anointed it.

She sighed, possessed of weird thoughts, obeying her body's urgent command to rub herself furiously. The music rose and fell, the dancers moving to the beat, as compelled as herself and filled with burning desire. It *did* burn. Her finger slid rapidly over the bump of her roused clit. Her other hand clasped her bare breast and rolled the nipple.

Oh, this is great, she thought. Why didn't I know about it till recently? Why didn't someone tell me? I've wasted years. Stuart should have known, but then, I suppose I can't really blame him. He wasn't interested enough to find out what turned women on, too eager to hide his own desire to hump a male arse.

31

It's of no consequence. I'm here with my greedy clit. It demands that I go on and on, massaging it, rubbing it, first one side then the other, tantalising the head with the merest touch, then unable to wait any more, part of the dance, longing to orgasm. I must! I *must!*

She gasped. The sensations gathered at the base of her spine, in her womb, radiating to the tips of her toes and back again. She sparked. She fizzed like fireworks. She came.

Falling back against the cushions, she watched the gangster putting the heroine through her tango steps, but now they were in an abattoir, their precisely positioned feet moving through blood. The phone shrilled and Laura turned the sound down as she reached for it.

'Hi there. It's me ... Cheryl. Are you all set for tomorrow, trawling the estate agents'? Shall we have a coffee first? How are you?'

'I'm fine; and you?'

'Fan-bloody-tastic!' Cheryl chortled. 'You'll never guess what I've been doing.'

She sounded so exhilarated that Laura could only draw one conclusion. 'Shagging?' she said.

'Too right!'

'Congratulations.'

'I'll tell you all about it tomorrow. Bye now.'

Laura put down the cordless phone and raised the sound level a tad. Then she settled down to watch the tragic, but satisfying, end of the movie.

The restaurant was spacious and verdant. There were exotic plants in jardinières at intervals along the walls and, sprawling and jungly, cascading from indoor water-features.

'The designer is obviously green and there isn't much on the menu to tempt the taste buds of a carnivore like me,' Cheryl said, walking in with Laura.

They had been whisked up in a glass-sided lift to this recently opened and ferociously expensive eating place on top of the new shopping mall. She had chosen it because it was a stone's throw from a road where several estate agents had their offices. The time for dallying was long past. Their money was in situ. Now came the serious business of finding suitable premises.

Lunch was not on the agenda and they sipped demitasses of strong black coffee and thumbed through a stack of leaflets sent to them by eager beavers hassling for a quick sale. Photos of houses – detached or terraced, each an already established hotel. There were two on the cliff road, boasting wonderful views, and some on the seafront where convenience to the town was stressed. The blurb came with them, giving glowing accounts of their amenities.

'Nothing there that grabs me,' Laura said.

'Me neither,' Cheryl answered, visualising a long, hard slog before they finally got settled.

'There's a couple more agents to see,' Laura put in, and Cheryl was struck by how attractive she looked. She'd shed years since leaving Stuart.

Cheryl yielded to the impulse to tell her all about Mark. 'I got laid yesterday afternoon,' she burst out, and desire grabbed at her, fired by memories.

'So you said. Was it Mark?' Laura replied, with no change of expression.

Cheryl was a little disappointed. She had expected a stronger reaction – shock, perhaps; envy even. 'Sure, Mark. We had lunch and went back to his house.'

'Did you enjoy it?'

'It was a blast. To tell the truth, I was a little scared at first You know . . . a different man.' Cheryl lowered her voice. 'A different cock. But it was all right. I've kind of broken the ice.'

'And you're ready to try others?'

'Why not? There's a whole wide world full of fuckable men out there waiting for me,' Cheryl declared, with a defiant grin. This faded. She couldn't fool Laura, and she knew it. Her bravado wilted and she shrugged her shoulders, adding, 'It really was fine with Mark. I think he'd like to carry it further, but I'm not sure.'

'I think you've enough on your plate for the moment. I know I have,' Laura said sensibly, then pushed her cup away. 'Come on. We can't put it off any more. We're shopping for a hotel . . . remember?'

The first estate agent's they came to was situated between a shoeshop with nothing in the window but a single boot placed on a small gilt chair, and a toyshop filled with Steiff-lookalike teddy bears in sweaters, beautifully dressed Victorian reproduction china-headed dolls and elaborate doll's houses.

Gilt lettering proclaimed that the estate agent was Dewhurst and Marshal, established 1880. They peered in at the windows and almost immediately saw it. It seemed to jump out at them from among the photos of the many properties for sale.

'Look at that!' squeaked Laura.

'Wow!' was all Cheryl could manage, staring at the jumbled impression of tall chimney pots, towers, mullioned windows and a gabled roof.

She read aloud the details printed alongside the photograph. 'Fine old school, once owned by the LEA. Many reception rooms, bedrooms and dormitories, a library, an assembly hall, several bathrooms and kitchens, gamesrooms, a swimming pool, and extensive grounds with tennis courts, etc. Needs some renovation and updating. Early viewing recommended.'

Laura grabbed her arm, her face alight with excitement. 'Come on!' she urged. 'What are we waiting for?'

They stepped into a cramped office where a pretty brunette sat at a desk buffing her nails, one knee crossed over the other. There were photographs of houses pinned to the walls, along with those of flats, shops and apartments to rent or for sale.

Cheryl stared at the young woman and she stared back. Then she smiled brightly and said, 'Good morning. My name is Daphne and I'm Mr Dewhurst's personal assistant. How may I help you?'

'I'm Cheryl Barden and this is Laura Tilford. We're planning to open a hotel and are interested in having the

34

details of a house in the window. The one in the middle. The old one,' Cheryl said breathlessly, in a panic in case it was already under offer.

'Oh yes, madam. I know it,' Daphne answered.

As she stood up, Cheryl noticed that she was wearing a short skirt and dark stockings. Her white blouse strained over a pair of pronounced breasts. Cheryl had the urge to touch her, appreciating how men would want to caress those big boobs and neat backside. She was astonished by this alien thought.

'It's still on the market,' Daphne continued. 'Very large, and there's a lot of land with it and stables and things. Were you looking for something that big? Historic, of course, but it does need doing up. Excuse me a minute. I'll get the details. Perhaps you'd like to talk to our Mr Moor? I'll buzz him.'

'Thank you,' Cheryl said, and smiled across at Laura who gave her the thumbs-up sign.

Cheryl was wrestling with her reaction towards Daphne. She had always been strictly heterosexual, apart from a crush on a teacher and a possessive relationship with Esther, her best friend at school. This had never developed further than comparing notes on their budding breasts and sprouting pubes. Their interest in one another had dwindled when they started dating boys. So why had she been overtaken by this aberration – this sudden lust for Daphne?

A balding, middle-aged man materialised from an inner sanctum, followed by Daphne. He was carrying some papers. His eyes scanned Cheryl, switched to Laura, and then back to Cheryl as he said, 'Ah, Mrs . . .?'

'Barden. And this is Mrs Tilford,' she said crisply. He was unprepossessing, with that patronising air often found in salesmen, especially when dealing with female customers. She suspected that he wanked over dirty magazines. He looked the type.

'I'm Mr Moor, and I'll be only too happy to assist you,' he gushed.

I'll bet you would, Cheryl thought, and wondered

what it would be like to indulge her desire to take a bullwhip to men like him. The trouble was, they'd probably enjoy it.

After having given them a load of spiel, he offered to show them over the house. It was called St Jude's and he explained that it had been a college until quite recently when the Local Education Authority had had to close it through lack of funds.

Four miles from the centre of Westcombe, the agent's Fiesta turned right and Cheryl followed in her car. The narrow road wound down towards a picturesque, prosperous-looking hamlet of slate-tiled roofs and walled gardens. They passed the public house, the post office and general stores and the school from which yet another generation of children streamed to be greeted by their mothers.

'They all have cars,' Cheryl remarked, waiting while the patrol lady shepherded the kids across the road. 'It looks a rich area. Very snob-dobbery.'

'And church fêtes,' observed Laura.

'And jumble sales.'

'And tea with the vicar.'

'And one hell of a lot of wife-swapping.'

'Do you think we'll fit in here?' Laura asked doubtfully as the car eased forward in the wake of Moor's.

'I don't see why not. As hoteliers we're hardly likely to have time for taking part in village activities.'

'Not even the wife-swapping?' Laura teased.

'Give me a break!' Cheryl groaned, eyebrows raised in protest. 'Anyway, don't pre-empt. This may not be the one for us.'

Moor signalled left and his blue car swung into a side road between tall trees. Partly bare branches met overhead. In summer their thick foliage would form a secret tunnel. Cheryl could see it in her mind's eye. It was as if she had been there before, driving down the avenue with the sun striking through, forming a filigree of light and shade.

The lane ended in a pair of high, rusted, creeper-hung

36

gates. Two lions topped their solid stone supports. Weather-beaten and lichen-encrusted, they guarded the entrance. Cheryl stared up at them when she had scrambled out of the car. They stared back at her sardonically.

On the ironwork beneath them was a FOR SALE notice and the address and telephone number of Dewhurst and Marshal. Moor clambered out and took a massive key to the equally massive lock The gates creaked in protest as he leaned a shoulder against them. They opened fully.

'Come along, ladies,' he urged cheerily. 'Follow me.'

Twat! Cheryl thought uncharitably as she got back into her car. She swept between the gates and up an overgrown drive. It widened and, with a suddenness that took her breath away, she saw the house. It stood foursquare, seeming to have grown from the soil rather than built by human hands. The surrounding trees protected St Jude's from intruders. Huge, crumbling in parts, its towers were like lewd, stiff fingers pointing towards the sky. Arched windows, pinnacles and quoins, statues in alcoves, gargoyles perched on the broken guttering. It was everything Cheryl had hoped for – and more.

Laura was more cautious. 'It's in a mess, Mr Moor. I dread to think of the cost of renovations.'

'It's not as bad as it looks, Mrs Tilford,' he said, bobbing at her elbow. 'The wiring is sound, so is the roof. It's only been empty for eighteen months. It just needs refurbishing, that's all.'

'What about English Heritage?' Cheryl asked. 'I presume it's older than the nineteenth century and will be a listed building.'

'They'll have their say, I suppose, though the LEA didn't have any trouble,' Moor said as he conducted them across a weedy circular drive and up the wide steps that led to a monumental front door under an arch.

He succeeded in turning the key in the lock easily enough. 'It was stiff on my first visit, but we've had it oiled since,' he said chattily, opening the door. 'I came out with Mr Dewhurst himself, but he's away at present. Holidaying in the Channel Islands.'

Get on with it, you prat, Cheryl grumbled inside. Then she registered that he was nervous. Would his job be on the line if he didn't make a sale? He wasn't young and there must be many bright, up-and-coming candidates for his post. Or is it the house making him jittery? He's sweating and if I were an animal I'd be able to smell his fear. Maybe I can . . . it's sharp, with a cloying undertone, and it's mixed with arousal too. He's getting randy because he's alone here with us. Even his aftershave can't disguise it.

He stood back so that she and Laura might precede him through the impressive portal. Inside the porch were stone benches on each side and another door, a carved screen and then the Great Hall.

'It's like a bloody ballroom,' Cheryl hissed, forgetting not to swear in front of him.

'Impressive, isn't it?' Moor enthused.

Panelled walls, a stone floor, fireplaces at either end big enough to hold logs the size of a man, with canopies rearing towards the rafters. Their footsteps echoed as if they walked through a church. But it wasn't a church Cheryl was visualising. Nor was it a college, or even a hotel, though it would fit the bill splendidly. A cover-up maybe – a blind for something else. She trembled as the vision grew stronger. Was it possible? Could it really be? What would Laura think about it?

Moor showed them round the dining room, the library and reception rooms, the kitchens and upstairs, a veritable rabbit warren, with countless rooms that inspired Cheryl's dream. She needed to talk privately to Laura, *now*.

More rooms, more corridors, all vast and showing signs of disrepair. There were patches of mould on ceilings and walls, but all Cheryl could see was opulence, St Jude's transformed into a pleasure house. She was ahead of Moor and Laura, dashing along passages, opening doors, peering inside, her blood, nerves and heart responding to the atmosphere and the possibilities. Wonderful old house. She had to have it.

Downstairs again and into a side room. 'I'm told that this was the matron's office, in the olden days when it was a boarding school for boys,' Moor said, and smirked across at Cheryl.

'Was it, indeed?' she replied, catching his mood, turning it around. 'I suppose they were sent to her when they'd been very, very naughty. Did she cane them, I wonder? Did she have them take down their trousers and bend over her desk?'

Moor was sweating even more and she noticed that he locked his hands in front of him, as if trying to hide an erection. Dirty bugger, she thought, and the idea that was blossoming within her came into full bloom. Oh yes, we'll keep matron's office, she decided.

Laura walked in a daze. The potential of St Jude's overwhelmed her. The film set of *The Naked Tango* would fit into it over and over. Art deco, in all its decadent splendour. A brothel inhabited by businessmen and bored, rich women, whores, gigolos, pimps and gangsters, and she would be the all-powerful madam. But would Cheryl ever agree to this? Didn't she want to open a five-star hotel?

'We'll do both,' Cheryl said, as they retired to the car to talk it over before giving Moor an answer.

It had been confession time, and both had been astonished and delighted to find that their ambitions were the same. Each dreamed of owning a whorehouse, with fantasy rooms where every sexual desire could be satisfied.

'Those towers and dormitories,' Laura exclaimed.

'We can have Victorian rooms, where the girls wear tight corsets and frilly bloomers. And dark dungeons for punishment, and harems and geisha tearooms, and space-age scenes and everything under the sun,' Cheryl said, her voice ringing.

'And the Jazz Age scenario, with dancing and spanking and all things wild.'

'But we'll cater for ordinary guests too. I intend to hire

a chef who will give St Jude's a reputation for first-class cuisine. Oh, Laura, just think! What fun we're going to have. Independent, and bringing our visions to life. St Jude's, hotel and bordello. We'll make it beautiful, a haven for those who seek, shall we say, an alternative sex life.'

'I can't wait to get started,' Laura said. 'Come on. Let's go and tell Moor we'll put in an offer, subject to survey.'

'Ah, the obsequious agent,' Cheryl replied, opening the driver's door and getting out, all long legs and tumbling, unkempt hair. 'Did you see him when we were in matron's office? I wouldn't be surprised if he came in his pants. He liked the idea of naughty boys getting the cane, Laura, liked it one hell of a lot.'

'Our first customer?'

'Maybe.'

Chapter Three

*D*aughters! Who'd have 'em? Joanna grumbled to herself. Cheryl's problems were clouding her peaceful state of mind, brought about by a session in the sweat lodge, a full-body massage and the anticipation of sex with her latest lover.

I should be able to control myself and allow my inner being to become one with the cosmos during meditation, she fretted. Jesus Christ! I've been practising it long enough. But Cheryl's hang-ups had a habit of impinging, even more so during the months she'd been staying at Fell Tor. She didn't exactly fit in, a constant reminder of her stockbroker father, Giles Newman, whom Joanna had married when she was eighteen, had a child by a year later and left shortly after.

A smile lifted the corners of her mouth and, though her eyes were closed and her expression tranquil, she couldn't restrain an inner giggle as she thought: I went off with the raggle-taggle gypsies-oh. Or their equivalent, the hippies. And Cheryl came with me, until the divorce when Giles was given care and control and I was granted access. It wasn't fair. Just because he did everything by the book, whereas I never have done and never will. In a way I was relieved. With Cheryl safely ensconced with him and his new wife for most of the time, I was free to carry on my nomadic existence, living in a converted bus and finding my forte with oil-paint and canvas.

How fast the years have flown, she reflected, squinting through lowered lashes at the beautiful naked man seated opposite her. Deven, of the heavenly blue-black hair and lithe, olive-hued body. He had the face of a Hindu god, Krishna perhaps, and a large cock that curved upwards from its wiry nest as he sat in the Lotus position, his elegant hands folded serenely.

The air was spiced with incense, but even so she could smell him, the exotic odour of cinnamon that breathed out through his pores. Coupled with the perfume of his long hair, and the musky, masculine essence that rose from his genitals, it was enough to sway Joanna from her quest for spiritual harmony. It roused the root chakra that lay like a full-blown crimson rose above her sex, and made her clit pulse.

The throbbing of the tambour and the plucked strings of a sitar filled the garden room and ... be still, she counselled herself. You have the whole night ahead of you. Deven is yours for hours. A spasm of lust totally devoid of anything but sheer physicality shot through her sex. She struggled to focus her thoughts – a forest glade – that's it, see every sun-dappled tree – a cloudless blue sky, a path leading to a waterfall. Hear it cascading into a pool. Kneel on the bank further down and look at your reflection. What do you see?

Deven obscured the view. He grew larger and larger, blotting out the landscape, his cock rising like a totem pole from between his thighs, his balls heavy in their scrotal sac. Joanna lost the plot, returning to herself with a bang. She opened her eyes, looked straight into his divine inky pupils, and then drowned in them. Oh, Lord, she sighed. I've an awful feeling I'm falling in love again, and this is bad. I don't do love. Not the one-to-one variety anyway, which isn't to be confused with the other sort that embraces the universe and all it contains, blah-de-blah.

She'd lost count of how many times she'd been a victim

of her emotions, and certainly had no record of the number of men she'd fucked. But one had to be careful these days, and condoms put a damper on things. It had little to do with age or opportunity. In the circles in which she operated there was always plenty of the latter, and with her unlined features, voluptuous figure, artistic flare and wisdom she had never found herself short of admirers. Neither had her appetite waned, but she resented putting a rubber barrier between her and whichever cock she had selected for her enjoyment, and she missed the bursts of come laving the inside of her pussy.

She railed against the vagaries of fate. No longer likely to become pregnant, unless by a miracle or the intervention of IVF, sex for her should have been a breeze, but no: one had the threat of viruses with long names and unpleasant fatal effects. Bugger, she thought, as she stared at Deven serenely, holding his gaze and sending raunchy messages along the telepathic link between them, or so she hoped. How could one ever really tell whether all this mind stuff was no more than a load of crap designed to lure the gullible into parting with their money? She was suddenly filled with doubts and impatient with the techniques she had struggled to learn in order to extend sexual unity and bonding. So what? All she wanted right now was a straightforward shag.

She couldn't deny that there was much to be gained by tuning one's senses to that of the lover, while meditation and breathing could be used to extend the arousal so that a cock would stay erect for ages. She had become very proficient at contracting her muscles to milk a cock while her partner lay passive, but – and it was a big but – she had to admit that she obtained the greatest pleasure of all while using a vibrator.

Oh dear, she thought, entranced by Deven's limpid eyes. How unkind. He'd be upset if he knew, or maybe he wouldn't. He likes to watch me with my sex toys. But most men, and this includes those who call themselves enlightened, are paranoid in case a woman thinks their dick's too small. We may have the disadvantage of having a tiny organ that takes some finding, but it's a hundred times more sensitive. Thinking about it made her tingle and she pressed her bottom down on the Persian rug. Seated cross-legged, it was easy to make contact with her clit and the hardness of the floor, but it wasn't enough. She needed something that would bring her off instantly. For at least an hour she had been sitting there, tantalised by Deven's nearness, trying to harness her wayward thoughts – and failing.

She had blamed it on Cheryl and the phone call she'd had not long before she started the session. Her daughter had babbled on about an old house she and that waiflike creature, Laura, had found. They planned to buy it and turn it into a hotel.

'You must come and see it, Mummy,' Cheryl had enthused, and the use of that sobriquet for the maternal parent jarred. Cheryl had learned it from Angela, Giles's second wife, a snob whom Joanna despised and daydreamed of seeing lose complete control and turn into a raging nymphomaniac who couldn't get enough.

How could Cheryl possibly refer to her as 'Mummy'? Joanna gloomed. It had been irksome enough when she was a girl, and it now sounded positively mushy. Even worse had been that plonker Ashley who, when he could be bothered to speak to her at all, had called her 'ma-in-law'. In his mouth it had been an insult. Their antipathy for one another had been intense and entirely mutual. Best thing Cheryl ever did was leave the twerp, she concluded, trying to push away all other thoughts and plunge into Deven like an overheated sunbather hitting the sea. Pity Cheryl didn't make the break sooner, like me. I recognised that Giles was a geek from the off. Only married him because I was pressurised by my parents. Christ, the harm some well-meaning people do. They were worried by my ambition to become a Flower Child and longed to see me settled with a man who'd provide for me.

Giles wanted to control me and he couldn't. They hadn't been able to either. I must be a throwback or something. Maybe there was a black sheep in the family several generations ago. Where did I get this need to express myself through an odd view of the world, not exactly surreal, but heading in that direction?

Not always, though. I've captured Deven on canvas and he's so pleasing to the eye that I wanted an accurate representation of him. You might say, then why not take photographs? I have. I do. I work from them, but paints allow me to somehow capture the exotic juxtaposition of sexuality and mysticism that is the sum total of his parts.

She had painted most of her lovers, male and female, and these, along with her fantastic dreamscapes, had inspired a gallery to exhibit her works. For years she'd employed an agent who handled the business side of things. She had acquired Fell Tor for a song during a slump in the property market. A stroke of luck as it was now worth at least a million, a farmhouse dating from the fifteenth century, with a ruined castle and a lake at the back and several acres of land. There she had set up her community of like-minded spirits. There she had her studio. There she had offered her daughter a home. There she was about to have intercourse with the strikingly handsome Deven. He might well be a poser, and Joanna was cynical enough to recognise this, but what the hell? At least he wasn't a pathetic wannabe, like Giles, Angela and Ashley.

It was an entirely different matter to walk through St Jude's as its owner rather than a prospective buyer. A chill trickled down Cheryl's spine and doubt shadowed her enjoyment. Supposing it flopped and they had to sell up? They were putting every penny they possessed into the project.

'We simply can't fail,' she said aloud, addressing the echoing hall, the monumental main staircase, the cobwebs and the ghosts.

There was no going back. It was signed, sealed and delivered, every 't' crossed, every 'i' dotted. St Jude's belonged to Laura and herself.

Cheryl had come there alone, intent on seeing how quickly she could move in. Life at Fell Tor was getting to her. It was just too much. Though accustomed to her mother's eccentricities, it seemed that these were becoming extreme. She favoured flimsy, flowing robes, swanning around like the Queen of Sheba, painting when she felt like it, lazing when she didn't, and spending money like a drunken sailor. As for her latest conquest, an escapee from *The Kama Sutra* called Deven? Cheryl had already crossed swords with him, suspecting that he was after Joanna's property and basking in reflected glory. He saw himself as a guru, and treated Cheryl as if she were a recalcitrant child. It was more than simply annoying, particularly as she found him dangerously attractive.

Time to move on and, as she paced the Great Hall, she was planning where she would put her furniture when she got it out of storage. She and Laura had already discussed their living arrangements. St Jude's was so large that they could both have their own spacious apartments. These already existed: one had been occupied by the headmaster; the other by matron. After refurbishing, these would provide ample space where they could retire in privacy, entertain whoever they liked without fear or favour, and generally behave as if they were in separate houses.

Mark had found an architect, Arthur Huntley, who had been willing to deal with English Heritage and send in plans for their approval. Apparently, they already knew about St Jude's and had worked with the former owners to ensure that its outside appearance was in no way altered. They must be kept informed if any changes to the interior were proposed. Cheryl told Mark to tell his architect chum (one of the old boy network) that it was her intention to keep every fascinating feature, and the towers in particular.

She consulted Laura on everything but, with her lawyer's training, it was natural that she handled most things legal, with the help of Mark. He had been with her to view the property, depressing her with his doubts, misgivings and portents of disaster. She didn't confess that it was to become a bordello, besides a hotel and venue for business conferences. She guessed he wouldn't be too keen, for he was already showing a distinctly possessive attitude towards her, hoping to take up where they had left off as graduates. Not that she planned to take part in the traffic in flesh. At least, she didn't think so at this stage, envisioning organising the prostitutes and clients and taking the money.

She accepted Mark's lovemaking, gave what she could, listened to his warnings, thought about them, then dismissed them. Nothing was going to stop her and Laura fulfilling their dream. They had talked sensibly to Huntley, who was awaiting estimates from builders for the work involved in making St Jude's habitable, but on the side they were searching for an interior designer who'd carry out their specific instructions. The hotel, restaurant and guestrooms would be in perfect taste and left in the hands of the architect. The swimming pool would be updated, also the gym, and the games-room for table tennis and billiards. They planned to add a squash court and a luxurious massage and beauty parlour.

This was all above board, but there was another, secret plan. It was their intention to turn the towers into fantasy rooms. These had to be flamboyantly decorated in keeping with the sexual themes. The cellars in their foundations would become dungeons. The help of an expert in decor was needed, someone who appreciated the psychological quirks that lay behind the desire for punishment and submission. Cheryl was confident that the right person would come along.

It was a hot afternoon, and the coloured glass in the leaded lights threw brilliant patterns on the dusty floors as she circumnavigated the passages and rooms. The door leading to the East Tower creaked like something out of a horror movie as she opened it and let herself into a corridor that connected with what had once been a dormitory. It must have slept at least twenty boys. She strolled through the deserted space, thinking that she

47

could hear their voices. Kids always made such a racket that it must be imprinted in the ether. Maybe that's what hauntings were, impressions left behind, almost as if the walls acted like a videotape, or a sponge. She wandered across to one of the narrow windows and looked down on the overgrown grounds. At once her active imagination peopled it with hunky, suntanned gardeners in sweat-soaked vests. Their faded jeans fitted so tightly round their cocks that it was almost possible to ascertain their religion.

Yes, she decided, Laura and me had better start making enquiries and interviewing a few muscular landscape architects. It's going to be a long, hot summer. Laura hasn't tried out her new-found sexuality yet, and though I've had Mark, this isn't enough. I've known him so long that he's almost like family. I need to dip a toe in the water and fuck a stranger or two.

The heavy sensation gathered in her loins and made her tingle. She was wearing linen shorts that fitted so snugly round the crotch that she was aware of her bottom crack. Her crop-top was brief and, not long ago, she would have been too embarrassed to wear it, worried about looking ridiculous, but no more. Mark had injected her with a large dose of confidence. Now she was proud of her slim, brown legs and liked the way her terrain sandals set them off, making her feel adventurous, as if she were some feisty female guerrilla about to take part in a revolution in some combustible part of Latin America. She could almost feel the cartridge belt slung round her shoulders and the shooter at her hip. Maybe she would get the chance to act out this role when St Jude's was up and running.

She knew that, even with all available help, she and Laura would have to work like slaves to make their dream reality, but it would be worth it. There was another room above the one she was in, and she had plans for the West Tower too. They should be meeting places for those who required something extra, wanting to investigate the byways of perversion. She had started reading up on these activities and soon realised that she needed the assistance of someone already in the scene. Another task to add to the already long list that must be completed before St Jude's could officially open.

She plumped down in a stone window embrasure. It chilled her buttocks and chafed the back of her thighs, but she lifted one leg and rested her foot on the seat. The knowledge that she was quite alone in her kingdom sent excitement rippling along her nerves. She could do what she liked there. Strip naked and dance; lie full-length on the bench and allow the surface to scratch at her skin; or simply dive a finger into the side of her shorts and masturbate. That seemed the best bet.

The leg was too tight for comfortable manipulation so she unzipped the fly, pushed her hand inside her panties and slid a finger into her damp groove. The familiar dart of pleasure shot down to her opening. It spasmed and her pussy lips thickened, making her clit firm up.

She closed her eyes and leaned her head back against the window, fully prepared to indulge herself. Her finger moved sweetly over her cleft. At once the sensation began, warm, tingling, permeating her whole being. She gasped and her legs parted slackly. The panties and shorts were an encumbrance but she didn't want to stop the flow and remove them. It was simply too good. Her clit was a hard nubbin under her rapidly moving finger and she knew she was about to come. She closed her eyes and prepared to go with it.

Then she froze, her finger leaving her anguished clit as she heard a sound from somewhere above. It reminded her of that fateful day when she'd come home unexpectedly and found Ashley in bed with Yvonne Harper.

Pain knifed her at his heartless betrayal, and the waves that were building in her groin receded. She withdrew her hand and zipped up her shorts. She sat there with her head cocked at a listening angle, and heard another thump. At once she thought of spooks, then dismissed this as nonsense. More likely to be squatters. Pride of ownership swelled and she wanted them off her property. She cleaned her sticky fingers with a wet-wipe, but she could still smell the scent of her own arousal. She marched to the door and let herself into the corridor, then took the spiral staircase that wound aloft.

Her sandals made no sound on the treads and she reached the second floor. This was slightly smaller than the first but contained a corridor and bathroom and a dormitory that could cater for a solid section of boys. The windows and architecture matched that of the lower floor, and there was another storey, leading to a battlement. She'd ventured there once on a windy day, clinging to the parapet and viewing her land and beyond that the fields, forests and hills, captivated by its wildness. The tower was not a safe place for adventurous children or adults with vertigo, she had thought, and understood why the door had been bolted and barred.

But the noises were not coming from up there. They issued from the chamber on her right. She hesitated for only a second, then pushed the door open.

At first she was blinded by sunlight. Then she saw him. A large, bearded, dark-haired stranger who had a metal tape in one hand with which he was measuring the fireplace.

He swung round, took her in at a glance, smiled and said, 'Who are you?'

'I could ask you the same thing,' she returned, her heart thudding. She wished she had worn something more sensible. Shorts indeed!

'No sweat,' he answered casually, though continuing to eye her up and down. 'I'm Felan Boynton. Mr Huntley called me out to work on the renovation costs.'

'You're employed by a builder?'

'It's my company,' he replied, and put the tape down on the grimy mantelpiece.

A faint recollection stirred at the back of Cheryl's mind. Boynton & Son. Builders. She'd heard Huntley and Mark discussing them, among others. So this was he, or was he the son? Or maybe he had a son who was being trained up to join him? She found her thoughts fragmenting, too interested in him for comfort. She despaired of herself lately. Nothing with a cock was sacred. It's like someone has been lacing my tea with Viagra, she concluded.

He came closer and completed the furore in her belly. He was very tall, and built like a baseball player. Craggily handsome, he had piercing blue eyes and a dark beard that covered his jaw and upper lip, well trimmed and thick, but not bushy. She liked it. His hair was long, pulled back into a ponytail. She liked that too. Age? She decided on mid-thirties. Voice? Deep, and educated. He was certainly no peasant. Manner? Casual, jokey, but with a hint of impatience. He wouldn't suffer fools gladly and liked his own way. Was used to getting it, by the hard set of his mouth and the steely look in his eyes.

'Now you know who I am and what I'm doing here, maybe you'll tell me your business,' he said. This wasn't a polite request. It was an order.

For some reason that she couldn't quite fathom, Cheryl didn't want to say that she owned St Jude's and might soon have him on her payroll. She shrugged and gave a toss of her ringletted hair, knowing that the rich reddish shade glittered in the sun. The very air seemed alive with pheromones and she wanted Felan to give her one hell of a seeing-to.

'Slut!' muttered the condemnatory demon from inside her skull, ever ready to criticise.

'Bollocks to you!' she retorted mentally.

'I found a door unlocked and thought I'd take a look round,' she lied, lifting her eyes to Felan's. 'Old buildings interest me.'

'Me too. But aren't you trespassing?'

'And what about you?' she challenged, surprised to find that her fists had automatically clenched. He had thrown down the gauntlet and she wanted to make him regret tangling with her.

He stared at her mockingly and pushed an errant lock of hair back from his forehead. 'I've permission to be here.' He held out a bunch of keys and jingled them.

'Where did you get those?' she said, deciding that she didn't like him. He was far too sure of himself.

He gave a quirky grin. 'I was authorised by Mr Huntley and Mr Warfield.'

Bloody hell! Cheryl thought on a burst of annoyance. What right had Mark to bandy her keys about willy-nilly? He hadn't told her that a building technician was calling in there that afternoon. She felt affronted, as if Mark had somehow insulted her intelligence. She liked to be in control, most definitely. No one was going to make decisions for her or push her around any more. Those days were over.

'Who owns it?' she asked grittily, testing this brash, overconfident man.

He lifted his broad shoulders in a shrug. Cheryl noted the muscles rippling in his arms. The vest was brief and she could see that his chest was smudged with hair. 'It's been bought by a couple of women who're turning it into a hotel,' he vouchsafed. 'They've more money than sense, if you ask me.'

He had moved closer and she had a sudden, claustrophobic feeling. She wanted to step back but wouldn't allow this weakness. Instead, she squared up to him. 'No one *did* ask you,' she snapped pithily. 'Why shouldn't they make a go of it?'

'No reason, except that it's going to be a slog. What's up? Don't tell me you're a bolshy, ball-breaking feminist. I don't believe it. You're far too sexy.'

'Stop patronising me.'

'Would I?' He pretended to be hurt by the suggestion.

The bugger's making fun of me! Cheryl could feel her face flaming and hoped he'd put it down to the summer sun. In reality it was generated by the sheer masculinity of the man, and her wayward bodily response. Jesus! We might as well be living in the Stone Age. Me, Tarzan; you, Jane, she concluded. Get real!

But she was still new to the programme, not yet believing that anyone could really find her sexy. Ashley had done a thorough job of putting her down. It's like

I'm in rehab, she thought. Finding my self-worth. Hot on this came the panic. I've got to get out of here before I lie down on the floor with Felan and turn the tower into a jungle.

She turned to go but felt his grip on her shoulder, swinging her towards him. He stroked her face with the back of his hand. 'Why so defensive?' he asked softly.

'I'm not,' she lied, while every sense, each tiny, quivering nerve end came alight at his touch.

He was so tall. The top of her head only just reached the pit of his throat. And he pulled her against him, breasts crushed to his chest, belly jabbed by the spear-hard cock. She had two options: to scratch, bite and knee him in the balls, or submit to the pounding in her veins. It was foolish. *She* was foolish. He could be a rapist. A murderer. At the very least he was probably married and she had made a pact with herself – she'd never mess with married men. One thing he wasn't was gay. There was no mistaking the signals. Supposing his firm proved the most suitable to take on? She'd have to face him later as boss-woman.

That was in the future. This was now. She opted for sex.

One iron-hard arm encompassed her back. His other hand cruised between them and cradled her breast. It was easily contained in his palm. She felt him feeling to see if her bra was a front-loader. It wasn't, so he pushed it down and lifted a breast free, his thumb revolving on the crimped nipple. Cheryl exhaled and then his mouth stopped her breath. It was big, like the rest of him, his lips engulfing her, his tongue penetrating deeply, tangling with hers, exploring her gums, inner cheeks and teeth. His beard prickled, but it was exciting and novel. He was unstoppable. Not that she wanted to try. His were the most exciting kisses ever, making her inside quicken, making her feel like a teenager at a drive-in movie with her first beau, indulging in necking and petting.

Reality struck. He was insistent and they weren't a

couple of kids but two mature people who knew what they wanted. His hand went from her breast to her mound. He opened her shorts and she felt the brutality of a stranger's hand between her legs. The same as Ashley's and Mark's in essence, but somehow alien. They'd hardly exchanged half a dozen sentences, yet he was examining her most intimate places and, what was even more alarming, she wanted him to finger-fuck her, to get her ready, prepare the way for his cock which, by the feel of it through the denim, was a substantial one.

He smelled of heat and fresh sweat that overpowered the deodorant at his armpits. His hair had come unbound and fell forward across his shoulders, strands tickling her face as he leaned over her. It was clean and fragrant, washed in a herbal shampoo, and her sense of the absurd, never absent for long, supplied the ad-man's irritating catch phrase, *'Because he's worth it.'*

Dignity? She didn't give a flying fuck! Age and decorum? Who cares? She was her own woman and could make her own choices. She chose Felan. Just for today, at any rate. She stood on tiptoe and raised her pubis, offering it to his hand. He clutched it, parted the avenue and dived a finger into the wet folds. He entered her and she bore down. His thumb was against her clit, working it. Her legs started to shake and she was far removed from St Jude's, mindlessly ecstatic.

His free hand clutched her arse and his finger homed in on her anus. She pushed against it, wanting to feel that invasion of the place where she was still virgin. The notion astonished her, and she felt the nether mouth yield to take his finger to the first knuckle.

'Are you up for this?' he murmured, his breath against her ear. 'Or shall we start with *this*?'

In an instant he had her on her knees. The floorboards were gritty and she was aware of discomfort. His jeans were unfastened and his cock protruded, thick-stemmed and fiery, the foreskin rolled back over the shiny red glans. She stared right at it, and her hand closed round it, then slid up and down, letting the jism act as a lubricant.

'Good slave-slut. Wank me off with your mouth,' he said, and a spasm darted straight to her insides.

No one had ever talked dirty to her before. She loved that edge to his voice, as if he were demanding that she be his slave. She wanted to prostrate herself before him and have him use her any which way. It was as if she could spend her life on her knees, looking up at him. She learned more about submission in that second than any amount of books could have taught her. All it needed was the right circumstances, the right man and the right tone of voice. But I'm into feminism, aren't I? she protested. Her body thought otherwise.

His cock was beating strongly in her face, a powerful weapon angled upwards. She wanted it inside her, needing its meaty length to fill her clenching pussy. He ran his hands through her hair and used it as a halter, drawing her closer to his crotch. He smelled musty, as if he hadn't showered that morning. Got up late, maybe, after a night with another woman? Cheryl was sure there was the taint of female sex mingled with his own scent. Or she might be wrong, and he'd merely jerked-off to a dirty movie on the X Channel. Whatever, it was the unmistakable odour of spunk. It added to her rising excitement.

She opened her lips and took him into her mouth. He tasted strong and she lapped at the salt bedewing his stalk, then inserted the tip of her tongue into the tiny eye, finding new pre-come. He growled and tightened his grip on her hair, pushing himself deeper into her throat. Cheryl wanted to gag but managed to stop herself. She wasn't skilled at sucking, more through lack of practice than reluctance. Mark was shy when it came to this, as if fearing to hand over control, and Ashley had never been one for experimentation when he was with her. Felan, it seemed, was eager to explore every avenue, totally uninhibited. She rejoiced, yearning to feel his mouth on her snatch, reciprocating the favour.

He stood there, his legs braced and slightly apart, as firm as a rock as she lavished pleasure on him. She relaxed her hold and pulled away for a moment, gulping in a great draught of air. She glanced up and saw that he had his head back, his snarling expression that of a man undergoing torture and his cock swayed persistently, seeking her mouth again. She closed over him, sucking him in deep, gradually milking the orgasm from him.

What did he think she was? A slapper who was anybody's? A casual bit of crumpet who needed very little persuasion? She didn't care. She plied her tongue as if she were one of the whores she intended to employ, and such sluttish behaviour aroused her. Now her taste buds registered something new as he began to ejaculate. Pull out or swallow? She let him spurt down her throat and took the residue on her lips as he half withdrew, a final burst creaming her cheeks, chin and neck. It seemed he would go on forever, but the last droplets fell and he returned his cock to his jeans.

She stood up and wiped her face on the back of her hand, then pulled a tissue from her bag. She couldn't look at Felan. Now that passion was spent he was once more a rather annoying stranger. Anyway, what could you say to a man who has just come in your mouth? This had been so raw an encounter, devoid of anything except the basic drive for orgasm. She was almost ashamed, stamping firmly on the tiny glimmer of self-satisfaction that warmed her. He had wanted her. OK, so it was purely the male drive to find an orifice and relieve the pressure in his balls. Yet, it had happened and he was a fine stud. He'd have no difficulty in finding an accommodating pussy. Was he anything more than an opportunist who had accepted what titbits life threw his way?

He bent to pick up his tools and backed away towards the door. The silence was almost deafening, but if she tried hard she could hear birdsong from outside the window. Her clothing was adjusted again, and she looked normal. Had anyone walked in they'd never have guessed what she'd been doing a few moments ago, but she was reminded by the odour of fresh come that wetted her hair.

'I'll see you on your way,' Felan said abruptly. 'Can't leave you here. Feel sort of responsible for the place.'

It was almost an insult. 'Still think I'm an intruder?' she said, bristling.

'I don't know what you are, apart from someone who gives bloody good head,' he answered with an impish lift of an eyebrow.

'Thanks a bunch!' she returned.

'Don't thank me. In my job I never know what's turning up next. That's the fun part.'

He was mocking her. Or was he? Did he often pick up women and have casual sex with them? The idea revolted her. She stalked to the door, saying icily, 'Don't think you're Mr Perfect. I've had better shags.'

His smile widened, even white teeth flashing against the darkness of his beard. 'I'm kidding. Don't have a heart attack.'

'I don't want to discuss it with you. I'm out of here,' she retorted, and plunged into the corridor.

He was behind her. She could sense rather than see him, feeling their isolation, trapped by the intimacy they had shared, be it never so briefly. The touching of bodies for a fraction of time in the midst of a cruel, uncaring world. A warmth, a flash of unity so that one didn't feel so alone. They reached the Great Hall and went towards the front door.

She wanted to say, 'Don't bother. I've got a key. This is my house,' but she didn't, waiting while he unlocked it and then descending the steps.

She didn't pause when he said, 'Can I drop you anywhere? My van's round the back.'

'No, thank you. I left my car in the lane.'

'Fine. I'll be off then,' he said, staring at her uncertainly.

She was glad to see that she'd rattled him and didn't bother to reply, turning on her heel and marching off down the drive.

* * *

'So, Ashley, what's been happening while I've been away?' John Dempsey went into the attack before the arrival of the first course. He believed in grabbing the day by the throat before it grabbed him. He fixed the man sitting opposite him with a gimlet stare, giving off an aura of arrogance and power as he added, 'Have you kicked that wife of yours into line yet?'

He was large and rugged, with iron-grey hair cut short about his bullet-shaped head and a face tanned by wind and weather, even more so as he had just returned from a regatta in Florida. Prominent businessman though he might be, his first love was striding the deck of his yacht, and he and Ashley were having lunch in the restaurant of the Westcombe Sailing Club. He patronised it whenever he could as he had invested a large sum of money in it.

Ashley cast him a reproachful look and fiddled with a pellet of bread on his side plate. He was slender and well dressed. His features were clean-cut and he was handsome in a refined way. He carried his forty-seven years well and kept himself in trim, a fine sailor and John's rival for trophies. John respected him for this and for his acumen, and used his computer company to help run his own complex business interests, but he couldn't do other than despise him for the way he had mishandled Cheryl. The man was an idiot to have let her find out about his dalliance with that tart Yvonne, who cuckolded the commodore on every possible occasion. Why, John had fucked her himself. In a way, she was to the sailing club what a common slag was to Westcombe's local lads – the town bike.

Seated at the damask-covered table near the window with its view of the sparkling bay, he could feel his cock expanding as he thought about that lush, big-bosomed woman with her penchant for kinky sex. He put financial deals first, these thrilled him most, but a close second were women – in most shapes, sizes and forms – and he was rich enough to afford the best. He loved their soft skins, their tits, their moans and sighs as he rogered

58

them, their abundant hair and capricious ways, and the sheer animal exuberance of them. He had wanted Cheryl and made his feelings plain, but the bitch had turned all prissy on him and had even told him to Foxtrot Oscar! He had never forgiven her the affront to his manhood, his status and position in the community. Didn't she realise that he would be Westcombe's mayor one day?

'Cheryl has gone,' he heard Ashley saying. 'Didn't you know that we're divorced?'

'What?' John sat up and, in so doing, rested one hand between his legs, having a quick feel of his prick. Cheryl was free? Probably missing being shafted. That's where I come in, he thought, but he said aloud, 'I knew you'd had a monumental row when she found you humping Yvonne, but then I went to the States and have missed out on the rest of it. I've been gone nearly a year, you know. Had to play it sweet with Raymond Golding, the Texas oil baron. Got the deal I wanted, but one of the stipulations was that I find him a property over here. He's looking for his roots; has some connection with the Pilgrim Fathers, or so he thinks. I've St Jude's in mind. I can buy it from the LEA for a pittance and sell it to old man Golding for a bomb. What about it? Is it still on the estate agent's books? I imagine it will be as no one would surely want to take on such a heap, unless they were stinking rich or had a screw loose.'

Ashley's face had turned pasty. He didn't even brighten when the toffee-haired, busty waitress sallied over with the starters and set them down. 'Thank you, my dear,' John leered, and patted her bottom. He had left explicit instructions that the sailing club staff should be comely.

He started to tuck in, white napkin spread over his bespoke tailored suit. Expensive clothes added to his confidence. He had his garments made in Savile Row and his shirts individually designed. No of-the-peg clobber for him. His shoes were Italian, his sailing gear obtained from the best sports shops. America had been something of a disappointment, with its lack of taste and attention to detail when it came to sartorial matters. That and its in-your-face women.

Then Ashley laid down his fork and, looking as if he wished the floor would open and swallow him up, he faltered, 'St Jude's has been sold.'

Just for a second, John lost his aplomb. He gasped and a section of prawn dropped from between his lips. 'Sold?' he spluttered, reaching for his glass of wine. 'Sold? Who the hell to?'

'My ex-wife,' Ashley replied, and John could have sworn there was a nasty little 'up yours' gleam in his eye.

'Cheryl? I'm gob-smacked! How come?' John regained control. He rarely let anyone see his true feelings. This showed weakness and put one at a disadvantage.

Yet underneath he was boiling with rage. That damned harpy! Bloody feminist who'd told him to fuck off! She'd had the fucking nerve to pip him at the post. And he had seen himself making millions, going into partnership with Golding, letting him have St Jude's as an English home, but building a village complex of costly houses, a school and a supermarket on the land. He had even planned a golf course.

'She's done it with her friend, Laura Tilford, who is also divorced. They've pooled the money they both got out of their settlements. I understand that they plan to open a hotel. It was all above board.'

'But I told that idiot Moor to let me know if anyone put in an offer,' John said, as he imagined roasting the estate agent over a slow fire.

'You were in America. I expect he tried to get hold of you, but couldn't. They had the cash. He had his orders to follow. It had been on the books for a while. Dewhurst and Marshal were wanting rid of it.'

'Don't make excuses for him, Ashley. I could go and see her, I suppose. Offer her more than she paid to get out.'

'She won't do it,' Ashley said, shaking his head. 'She's become damned unreasonable and won't have anything to do with me. Her bloody old crone of a mother is behind it all, I'm convinced.'

'You lost control of her, man. A woman like that needs showing who is master.' As John spoke, his cock jumped. He longed to have Cheryl tied up and at his mercy.

Last time he'd seen her she was a tad too plump for current fashion, but this hadn't bothered him. In his way of thinking size didn't matter, or shape or even beauty. It was the sexual energy that a woman gave off that intrigued him, and Cheryl had this in abundance. She generated warmth and the promise of fulfilment, with her ample breasts and rounded arse. Thinking of those globes of flesh very nearly caused him to spunk in his silk boxer shorts. He quickly diverted his thoughts to Moor, and what he intended to do to him – public humiliation wouldn't be enough.

The honey-blonde beauty brought across the main course: two fine fillet steaks and all the trimmings. The steward who managed the restaurant had reported in earlier, telling John that the club had scored points in a gourmet magazine and was getting itself a reputation for excellence. This was due to a newly appointed chef, a Londoner called Eddie who, in the steward's opinion, was good enough to have his own show on TV.

'Don't tell him,' John had advised. 'If he's that good, we don't want to lose him.'

He was irritated by the way Ashley picked at his food. He whaled in, as he always did when indulging his appetites, be they for food, alcohol or sex. He'd admired the expansive lifestyle of his American colleagues. Big steaks, a big country, roads to dream of when you had a fast motor under your hands, and that obsession for making money that drove them to have business break-fasts at seven-thirty in the morning. Anything went there, provided you didn't upset the Bible Belt, and this gave you plenty of scope.

'I ate buffalo out West,' he said, after spearing a piece of beef on the tines of his fork and then transferring it to his full-lipped, sensual mouth. 'And alligator in New Orleans. You ever been there, Ashley?'

'No.' Ashley shook his head and his appetite seemed to have gone. 'I've never been a great one for travel.'

'You should. It broadens the mind,' John pontificated. 'Maybe you'd have kept your woman interested if you'd been more adventurous.'

'I think not.'

'Didn't she like the old rumpy-pumpy?' John knew he could probe. Ashley wouldn't protest. He'd be feeling too guilty because Cheryl had frustrated John's plans. No one in that tight-knit circle who ran Westcombe liked to upset John. It wasn't wise. He had too much influence.

Jesus Christ! His hard-on was beginning to ache. That blonde bimbo was watching him from her place against the wall where she was ready to attend to the diners' needs. She was dressed in a short black skirt and blouse, with a frilly apron fastened round the waist. She had a fine pair of legs, with bulging calves, and her little high-heeled shoes set them off a treat. He'd noticed that, when she walked, her arse rolled. He'd like to stick his dick right up there.

John believed in old-fashioned values. He'd taken his pleasure with the lower orders since he was fourteen, the indulged son of a self-made man who'd sent him to public school and university, but John had never hesitated to pull rank when it came to seducing working girls. They were easier meat than upper-class ones, who expected commitment and possibly marriage. Heaven forfend! He had married, of course, twenty years ago, and Emily was meek, brow-beaten and well trained, producing the heir he demanded and two daughters, then immersing herself in charity work and the running of the sailing club's Ladies' Committee. She would make an ideal first lady.

'Cheryl was interested in sex before she had the children,' Ashley said, pulling John back from his absorption with his cock. 'Then she sort of went off it. That's why I fucked Yvonne, I suppose. And now it's transpired that Cheryl's involved with Laura.'

This was very nearly enough to send John over the edge. 'Are you saying they're lesbians?' he said.

'Well, no . . . I don't think so. There's never been any suggestion . . .' Ashley floundered.

'Bet a pound to a penny they are,' John rejoined, and he could feel the sweat breaking out in his armpits, making dark arcs in his blue designer shirt.

Oh, that tantalising dream of a couple of women frolicking in bed! He'd watch them at it, see them sucking each other's nipples and rubbing their mounds together, and he'd be invited to join them. By God, he'd show them what they were missing! Get a load of this, girls, he'd cry, and waggle his huge tool at them. Cheryl and Laura. He vaguely recalled that mousy little thing, but she had now assumed the glamour of a disciple of Sapphic sex. He winked across at the waitress. She dropped her eyes demurely but a knowing smile hovered around her red, Cupid's Bow lips.

'I don't know anything about their private lives,' Ashley said, and pushed his plate away.

They had dessert, and this was followed by brandy and cigars. 'I shan't let it rest,' John said, staring at him with rapier-sharp eyes.

'What?' Ashley said, choking a little on the rich fumes of Havana's best.

'St Jude's,' John went on, the blue smoke hanging between them like a mist.

'I don't see what you can do,' Ashley said feebly, devoid of sensible comments in the face of this clever, domineering man. 'The sale has gone through. The builders are moving in soon, so I hear, and renovations are in hand. She'll make a success of it, I'm sure. She's that kind of woman.'

'And her dyke pal, Laura?' John narrowed his eyes speculatively.

'I don't know her very well. They've been friends for

yonks, but I think you're barking up the wrong tree. I don't see them as lesbians.'

'Don't want to, perhaps. It poses too much of a threat to think that she might prefer pussy to having you shove your cock in her minge.' John was slightly drunk, and the fundamental coarseness that couldn't be erased by a couple of generations of wealth came to the surface. Underneath it all he was vulgar. 'I intend to do something about Cheryl. She's not keeping the bloody property,' he added nastily.

'Good luck to you. I wouldn't want to take her on, not as she is today,' Ashley said. He then put aside his napkin and prepared to leave.

When he had gone, John waved a hand towards the waitress. She shimmied across, her breasts jiggling under the prim, high-necked blouse. 'In a moment, I'm going to the ladies' toilet,' he said, speaking low, his flinty eyes mesmerising her. 'You'll be there, waiting for me. Lock the door so no one else uses it. I'll tap three times and you'll let me in. D'you understand?'

'Yes, sir,' she said, and had the grace to blush.

This is the way to do it, he thought when, later, he had her pinned up against the washbasin in the stylish, sugar-and-spice decor of the club's female restroom. No ties. No complications. Just shoving it in and out.

The girl was willing, pushing her breasts towards his hands, her blouse unbuttoned, her white cotton bra thrust aside. Her skirt was up round her waist and her knickers were down. John could smell her cheap perfume and the whiff of the body spray she used under her arms. But above this and through it was the pungent odour of her sexual juices. She was aroused, hitching her bottom on the washbasin, spreading her legs with a fine display of black stockings and showing him all her treasures. Her hair was fair but her bush was dark, fringing the rose-pink wings that rolled back from her clit. John fingered it and she squealed. He rubbed harder and she came. He pushed his cock in deeper and she folded her legs round his waist, holding him fast as she sighed and convulsed.

He could feel her hot pussy gripping him tightly and his climax tore through him, jetting his spunk into the condom.

The last thing he saw before being engulfed was the mocking face of Ashley's ex-wife, jeering at him for losing St Jude's.

Chapter Four

*T*he builders' tenders had come in. The architect had forwarded them to Mark for consideration before a final decision was made. Among them was one from Boynton & Son.

'It's by far the most reasonable, and they've a solid reputation. Not cowboys,' opined Mark over coffee in Laura's flat. 'I know Huntley's in favour of them. I'd have preferred to have left the choice to him, but I know you want to be in on everything.'

'Hum, I'm not so sure,' Cheryl said, from the depths of an armchair. 'I've heard that Will Hewitt runs a tight ship. Why don't we suggest to Huntley that we give him a go?'

'Because his price is sky-high,' Mark explained, in his calm, reasonable way.

'What about this other? Here.' Cheryl shuffled about among the letters, extracting one and handing it to him.

Mark looked down his thin-bridged nose at it. 'Dobey and Co? Well, I've heard that they're about to go bust.'

'So that really narrows it down to Boynton,' Laura observed, wondering why Cheryl was so edgy. She'd been short-fused for several days now, but wouldn't say what was bugging her. Man trouble? Had she had a falling out with Mark? Laura wondered, but he seemed to be OK. Yet she was sure there was something amiss.

There was much too much going on for her to waste energy on the pros and cons of Cheryl's moods. Maybe it was nothing more than PMT. Laura was impatient for the refurbishment to start. This flat was all very well, but it was small and inconvenient. She could have taken something better but wanted to hang on to her money. St Jude's was like a mighty sponge, absorbing cash by the ton. It was essential that it was completed quickly and start operating. She was already working on the spread for the *Westcombe Star*. She planned to have someone in to set up a website for the hotel, some earnest computer nerd who'd show her what to do. It had taken a while to shuck off Stuart's influence and become her own person, but she was getting there.

He hadn't raised much protest when she told him that she knew about his affair. He'd admitted that it had been going on for ages. He'd even apologised for marrying her in the first place, but had done it to try and convince himself and everyone else that he wasn't homosexual. He'd kept up the pretence for years, but it had become more and more difficult. The Internet chat rooms had proved a godsend. Now he could contact others with a similar sexuality. He begged her to understand and forgive him.

She struggled to be fair, read up about gays of both sexes and forced herself to rationalise her feelings. She could understand him now, but as for forgiveness? It was early days yet. When I fall in love, she promised herself, when the sun shines on my parade again, then I'll be able to forgive if not necessarily forget. Her children had proved much more liberal-minded. She'd only spoken to them by phone. Harry was still in some far distant reaches of the Himalayas, and Vicky queen of the campus in Maryland. Fat lot of comfort they've turned out to be, she thought, they didn't seem concerned because their father was on the wrong bus. They wished her well in her hotel venture but were deep into their own agendas, and this is how it should be, Laura concluded. They don't owe me a thing.

'So, what d'you want me to do?' Mark's voice interrupted her thoughts.

'Why don't we meet them all?' Laura suggested into the protracted silence that followed. Cheryl seemed unable or unwilling to make any worthwhile contribution.

'That seems a colossal waste of time,' Mark said, frowning slightly. 'After all, we have the estimates and Huntley's recommendation, and should be able to decide from this.'

'You know Boynton, I take it?' Cheryl asked crisply.

'Yes. I know Felan Boynton. I've had clients who have employed him and found him easy to get on with, honest, quick and trustworthy.'

'Oh, saintly builder! Someone fetch him a halo, quick!'

Laura was surprised by the vehemence in Cheryl's tone, then further perplexed when, as if calling the meeting to a close, she gathered up her belongs and got to her feet. She glared at Mark and headed for the door.

'So that's it, is it? We're agreed on Boynton?' he called after her.

'Do what the hell you like. It's your shout,' she returned acidly, without turning round.

'On the contrary. You're the one paying the bills,' he retorted, and it was the first time ever that Laura had seen him ruffled.

'And me,' she put in timidly.

'And Laura,' he added loudly to Cheryl's retreating back.

'I really don't care,' Cheryl said, pausing with her hand on the doorknob. 'The sooner the place is finished, the better I'll be pleased.' And she swept out.

Laura and Mark exchanged a glance and he shrugged, saying, 'All right. Are you in agreement?'

'Yes, and so will she be when she's calmed down. I can't think what's rattled her cage.'

When he had gone, Laura prepared for a shopping trip. Cheryl had left her to organise staff for the hotel, and sort out costumes and decor for the secret sexual extravaganzas and find harlots willing to participate. Either gender would do, or even ones that weren't quite sure. It was no mean feat, but she was better with people than Cheryl. Worried about where to start, she had decided to go to London and tackle Soho, pornography's heartland. She'd seen a shop called Don't Be Shy on a late-night Channel 5 programme. It was said to be a place where women could browse among naughty underwear and sex aids without being hassled or embarrassed. Men weren't allowed to enter its select precincts unless accompanied by a female.

What am I doing here? Laura asked herself, stuck in a traffic jam when she entered the City via Richmond. This isn't me, is it? Stuart always drove if we visited London. Remember taking the children to the Tower, and the Natural History Museum? And all the time he was living a lie, wanting to dash off to places where he could cruise for gay lovers. He'd be the active one, she supposed, not passive. What was it they called it in gay parlance? The top. That was it.

An impatient hooting reminded her to drive on. She wished she'd come by train, though they were unreliable. She wished she'd taken a coach, but this took hours. She wished that she could turn back the clock and find her marriage stable after all, not this chaotic mess.

Greatly daring, for this too was a one-off, she had phoned and booked into the Dickens Hotel for the night. Now she left her car in its allotted parking space and took a bus from Knightsbridge to Soho. The streets were crowded with shoppers and tourists and sightseers. There was a large percentage of foreigners. London had changed since she was there last. Fashions had changed too, and she felt overdressed in her cotton trousers and loose jacket. The men wore jeans and T-shirts, their hair shaved like inmates of Alcatraz. It was a style she deplored, making them look hard which, presumably, was the effect they were after. They favoured piercing –

eyebrows, lips and noses. She dreaded to think what went on under their clothes.

Then there were the executive types in expensive, lightweight suits, casually cut for the warm weather. They too favoured crop-cuts, or maybe curtains with a fringe parted in the middle and drooping over their foreheads. The younger element among the women were skimpily dressed; short skirts, camisole tops with their bra straps showing, wedge-heeled shoes, chunky jewellery. Their make-up was exaggerated, their hair tousled and streaked or pinned high with sparkling slides. They were bold. They were feisty. They believed in girl power. Everyone carried a mobile phone. Many of them were talking into them as they stalked the pavements.

I'm out of date, Laura mourned, even now when I've tried to tart myself up. You can't stop the march of time. I'm supposed to be in my prime. Someone said, life begins at forty. So here goes, and she stepped out boldly, finding Wardour Street and Compton Street and all the little alleys that branched off each side. It was there that she located Don't Be Shy. It had a tiny frontage with one bow window, flowers in wooden tubs and an old-fashioned door with a bell that tinkled as she entered.

Oh dear, Laura thought, listening to it. There's no retreat now.

But far from being besieged by an assistant demanding to help, no one bothered her. There were two other women browsing among the dazzling array of goods, and another seated behind a counter. She had flaming red hair, big breasts and shapely legs, and was wearing a halter-necked see-through top and skirt with the minimum of lingerie underneath. She gave Laura a friendly smile, then continued thumbing through a catalogue with a flash of long, purple-lacquered nails.

Laura was overwhelmed. There was so much to look at, such a range of outlandish clothing, the walls festooned with black leather bustiers and miniskirts, red PVC catsuits, split-crotch panties, peephole bras and fancy suspender belts. There were moulded rubber corsets with tight lacing, and silk stockings, some plain, others fishnet, and shoes of all description – courts, wedges, sling-backs and thigh-high boots with spurs and buckled straps. All had stilt heels. Alongside this cornucopia of silk and leather bliss hung harnesses and bondage trappings. Laura could only guess their purpose. Not only these, but also muzzles and reins and snaffles and bits. A glass-fronted cabinet contained alarming implements – whips and canes, tawse and paddles, gags, nipple clamps and blindfolds.

She knew she was goggling but couldn't help herself. It was as if she had come across a sadist's private stash. Her pussy began to spasm and, when she went over to examine the array of dildoes, the longing to have one buried within her was almost uncontrollable. She'd never used one, but she had been thinking about it. Now she was spoiled for choice.

'They don't have to look like cocks to do the job,' said a voice at her elbow, and she spun round and found herself gazing into the redhead's amber-coloured eyes.

'Don't they?' she faltered, feeling herself blushing.

'Oh no. We specialise in all types. What are you looking for? A vibrator or a dildo? A vibrator just vibrates, and a dildo doesn't. Both can be used for penetration or on the clitoris, or made into a strap-on.'

'I see,' Laura gulped, not fully understanding and too embarrassed to ask for enlightenment.

'A plug-in vibrator is excellent. You don't keep running out of batteries, but if you're going to use it internally then it must be safe. My favourite is this one,' said the redhead, and picked up a pink wand with a top like a dish-mop. She switched it on and the head rotated. 'Then there's the Tickler,' she continued, and produced an object that looked like a tongue made of red jelly. At the flick of a button, the tongue moved from side to side or up and down.

Laura was mesmerised. How would it feel to have that obscene thing palpating her clit? She was shocked, but her pussy ached and her knickers were damp.

71

'How weird,' she managed to stammer.

'Never tried one? I can assure you, this is the best for cunnilingus. Better than men – it doesn't get tired and its jaw doesn't ache and it isn't thinking about its own climax.' She held out her hand and added, 'My name's Bronwen – Bronwen Davis.'

'I'm Laura Tilford.' It might be a foolhardy move, but curiosity and lust overcame Laura's wariness about giving her identity away.

'You don't have to worry about being here,' Bronwen assured her. 'We cater especially for women who aren't familiar with toys. Ask any questions you like. Handle the vibrators. I test new additions to the range myself. Want to make sure they're buzzing beautifully. Care to try them for sound? I expect you're wondering if they're dead noisy, like someone's using a pneumatic drill, and are you going to have to switch on the vacuum cleaner to disguise it.'

'You own the shop?' Laura was surprised by the firm handshake, and reduced to blancmange inside by the feel of that smooth, warm palm clasping hers. She was glad to change the subject, but couldn't stop staring at the Tickler, the dildoes and the vibrators.

'I'm the manageress.' Bronwen shot her a sharp, golden stare. 'Are there any clothes you want to try on? We have a changing room over there.' She looked across to where a girl with a Mohican crest and tribal face-paint was serving a customer. 'Kat, keep an eye on things out here. I'm helping this lady.'

'OK, Bron,' the girl answered.

'Oh, I don't know . . . I came in to look . . . I need to find out, you see . . .' Laura stammered.

Bronwen smiled and said, 'Of course. I understand. What size are you? A twelve?' And she leafed through the stands, hauling forth this outfit and that. 'This is a popular number. We call it the Boudicca. It'll make you feel like a gladiator.'

Laura wasn't quite sure if this was what she wanted to feel like, but then she remembered the call of duty and her purpose for being there. She might as well go the whole hog. 'All right,' she said, and followed Bronwen into an alcove.

It was small, with a full-length mirror at the back. Rings jingled on a pole as Bronwen drew the curtain across. Laura's heart thumped, drowning out the sounds of the shop and even her own thoughts. Bronwen's perfume was pungent, a mixture of jasmine and roses and her own personal body scent. Brushing close to her, Browen reached for the coat-hook, hanging up a crotch-strap and a thick smooth collar studded with silver bullets.

'Undress,' she said, so matter-of-factly that Laura obeyed her.

'Shall I keep my panties on?' she asked nervously when every other item had been discarded. 'I mean . . . I don't want to mark the clothes.'

'With pussy juice? Are you that aroused?' Bronwen said, smiling widely. She bent with smooth agility and felt between Laura's legs. 'Ah, yes. You're very wet,' she went on, and Laura was stunned by the erotic feelings surging through her at the touch of that slim, purple-taloned hand.

One finger eased aside the pantie leg and touched Laura's sparse, brown bush. Each individual hair sent shock waves to her clit. Laura stood still, holding her body stiff, fighting this rush of sensation that was alien to anything she had had before. She'd never felt sexy with a woman. Not at puberty, or even with her best of friends. It hadn't been part of the equation. She desired men, didn't she? Real men with big todgers. Men who would make her feel frail and feminine, adored and revered. The fictional heroes of her imagination, the mainstay of romance.

Bronwen withdrew her hand and said, 'Don't worry about it. This costume has no crotch to it anyway.' And she helped Laura into a gold-leather and chain bodysuit with a tiny skirt that ended just above her thighs.

It was snug fitting and jacked her breasts high, the

nipples jutting over the top. Bronwen knelled and had her slip out of her sandals and into a pair of matching boots, lacing them at the outer sides. Laura almost lost her balance on the six–inch heels. She stared at herself, amazed by her reflection. She looked raunchy, barbaric, totally unlike Laura Tilford, mother and ex-wife.

The gold leather was laced tight, and the restriction pulled in her waist and exaggerated her breasts and hips. It drew the eye to the fuzz on her mound, and the dark cleft that disappeared into the mystery beneath. The boots came up mid-thigh and they too seemed to attract attention to her pussy. The high heels added to her length of leg, making her feel as tall and graceful as a man-nequin about to pace the catwalk.

This was heady stuff, refuelling ambitions that she had thought were well past their sell-by date – the dream of being a model, an actress, a movie star. But now with a flash of insight, she saw that St Jude's would allow her to play-act. It was the ideal place for making fantasies come true. Not only for the clients she hoped to attract with clever advertising, but for her and Cheryl as well. Life begins at forty? There was never a truer word.

'It suits you,' Bronwen complimented, and produced a wig. It was everything Laura had ever wanted, envying those who Nature had blessed with thick, curly hair. 'Here. Let me,' Bronwen offered, and swept back Laura's own straight, highlighted locks, then carefully settled the wig in place. A tweak here and there, and Laura was transformed. It was miraculous. The glorious mane fell almost to her waist in a cascade of layered ringlets.

'Gosh,' she murmured, her face framed by curls. She was hardly recognisable and it affected her whole stance. She felt suddenly at ease in the spiky heels, bracing her legs, never mind that her bush was on display. She drew in her ribs and lifted her breasts high. She was beautiful!

Bronwen looked pleased with her handiwork. 'It never ceases to amaze me,' she said. 'The change in women, I mean. Get them in costume, do their make-up, supply them with a range of wigs and they take on a new identity.'

'I can't believe it.' Laura knew there was a pleased smile tugging at her lips, but she couldn't stop it. 'I thought I was too old.'

'Never,' Bronwen exclaimed stoutly. 'You've a lovely figure. Are you ready to try some of my other treats?' and she held out the vibrating tongue teaser.

'I don't know . . .' Laura faltered, but Bronwen was on her knees in front of her and the tickler was wagging. The temptation to lift her pubis towards its red tip was too enticing to resist. Laura cried out as it contacted her swollen clit.

'Don't worry. Just enjoy,' Bronwen murmured, holding Laura's lips apart with her free hand. 'Play with your nipples. Triple the pleasure.'

Laura lifted her breasts in both hands, feeling the leather, the underwiring of the cups, and the upper swell that exposed her brown nipples. Her thumbs revolved on them. The feeling intensified that churning in her belly. The mock tongue lapped at her, and Bronwen held it in place, knowing the most responsive spots. It licked each side of Laura's bud, then traced the stem back to where it spread out and joined that special band of muscles deep within her sex.

'Ah . . . oh,' Laura groaned, and was close to the finishing line, her orgasm gaining momentum.

She started to scream, forgetting that there might be people in the shop. She imagined herself in a leather harness, trapped within it, and it was as if those straps were reins controlling her sexual response. She mentally let them out, and came violently against that probing, artificial tongue. She tensed, arched, then relaxed, drifting, her pussy convulsing round the three fingers that Bronwen had inserted deep inside her.

'Good, eh?' she said, smiling at Laura as she rose to her feet, her miniskirt slipping down an inch, covering her black satin crotch. 'Now I'm wet too.'

Laura leaned against the wall, lost in a sensuous haze.

75

Bronwen's words made her feel guilty. 'You want to climax?' she said, and found herself longing to touch her intimately.

Bronwen chuckled. 'I'm hot, but then I usually am. But I'm quite used to giving pleasure and not necessarily getting it. I was a call-girl and whore before working here. Even now I turn a trick or two.'

Laura came back to earth with a bump. 'You've been on the game?' she asked.

'Yes. Why? Does it fascinate you?' Bronwen drawled, seated cross-legged on the bench and running her hands down her perfect thighs. 'If you've got it then flaunt it, I always say. I needed the money. Still do. Got a kid at boarding school and the fees are crippling.'

'No, it's just . . . well, I'm looking for an experienced person to help me run a brothel,' Laura blurted out, wrestling with the idea of this glamorous woman being a mother.

It was Bronwen's turn to look surprised. 'You're kidding me.'

'No. I'm serious. Why?'

'You don't quite cut it as a whorehouse madam.'

'I'm not. Leastways, not till now.'

'You'd better tell me all about it. Get dressed and we'll go into the office. Kat can bring us coffee,' said Bronwen decisively.

The upshot was that Laura told her everything, and it seemed so right to be sitting there surrounded by all the paraphernalia of porn and discussing the possibility of opening a house of ill-fame under the guise of a respectable hotel.

'I think it's bloody great,' Bronwen enthused, swivelling in the leather chair in front of the computer desk. 'I could manage it standing on my head. Imagine the scenarios. The Naughty Nineties. Arabian Nights. Dominatrix and slaves. Submissives and masters. Bad girls being spanked and rude boys flogged. I love it! We'd have Roman orgies, of course. Victorian stays and open-crotch drawers, harem outfits, Greek tunics and gilded

76

armour. We'll need feather boas, slinky silk purple knickers, and ones in pussy pink, hot red and not-so-pure white. And that's only for starters. There'll have to be leather caps, leather restraints, clips for tits and pussy lips, large-sized basques and gear for men who want to wear women's clothes. Not forgetting the floggers and rods for CP.'

'CP? What's that?'

'Corporal punishment. Wow, you'll be learning a new language,' commented Bronwen, amber eyes dancing.

'So I shall. That's wonderful. You're an inspiration,' Laura breathed, perched on a corner of the table where she could watch Bronwen's animated face and enjoy the movement of her large breasts under the diaphanous bodice. Her clit tingled from the recently enjoyed orgasm, and she hungered greedily for more. Then she added, 'But you can't get involved. You work here.'

Bronwen cast her a shrewd glance. 'I might be persuaded to leave, if the offer was generous. I must say, a spell in the country would be refreshing.'

'I don't know a thing about you,' Laura said, regretting her impulse. 'Anyway, I'd have to talk it over with my partner.'

'Fine. I'm not about to rip you off. Here's where I live and my telephone number. It's kosher. This isn't going to be an immediate move, is it?'

'No. There's lots to do at St Jude's. I don't think we'll be opening till autumn.'

'What if I come round and see you tonight? I'll bring a colleague. Give me the name of the hotel where you're staying.'

'What d'you reckon, Luke?' Bronwen said, straddling his lap, facing him. He lounged in the computer chair. His legs were spread, his zipper open and his cock buried in her depths.

'Sounds like you're bonkers,' he said unsteadily as she moved up, letting him almost slip away, then quickly bouncing down till her pussy sucked him in and her clit

77

rubbed against his cock-root 'Why leave a cushy number like this? I like living in the city. Who needs green fields and farmers . . .?'

'And the sea,' Bronwen reminded, angling her hand between their bodies and rubbing her bud briskly. 'London's OK, but let's face it, we're never going to make much in this dump. If it was ours, maybe, but there's no chance of that unless we win the Lottery.'

She knew he'd agree to whatever she wanted, putty in her hands when it came to the crunch. Her slave? Sometimes. But when the mood took her, she became his. He knew the score, swung both ways and would be invaluable in Laura's bordello. Women grew wet at the sight of him. Men of a certain persuasion lusted after his slim-hipped, boyish, swarthy looks. He had the capacity to be all things to all persons. As for herself, Bronwen supposed that she loved him in her own fashion but would never give herself wholeheartedly to anyone. She always kept a little piece back. That way it was possible to avoid being hurt.

They lived together, and whereas she felt nothing for her punters, simply performing a service as professionally as she was able, taking pride in it, when she was with Luke she burned up with passion. His tight-muscled buttocks fitted her palms so neatly. The hollows in his flanks were a delight to view. He smelled right, of fresh young sweat and expensive body spray. Luke never stinted himself when it came to spending on luxuries. He looked on them as necessities. Clothes, hair stylists, dental cosmetic treatment; he'd go without food rather than skimp on these. And Bronwen understood. His body was his stock-in-trade, exactly like hers. And his greatest asset of all? He was extraordinarily well hung.

Sometimes she said to him, half joking, half serious, 'Hey, donkey dick! We could make more money selling you to porn producers.'

She wasn't jealous when he went with others. Just as long as it was a sexual, monetary exchange, not emotional. They saved this for each other, sharing their hopes and dreams, looking after one another, caring friends as well as lovers. It was a mean old rat-race out there, and unity helped them to survive it.

She lowered her face to his and looked into his brown eyes. He had unfairly long, curling, sooty lashes. She ran her tongue over his lips, first the corners, then the slightly pouting middle section, and kissed him, penetrating his mouth, just as his iron-hard cock was plumbing the depths of her lower one. He tasted of peppermint. And her arousal rose to an even higher level. Using her arms, she levered herself into position, ramming down hard. Even so, when she removed her thumb she couldn't quite obtain the friction she needed on her clit.

Luke understood. He inserted a hand under her, found her pleasure nodule, and rubbed it. Bronwen braced herself on one arm and fingered her breasts through the flimsy top, feeling the heat radiating from them. He thrust upwards, but he didn't stop massaging her button and she could feel her climax rising to a peak. It broke, pouring over her in giant waves of bliss. Luke cried out and his upward jerks increased. She felt him coming inside her and she continued to ride him as the last contractions shivered through her loins. She fell forward, arms round his neck, her face buried in his night-dark hair.

'That was wicked, babes,' he murmured, his breath tickling her ear.

She was unwilling to return to everyday problems, but it had to be done. Sitting up, she swung a leg over his lap and got to her feet. 'So, are you up for this?' she asked, hands to her hair, pushing the tumbling curls in place.

Luke put his deflated member away, tucked in his shirt and zipped his flies. He grinned at her. 'OK. If that's what you want.'

'I haven't made up my mind yet, but I have arranged to meet Laura early evening. You come too, and we'll suss it out.'

'Whatever,' he said, and they went back to the shop.

79

It bustled with late-afternoon shoppers, and Bronwen watched him as he switched on the charm. He had the knack of making the ladies feel as easy with him as the female assistants. If he puts this into practice when he meets Laura then we're home and dry, she thought.

I could get used to this, even grow to like it, Laura mused as she went up to the reception desk, signed in and collected her key. A spruce, uniformed pageboy was there to carry her bag, and they were whisked aloft in the elevator to the third floor where he conducted her to her room. She tipped him, probably too generously, but she didn't want to appear mean.

A sense of adventure tingled through her, and a feeling of achievement. She'd done it. Driven through London and found Don't Be Shy, had even had a sexual experience with the manageress. She could hardly credit it, but the evidence was there every time she moved – the smell of her juices wafting from between her legs. And now she'd stalked into the hotel as if it was an everyday occurrence and was installed in one of its expensive rooms, not *the* most expensive, but certainly pricey. Such extravagance would have alarmed her not long ago. She and Stuart had been comfortably off, but she'd done even better since they'd gone their separate ways.

She hadn't been too star-struck to look over the place with a professional eye, and would have liked to have seen the kitchens and other bedrooms, including the bridal suite. She intended to take notes, but just for now it was impossible to concentrate on anything so mundane. All she could think of was Bronwen and her promise to call.

She unpacked her overnight bag and checked the room out. It had a double bed, a television, the phone, a small fridge containing miniature bottles of spirits and a carton of milk. The unit nearby housed a kettle, a coffee-maker, sachets of tea (herbal and Indian), drinking chocolate, sugar and little tubs of cream. The writing desk was equipped with notepaper bearing the hotel's logo, and there was a directory of things to see and do in the City. The drawer of the bedside table contained the obligatory Bible. A built-in wardrobe with a mirror frontage was positioned opposite the bathroom. This had a shower stall and bidet as well as the usual facilities.

We must do the same at St Jude's, she decided. There are bound to be fitters who specialise in this sort of thing. I really should phone Cheryl. But for some inexplicable reason, she was reluctant to speak to her yet. Her mind and body were still reeling. She needed to compartmentalise her feelings about Bronwen, and come to terms with the turn her sexuality had taken. She was hungry too, having eaten nothing except a service station bun since leaving Westcombe. She glanced at the hotel tariff. Too early for dinner but not too late for tea. She headed for the restaurant.

A woman alone still had the power to turn heads, even in this day and age, she discovered. She knew that she looked attractive, and her recent encounter had heightened her colour and put a sparkle in her eyes. She found a table and ordered a toasted cheese sandwich, iced fancies and a pot of tea. The hum of light conversation around her, the conservative decor and refined ambience had a soothing effect. She sipped her tea from a fine bone china cup and reflected on her situation. Bronwen's number was in her address book. All she had to do was take out her mobile and ring her, cancelling their arrangement. She could say she had spoken to Cheryl and they'd decided not to take up her offer.

But something inside her was reluctant to lose contact with the strong, confident hooker. They needed someone like her most desperately if they were to carry out their plans for St Jude's. Where else might they find such a knowledgeable treasure? The more she pondered on it, the more convinced she became that this was the right course.

'Is everything to your liking, madam?' asked the waiter who had served her.

It was as if scales had been taken from her eyes and

everywhere she looked it was to see personable men. He was of medium height and lean build, and had a fascinating accent, Greek probably, or Italian. There was a decided twinkle in his eyes as he looked at her and, though deferential, she was aware that he was flirting with her. Oh, Bronwen, she thought, scandalised but happy, what have you done to me?

'Yes, thank you,' she answered, glancing up at him. 'Everything is fine.'

'Is there anything else I can get you, madam?' he said and, though his question was innocent enough, she sensed hidden undertones that made her cheeks burn.

'Not at the moment, thank you,' she answered, glad to find that her voice was steady.

'You can always ring for service from your room,' he reminded meaningfully.

'Thank you,' she said again, wondering if he would know if she rang through and make sure that he was the one to deliver.

Gorgeous young foreigner, with your neat bum and promising cock bulge, do I want you in my room? she asked herself. I know what the end result would be and I'm not sure if I'm ready for this yet. Is it in my nature to toss-off strangers? Or have them bring me to orgasm? I've already done it once today. My God, what's got into me?

He went away, and she glanced at her watch. It was five o'clock, and if she hurried she could take a shower and change before Bronwen arrived. She had promised to bring a friend. Laura speculated about this as she showered, washed her hair and then looked out clean underwear, a skirt and T-shirt. She was disappointed by her image in the mirror, missing the brazen hussy of the changing room. Plain Laura Tilford didn't please her any more.

She had a plastic bag containing the Boadicia costume she'd purchased, along with the boots and the wild wig. She didn't like to dwell on what she'd paid for them or even if she'd ever wear them again. I can put it down to business expenses, she thought. Research, if you like. At least I shall be able to show Cheryl as an example of the items we require.

She jumped when the intercom beeped. 'Mrs Tilford, there's a Miss Davis in reception. She says you're expecting her,' said the disembodied voice of the desk clerk.

'Ask her to come up,' Laura answered with what she hoped was admirable aplomb.

She put down the receiver and dithered, making an entirely unnecessary adjustment to her hair and dabbing powder on her nose. A squirt of perfume followed – one that she had paid over the odds for in the hotel foyer gift shop. It rocked the room. She sat on the dressing table stool, then tried the sofa by the opened window. The traffic had died to a steady rumble to which her ears had already become accustomed. It was too hot to keep the casement shut. English hotels never had got the hang of air-conditioning. She'd add this to her list. She searched through the brochure, trying to find out if there was a swimming pool. She couldn't track one down and made a mental note to ensure that the one at St Jude's was in working order. Essential for her own well-being, never mind the clientele.

Though on the alert, she jumped when the summons came. She went to the door and opened it. Bronwen was framed in the doorway and beside her was a young man with film-star looks – a dark young man who reminded Laura of the waiter, a lithe young man with the physique of a dancer.

'Hi there, this is Luke Dowling,' Bronwen said, stepping over the threshold. 'Luke, meet Laura.'

Formality over, she made for the chintz-covered couch, sprawled across it and lit a cigarette. Luke smiled at Laura and took her hand and planted a kiss on the back. Such an old-world gesture knocked her off kilter, and the down on her arms and legs rose at the touch of his firm, full lips. A very smooth operator indeed!

'Honoured to meet you, Laura,' he said, straightening up, and the warmth in his eyes made her feel special.

'Bronwen said you were lovely, but that was an understatement.'

Laura was bowled over, though a cynical side of her warned that he was just too perfect. She withdrew her hand and surreptitiously wiped it down her skirt. 'Bronwen has told you of my scheme,' she said, trying to sound like a prospective employer.

'Yes, indeed,' Luke replied, and he seemed nonplussed, as if thrown by her cool, expecting her to drool over him. But he still smiled at her and retained his dignity, even though he was sporting a massive hard-on under his chinos.

Laura speculated on what Bronwen had told him about her. Had she mentioned how she screamed when she climaxed? And did he guess that she had the potential to be insatiable, one orgasm not enough? 'Won't you sit down?' she asked, playing the hostess as she had done countless times when Stuart entertained business associates. 'Can I get you something to drink?' She had a mental flash of the contents of the fridge.

'D'you have a beer?'

'I think I saw a can or two,' she said and opened the door.

The light came on and the miniature bottles stood in a row. Beneath them were tins of lager.

'That'll do me,' Luke said.

'A gin and tonic, please,' said Bronwen.

Laura poured one for herself too, adding ice. Bronwen smiled encouragingly and said, 'Luke works with me. I've told him about St Jude's and he's interested. You could do with a male around the place. He'll organise bouncers and help to keep things flowing sweetly. But as I said earlier, we need to talk money.'

'Of course, but I've yet to put the idea to Cheryl . . . we own it jointly. She's given me the job of staffing it but will want to know the financial ins and outs.'

'Naturally. But you do realise that you'll have to be careful, don't you? I suppose you're aware that if two persons are selling sex under the same roof then the premises are regarded as a bawdy house, illegal and likely to be raided by the police?'

Laura gulped and said, 'No. I didn't know this.' Suddenly all her bright plans threatened to disappear down the pan.

'It's OK.' Bronwen patted her hand. 'We get round this one by turning it into an exclusive club that costs to join. We even have membership cards printed and open a bank account. That way, we avoid the actual handing over of cash, and the girls or guys are hired as entertainers. I suggest you open the club for a weekend here and there, not regularly, and concentrate on off-peak periods.'

'I see. Right. I'll tell Cheryl,' Laura agreed.

'Leave the arrangements to me, and I'll spread the word discreetly. Let me sort out the costumes and gear. It'll be worth your while as I can get it trade. You'll save a fortune on that alone. As for my choice of performers – maybe you've not had a strong enough example of what I can do. Luke and I will put that right, won't we, tiger?' Bronwen said, narrowing her eyes at him and easing her skirt above her pubis. She wasn't wearing knickers and her foxy bush was on display.

'I've brought you a present,' she continued, and hauled a package from her shoulder bag.

It contained a pair of shoes. They had a sexy strap round the ankle and several more around the toes, but were backless. Laura tried walking on the impossible heels, pacing the carpet and nearly falling off, till she got the hang of them. They were higher even than the gold leather boots.

'Thank you,' she managed to murmur.

'I shoved in a couple of other things too,' Bronwen said, and rummaged further, pulling out the bullet-studded collar Laura had seen in the changing room. Bronwen handed it to Luke who fastened it round her neck, buckling it snugly.

'Isn't that uncomfortable?' Laura asked, confused by the contented expression that crossed Bronwen's face, and the way she fell to her knees in front of him, while he clipped a lead to the collar and gave it a tug.

He hauled her up, using a stranglehold, and Laura twitched as she watched them performing this harsh charade. Luke pillaged Bronwen's mouth with the crude hunger of a barbarian. His hands were rough as he pushed down her shoulder straps and bared her breasts. In a short while she was nude, and he thrust her, belly-down, on the bed and tethered her wrists and ankles, using cords from her bag.

Laura couldn't move. Seeing Bronwen naked was enough. She wasn't used to viewing the body unclothed and was thrilled yet embarrassed by the large breasts and flat belly, the flaming pubes and creamy-white skin of the natural redhead. Whatever ritual was being enacted in the hotel room, there was no way she could prevent or interrupt it. Each move followed one upon the other as if choreographed. There was a kind of savage beauty in the way Luke stuffed a pillow under Bronwen's hips to raise her buttocks high, and then wound his belt round his hand for greater purchase before bringing it down across her rump.

Laura felt the blow as if it had struck her own hind-quarters. Pure imagination. In real life no one had ever struck her like that – but it was as if some ancient race memory stirred and she was catapulted back in time to a moment when a strong, powerful man had punished her and roused her and become her master. Hardly aware of her action, she reached down and grabbed her hungering crotch through her skirt.

She saw Luke's arm rise again, heard the whistle and the crack as leather hit tender flesh. Bronwen's arse cheeks bore crimson welts and she bucked on the bed and tugged at the restraints, but her wrists remained tethered. Her Titian hair was spread across the pillow, her face pressed to one side, tears running from the corner of her eyes, but her moans were ones of need, not anguish. Her pussy pouted between her thighs, wetness glistening on the crisp fiery hair. Luke dabbled his finger in this and anointed her anal hole, then pushed it in to the first knuckle.

Bronwen grunted, then pleaded, 'Go on. Fill me. Stuff me. Do it. Do it!'

He silently denied her, wiped his finger in her hair and belted her backside twice more. He looked at Laura, and she stopped masturbating, shamed to have him see her. He grinned and, deliberately facing her, unzipped his chinos and lifted out the largest cock she had ever seen in fact or photograph. It was fully erect, a strapping weapon, so thick and long that she couldn't think how it could be contained within a woman's pussy. As for anal penetration: it didn't bear contemplating.

He stroked it lovingly, pulling down the loose ridge of foreskin to expose the shiny purplish knob, then he slid it back up again. Under the pressure, his cock gained in girth and length, thick, pulsing, aggressively, almost offensively feral. Despite herself, Laura wanted to touch it. His smile deepened and he said, 'Bronwen needs you. Frig her.'

Laura scuttled over to the bed, kneeled beside it and slid her hand under Bronwen's belly. The softness of her skin was amazing, and her smell was like falling into the ocean. She felt the lovely nest of pubic hair and then it was like touching her own parts, except that the clit was prominent, hanging down like a miniature cock.

Bronwen moaned and turned her head. 'That's right,' she said huskily. 'Rub it for me.'

Encouraged and even proud to know that she was doing it right, Laura settled her middle digit into a steady back and forth rhythm. It was like masturbating herself. Luke kneeled on the bed behind Bronwen and inserted his protected and lubricated cock into her cunt. He took his time, entering inch by inch, and Bronwen lifted her hips towards him, and Laura gained greater access to her clit.

She was bathed in sweat and wished she were naked too. Her nipples ached, her bud thrummed and she prayed that they would attend to her needs once their own had been fulfilled. Luke gave a last thrust and his cock disappeared like a cork in a bottle. Then he started to propel himself in and out, and Bronwen set up a caterwauling that Laura feared would be heard by other hotel guests. She wished she'd had the forethought to turn on the telly.

She rubbed fast and furious and felt Bronwen shiver and wondered if she'd climaxed. She was left in no doubt about his when Luke flung back his head and gave a sharp bark, thrusting madly, then collapsing across Bronwen's back.

Bronwen stirred, then said, 'Get off, you great lummox,' and winked at Laura. 'Thanks, love. You did it just right.'

Luke rolled off her, lying flat on his back on the bed, an arm flung over his eyes. His latex-covered cock had reduced in size, but it was still of a length that many a man would have envied. The air was redolent of sex. Laura could smell Bronwen on her fingers. Her body throbbed. She wanted fingers or a mouth on her. She couldn't come without that stimulation, but she wanted to be impaled on Luke's monstrous prick as well. They would understand. They were bound to. They were both watching her now, and she didn't want to have to beg.

Then Bronwen said, 'Undress, petal. Come and lie with us.'

She did, stripping with hardly a second thought. Then she was on the bed and feeling Bronwen's tongue on her nipples, the smell of her rousing profound lusts and desires. For a moment she wanted to crawl inside her arms and stay there, being held and petted, but Bronwen had other treats in mind. She moved so that Laura could reach her cleft, then gripped her buttocks with her long nails and pulled her over her face. Her mouth sucked at Laura's sex, and her tongue flicked the swollen bud. Laura rubbed the wet folds of Bronwen's cleft, but could hardly concentrate on it, chasing her own completion, demanding more from each stroke of Bronwen's tongue or movement of her mouth.

Luke suddenly focused on Laura's pussy, and she felt herself expanding to take his cock. She was so wet and ready that it went in with ease, filling her up and nudging the end of her passage. As he worked it in and out, she could feel her inner muscles grabbing at him. The double sensations built, a clitoral climax rising ecstatically, and her pussy clenching round that monumental dick. She yelled, neighbours forgotten, coming in a welter of pleasure.

She came out of it reluctantly, cradled in two pairs of arms, and with the legs of her new playmates and possible members of staff tangled with hers.

Chapter Five

Never one to let the grass grow under his feet, Mark convened a meeting with each builder in turn, arranging for these to take place on the following day. Laura was still in London; Huntley was otherwise engaged and Mark was open-minded, so it was down to Cheryl to make the final choice.

She wasn't in a particularly good mood. Living at Fell Tor was tedious. Deven was coming on strong. If he didn't stop laying on the charm as only a man who had studied tantric sex along with every other variation under the sun could do, she was certain that she'd succumb to temptation and screw her mother's lover if she didn't remove herself soon. I've heard of share and share alike, she brooded, but this is ridiculous. Is it what Deven wants? Mother and daughter in the same bed? Was this the ultimate in cosmic turn-on? Bosh, she concluded irritably. Bosh and codswallop. He's no more a spiritual being than any other virile male whose cock tingles at the scent of pussy. I know this, and Mother knows it, but this doesn't stop either of us falling for his shenanigans.

Besides which, it was essential that she take charge of her own destiny again, making decisions about what she ate and when, who she spent time with or not. In fact, living under her mother's aegis was proving every bit as irksome as she had suspected it would be.

I need to move out, she resolved. I could rent a flat, like Laura, but there's no need of this if the workmen start on my St Jude's quarters pdq. With this thought uppermost, she interrogated the first of the builders, a middle-aged, balding, dungaree-clad man called Will Hewitt. He was Westcombe born and bred, the sort who might inspire sentimentalists to refer to him as 'the salt of the earth'. Though thorough and undoubtedly reliable, he lacked imagination, and Cheryl had to agree with Mark that his estimate went through the roof.

The next candidate was from Dobey and Co. As soon as he set foot in matron's office, where the interviews were taking place, Cheryl took an instant dislike to him. She very much wished she didn't, hoping against all hope that she wouldn't be forced to employ Felan Boynton, but the antipathy was too strong to be ignored. Dobey's representative was a know-it-all, and she could well believe that the firm might be teetering on the brink of ruin. Mark wasn't impressed either.

'Neither of them seem clued up about old buildings and their special requirements,' he opined, as the door closed behind Dobey's man. 'That leaves Felan Boynton.'

Despite herself, excitement ripped along her nerves and stabbed her groin at the mention of his name. Preparing for this, she'd been circumspect in her manner of dress. Nothing garish or give-away – a simple, stylish, boss-lady outfit comprising of an A-line, mid-calf skirt and a tailored shirt-blouse. She'd pinned up her hair and been discreet with cosmetics. Felan was in for a shock when he realised that the woman he'd fucked in the tower was the same person who'd do the hiring and firing. The prospect of seeing him again enraged yet aroused her. If her outer garments were modest, her underwear wasn't, and every time she so much as thought about Felan the gusset of her black silk panties was dampened by fresh juice. It annoyed her profoundly, for she had been trying to convince herself that he meant nothing to her, even though she had been using him as her favourite masturbation fantasy for the past few days.

Exerting supreme control, she didn't turn her head, keeping her back to the door as she heard it open and Mark say, 'Come in, Felan. Nice to see you again. How are tricks?'

'Mustn't grumble.' The deep timbre of his voice played havoc with her nipples. They crimped wantonly under the lace bra and prim blouse. Her clit engorged, poking from its folds and trying to rub itself against the silky panties.

'Your estimate seems a fair one,' Mark continued, and then added, 'This is Mrs Barden, part owner of St Jude's.'

There was no escape. Cheryl turned in her chair and faced him. It was like a blow between the eyes. She had thought she'd forgotten just how attractive he was. Not so. He was impossible to forget, so large, so dark, forceful and masculine.

His astonishment was quickly followed by amusement. 'You,' he said. 'You are Mrs Barden?'

'Yes,' she replied. There was nothing more to add.

'You two know each other?' Mark was obviously mystified.

'We met once, by chance,' Cheryl said quickly. Her hackles rose. She didn't owe him an explanation or Felan either, for that matter. What she did was entirely her own concern.

She refused to back down, holding Felan's questioning gaze with her own, struggling to remain deadpan.

'As I've already explained to Huntley, there's a mass of work to be done to get the place together, and my costing is as accurate as I could make it, give or take a few quid if we hit any snags,' Felan said matter-of-factly. Then he went on, 'As I told you the other day, Mrs Barden, I'm interested in ancient houses and will enjoy restoring this one.'

All Cheryl could think of was his thick cock in her mouth and the taste of his spunk as he came. She ached to do it again, and to feel it inside her, his work-roughened fingers on her, bringing her off as he pumped away at her. Her face was hot, her skirt sticking to her buttocks against the worn leather seat of the chair that must once have belonged to matron. How would Felan react if she told him about her plans for the towers?

If she agreed to take him on then there would be no relief from the lust he engendered. She wished it were anyone else but him. He was a domineering person, a full-on male who would expect his way on every issue. Normally she relished a fight, but she was reluctant to tangle with him. He knew precisely how to bring about her climax. Had done so in the tower, had had her shaking and moaning under his artful fingers. This gave him an unfair advantage. How could she issue orders to someone who had plugged her mouth with his cock? Wouldn't he remember how he had invaded her? Wouldn't he be laughing up his sleeve? Authority would be nigh impossible to maintain.

Mark was sitting there with a bland expression but, nobody's fool, she had the distinct feeling that he was on to them. Not perhaps guessing the whole truth, but suspicious nonetheless. No one with an ounce of sensitivity could fail to be aware of the charge in the atmosphere. The sparks were almost visible.

They were waiting for a response from her and for the life of her she didn't know what to do. Then Mark came to the rescue, saying, 'Of course, there are a lot of details to go into. The pool, for example. It needs re-tiling, and the filter system is antiquated . . .'

'I want my apartment done before anything else. I need to move in right away,' she said, her voice high-pitched with nerves.

Mark raised an eyebrow at her vehemence, but replied calmly, 'OK. Whatever. I suggest that Felan takes a closer look at it, then he can tell you how long it's going to be.'

'Oh? So it's a foregone conclusion that he gets the contract, is it?' Try as she might, there was no way she could control that shrewish tone. Just when she most needed to be dignified, she was acting the spoiled brat.

'It's up to you,' Mark answered, lifting his shoulders in a shrug under his draped cream linen jacket. 'You're the one paying the piper. But, personally speaking, I can't see what objection you can possibly have. The price is right, and Felan's reputation is second to none around here.'

'Laura,' she brought out, clutching at straws.

'As I understand it, Laura's happy to leave it to you. Seems to me it would take an alien invasion to get her rattled.'

Fuck! Cheryl swore inwardly. There was no putting it off any longer. She had to come to a decision.

Felan stood there coolly, hands thrust into the pockets of his baggy blue jeans. They were upheld by a pair of wide yellow braces printed to resemble tape-measures. The coppery hue of his bare arms and chest was made even darker in contrast to his white vest. His muscles were those of a man who worked hard physically and didn't need sessions pumping iron. He looked clean and wholesome, good enough to devour whole. She found it hard to think further than that.

She capitulated suddenly. What the hell! Bravely she told herself that she'd be able to manage him, drain him, chew him up and spit out what was left. Brave talk and a load of crap and she knew it, but she was too confused to argue further. She wanted Laura there, but all she'd had was a garbled phone call late last night. Something about having found a lady of experience who was willing to come to St Jude's and take charge of the whorehouse arrangements, only it wasn't to be called that any more. It was to be an expensive club. Too dangerous otherwise, and they'd risk being closed down and probably arrested. The woman's name was Bronwen and there was a man too, someone known as Luke. Laura had invited them down to view the place. She had rabbited on about leather gear and S&M, and Bronwen's wonderful grasp of the essentials of deviant sex.

Not wishing to spike her confidence, Cheryl hadn't reminded her that it was early days yet. There was a lot

94

to do before St Jude's could hold its first orgy. It seemed like she was being railroaded into action. First Laura and now Felan.

'Is that it then?' he said briskly. 'If you're going to mess me about, then I've another prospective client to see.'

'Is it, Cheryl?' Mark asked, uncrossing his legs and preparing to get up. 'I too have an appointment at two-thirty. I'm afraid I shall have to leave you to it. Shall we give the job to Felan?'

'I suppose so,' she muttered ungraciously.

'Right. Fine. Then you'd better take me to your apartment for a quick look,' Felan suggested, the simple statement heavy with innuendoes.

Mark came across and kissed her cheek before leaving, saying, 'I'm sure you're doing the right thing. I'll see you tonight . . . for dinner . . . remember?'

'I must talk to Laura,' she demurred, reluctant to face him in the privacy of his home where he might start asking awkward questions concerning her acquaintance with Felan. She had to keep reminding herself that he wasn't her husband, nor likely to be in the near future.

'All right. Give me a ring later and we'll take it from there.'

Silence descended like a funeral pall once she was alone with Felan. Then, 'Why didn't you tell me you were the owner?' he asked, with a stabbing glance from his intensely blue eyes.

'It was none of your business,' she retorted crossly. 'It still isn't. You're engaged to work here, no more, no less.'

His grin mocked her as he said, 'OK, ma'am. Let's go to your rooms, shall we? Or would you rather we had a chaperone?'

'You think I'm afraid of you?' She pushed past him towards the door. Ice on the outside, she was boiling within, wanting to stop at his side, to embrace him with her arms and fling one leg up round his hip so that she might grind her hungry pubis against his thigh.

He stood back, then walked behind her into the

95

passage. 'No, not of me. Of yourself, perhaps,' he murmured and, to her horror and melting delight, ran an impudent finger all the way down her spine, stopping only when he reached the waistband of her skirt.

'Get your hands off me,' she said grittily, and stalked ahead of him, putting as much space as possible between them. She heard him laugh and wanted to swing round and slap his face.

They took the magnificent central staircase that curved aloft. Its handrails bore a sheen left by the hundreds of palms that had touched it across the years. The treads were wide and shallow, and their footsteps echoed in that lofty space under the curved dome.

'I'll carpet the stairs,' she said, thinking aloud.

'Vandal!' he retorted crisply. 'You'll destroy the look of it. The wood needs sanding and polishing, that's all. The grain will come up a treat.'

'It's too noisy. Anyhow, Laura and I say what goes.'

He pulled a face but said no more till they arrived at the door leading into the vestibule of the former headmaster's suite. 'I've already made notes about this,' he commented, pacing down the hall and into the spacious sitting room. 'It's too dark, too gloomy. I think a pale dove-grey for the panelling and white for the ceiling, with perhaps a dash of Wedgwood blue for the cornices and mouldings. It was once fitted with chandeliers and these should be replaced. Just the two of them, hanging from those medallions ... we'll pick them out in blue too, and add wall lights and standard lamps with heavily fringed shades.'

'Oh? I rather fancied central spots,' she said on impulse. She didn't and knew they wouldn't be in keeping but was determined to raise objections.

He winced. 'Definitely not. You can have them in the kitchen if you must, seeing as how this needs modernisation, but even there I must insist on lime-washed oak for the units with cathedral doors, a Belfast sink and a cooker that resembles a range.'

'It'll have to be gas. I can't cope with solid fuel.'

'The place is oil-fired. There's no gas out here, only electricity.'

'It doesn't matter to me. I shall have most of my meals sent up from the main kitchen. I've done my share of cooking over the years and I'm sick of it.' She was voicing an old resentment.

His hands came up, fending her off. 'Hold it right there. Don't unpack your emotional suitcase on my bed.'

'I've no intention of doing so,' she sparked, face hot, sex hot, angrier than she'd been for a long time.

He smiled and his eyes softened. She wished they wouldn't. It made it harder to hate him. 'You must let me cook for you. Actually, I quite get off on it.'

'Do you wash up after yourself? I'll bet you don't,' she accused, remembering times when Ashley had taken it upon himself to play the chef, and the bitter recriminations that had followed when she saw the state of the kitchen.

'Come along and see,' he challenged.

'Hadn't you better ask your wife before you start handing out invitations?'

'I'm divorced,' he said evenly. 'I live alone.'

With that question out of the way, she started to extend more feelers, though in denial about her rabid curiosity. 'In Westcombe?' she asked, but casually, moving across to examine the walls, as if the state of the tattered paper was of overwhelming concern.

'Not far from,' he vouchsafed, and she was aware of the warmth of his body as he came up behind her, so close that she could feel his breath tickling the back of her neck. She wished she hadn't pinned up her hair. It left her nape too vulnerable.

Involuntarily, she braced her arms against the wall, hands flat, registering the damp coldness that permeates unused rooms. It made his body heat all the more alluring. She caught a whiff of freshly showered male genitals, coupled with a hint of Eternity. It pleased her to think that he might have spruced himself up for the interview, even though he didn't know about her.

'I'll bet you're glad you made the effort.' She spoke without meaning to.

She felt laughter rumbling in his chest, felt his arms close round her ribs and his hands cup her breasts. His solid cock was boring into the small of her back, and a pair of strong thighs touched her buttocks and upper legs. He lowered his head and she shivered as his lips caressed her skin in that erogenous zone where her shoulders joined her neck. Goose bumps stippled her limbs, and her clit thrummed in time to the throbbing in her breasts.

'Because of you? I don't think so, Mrs Barden.' He chuckled, his breath tickling her ear, the rasp of his beard adding its own seduction. 'Put it down to the hope that I might get lucky again.'

His mockery proved her salvation. She stiffened, pushed his hands away and slid along the wall. Turning, she snarled, 'We came here on a mission, Mr Boynton. To view the apartment and make a plan for its immediate redecoration. I want to be able to take it over a week from today, so you'd better get a move on.'

From then on it was business all the way. She threw out ideas and he made notes and sketched. They debated; they even argued, but it was a strictly client-and-builder relationship, nothing more intimate, not even when they were discussing her bedroom. She knew what she wanted. A late-eighteenth-century-style tester bed would set the tone and all else would follow – striped wallpaper, a lot of gilding, Venetian mirrors, plaster Cupids and all the luxury and decadence of a period that had given England the Regent's Pavilion at Brighton.

'I shall go to auction sales,' she declared.

'I trust you have a substantial wad set aside for this,' he remarked.

'Let me worry about that. All you have to do is follow instructions.'

'Yes, ma'am. Certainly, ma'am,' he said, ducking and tugging his forelock.

She pulled up short, standing in front of him defiantly and saying, 'This isn't going to work.'

He eyed her speculatively, a sardonic expression on his face. 'It will.'

'It won't, unless you start taking me seriously.'

'I do,' he protested, his arms wide-flung. 'I'm seriously reminding myself that you're Mrs Barden, my new, important customer with money to burn, not the trespasser who gave the best head I've ever had.'

'Stop it!' she shouted. 'I don't want to think about that.'

'But you do, don't you? All the time. So do I,' he said, devoid of humour now. 'The solicitor. Is he humping you?'

'You've got a nerve!' she cried, exasperated. Then she changed the subject. 'Let me see those colour charts. The selection is huge and exciting. I love it. I'll have this place looking like a palace.'

With a supreme effort she managed to maintain a strictly working rapport between them for the next hour or so, though still the tension bubbled away like a potent brew about to explode. It didn't and Cheryl left later, knowing that the colour scheme had been decided on and Felan was off to the wholesaler's to buy paint and every other requirement. He had promised to get his team together and make a start in the morning.

Seated in her car, she called Laura on her mobile. There was no reply. Jesus God! What was keeping her, Cheryl thought impatiently. Bronwen and Luke must be something else. What was Laura doing? Fucking them both?

Westcombe was swarming with visitors, though the season was not yet in full swing. Early June and several weeks to go before the schools broke up and parents and children invaded the beaches in boisterous hordes. It was best avoided at this time. Though package holidays abroad in the sun were the norm, there was still a hard core who insisted on a traditional seaside holiday in England, risking rain, gales and torrential flooding.

Cheryl dropped by at Laura's flat. There was no response to her repeated assault on the doorbell. She gave up and drove back to the countryside and Fell Tor. She might not like it much but at least she could take a shower and cool off. There were so many emotions battling for airspace in her mind, and she couldn't shake off images of Felan. As the road gave way to narrow lanes, then wound up to the broader reaches of moorland, so she was aware of the need grinding away inside her and, as she parted her thighs to manoeuvre the brakes, the odour of sex juice wafted up from her cleft. She resisted the urge to pull into a lay-by and surrender to the rampant desire for orgasm. Instead, she promised herself that when she reached her bedroom she would spend the afternoon indulging with her favourite vibrator. That would banish Felan's ghost. Or would it?

'What d'you think?' Laura asked nervously, when she managed a moment alone with Cheryl.

They had left Bronwen and Luke in the towers, which they were going over like pointers scenting game. Bronwen emitted little shrieks of delight every so often, particularly when they explored the basements.

'They seem to know their business,' Cheryl said guardedly. 'Tell me again how you came to meet them.'

Laura went through the story, from finding Bronwen in Don't be Shy, to the moment she and Luke had visited her in the Dickens Hotel. She blushed as she went into intimate details but managed to keep her voice steady. Cheryl nodded and listened without comment, boiling the kettle in the cobwebbed, semi-subterranean kitchen that had once produced meals for a hundred students. She had brought along crockery and a tray, a jar of coffee, sugar and powered milk.

'So, you trust them?' she said.

'Yes, I think so. We're going to have to take all members of staff on trust, aren't we?'

'Well, no. We can use agencies to find maids and waiters, gardeners and groundsmen and a cook and a housekeeper, and they'll all have references,' Cheryl pointed out, pausing with her shoulder against the door, the tray balanced on her hip. 'But I don't know of a similar service concerning applicants for a whorehouse, do you?'

'That's why it was so lucky, me running into them like that,' Laura insisted, and trotted behind Cheryl as they returned to the East Tower. 'And her advice about turning it into a club was so sound. I'd never have thought of it, would you?'

'Well, no, but I do remember reading about police raids on houses of ill-fame, and the owners facing hefty fines. I guess I thought we could get away with it, under cover of a respectable hotel. You're right. It's fine to have sensible advice from someone in the know,' Cheryl agreed.

'A pity more of the work hasn't been done yet. I hope it doesn't put them off,' Laura said.

She had met the black-browed builder Felan, found him a hunk and wondered why Cheryl seemed agitated around him. Not wanting to delay, she had invited Bronwen and Luke down for Saturday over into Sunday. She had a spare room and had been looking forward to seeing them again. This was their first glimpse of St Jude's, on a sunny afternoon likely to impress any city-dweller. The jungly garden, the overgrown summer-house, the large proportions of the rooms and the grandeur that was becoming more apparent under the skilled attentions of Felan's team had Bronwen goggling, while Luke strolled around, regarding everything through narrowed eyes as if making an inventory.

'It's the towers that'll be your special province, if you decide you want to join us,' Cheryl said, when the coffee had been handed round. 'The basics have been done.'

'The cellars have massive potential. That'll be the hook. You've got to call in a designer with a special understanding of fantasy needs,' Bronwen broke in. 'And I know just the geezer.'

'Alroy,' said Luke, leaping on the window seat and bracing his hands against the stone mullions, staring down the long drop to the terrace.

101

'That's our main man. He's brilliant. And knows every inch of the scene. He'll come up with designs and you'll be amazed. He's the best.' Bronwen joined Luke on his perch, and Laura thought they looked like a couple of brilliantly plumaged parakeets.

She glittered, and so did he. They had managed to get a tan, basking spreadeagled on the flat roof of their apartment, then topping it up in the local solarium. Laura had noted Cheryl's surprise when they had first met. The workmen had finished at noon and she had been waiting at St Jude's to show them round. Bronwen wore a brief cotton slip, orange flecked with gold, her bountiful breasts and long legs displayed unselfconsciously, her fiery hair brushed up at the back, then cascading into ringlets around each ear and at the tender nape of her neck. Diamanté clips added their white-hot flash. The highest of high-heeled sandals were strapped across her toes, and she had put them on when she reached Laura's flat, having driven down from London barefoot.

Cheryl had done a double take when introduced to Luke, that boyish version of John Travolta. This amused Laura, knowing the effect he had on herself. If she had the equipment, she knew she'd have a permanent hard-on in his company and guessed it would be the same for Cheryl.

'You'd like me to ring Alroy and get him down here?' Bronwen asked, landing like a cat beside Cheryl.

'Maybe. I can't very well ask my workmen.'

'Leave it to me, Cheryl. I'm full of ideas for the place. Alroy and me have worked together on projects before. A couple of strip-joints, a couple of private pads . . . you know the kind of thing.'

Cheryl nodded, though Laura knew she was as much in the dark as herself. What had they let themselves in for? 'Is it possible to run the hotel and "club" in tandem? Won't we be rumbled? What about staffing and cleaning it?' she asked.

'I see no prob,' Bronwen remarked, sipping her coffee, sherry-coloured eyes skimming the room. 'You'll advertise St Jude's in the normal way and attract straight guests, but leave the other half to me. I know the right spots to circulate news of a fabulous club, where, for a price, anything can be arranged to fulfil the discerning person's every dream.'

'Nothing crude,' Cheryl insisted.

'Would I?' Bronwen placed a hand on her breast, big-eyed. 'I understand these things, Cheryl. In a throwaway culture, things that are timeless and enduring have a great appeal. You'd be surprised at the number of men who want to wear frocks and pinnies, or dog-collars and leads and be bullied about by a dominating mistress.'

'They love reverting to the prep-school and the cane,' Luke said, and landed lightly on Cheryl's other side. He smiled at Laura and held out an arm. 'We've already shown Laura what we're made of, haven't we, love? Shall I get out my todger for Cheryl to play with?'

'Not yet. Fetch up the case, Luke,' Bronwen ordered.

'Right on, babes,' he said good-naturedly, and disappeared.

'I've brought some of the stuff we'll need for here. A substantial wardrobe is essential. Clients like to pretend, you see. If they wear masks and different gear to their own, then they can become whatever they like . . . submissives, dominants, tarts or whoremasters, even ponies if they want. Ask Laura how she felt in her gladiator gear.'

'She's already told me, shown it to me . . . even put it on,' Cheryl said, and Laura sensed that she wasn't yet convinced.

'Your turn now,' Bronwen cried, and she took the case from Luke as soon as he came back, plonked it on the window seat and sprang the catches. She opened the soft top and started to shake out silks and feathers, leather and PVC, thigh boots and stilettos.

Cheryl shook her head and backed away, but then Bronwen unearthed a wasp-waisted corset. It was made of black satin, kept rigid by whale boning and edged with scarlet net. Next came a bustle, several frilly petticoats, suspenders, stockings, a rustling taffeta skirt and a low-cut velvet bodice.

'You should dress right when you're being the club's hostess,' Bronwen said, smiling and holding out the garments.

Cheryl looked at Laura, who nodded in answer.

'It'll be fun. I promise you.'

'Don't mind me,' Luke said, taking a ringside seat. 'I've seen more minges that you've had hot dinners.'

Laura half expected Cheryl to refuse point-blank, but instead saw her taking off her shorts and T-shirt. She admired her figure, for she was slimmer than she'd been for ages, honed too, as if she'd been popping an exercise tape into the video machine and working out. Taller than herself and golden brown all over. Swimming and sun-bathing nude would be encouraged at Fell Tor. I must do it too, Laura resolved. Despite what they say about exposing yourself to the rays, there's nothing quite like a tan for making you feel pampered and expensive and glamorous.

'Panties and bra too, Cheryl,' Bronwen encouraged, and, keeping her back to Luke, Cheryl removed the last barriers between herself and total nakedness.

An expert, Bronwen soon had the corset round her and was straining on the back lacing. Cheryl's breath rushed out and her waist diminished. Her breasts rose above the ruched edging, and her hips appeared to be wider.

'God, that's tight!' she exclaimed.

'Has to be. That's part of the charm,' Bronwen insisted and, while Cheryl rested one hand on her shoulder for support, she rolled first one then the other of the sheer stockings up her legs and fastened the welts to the suspenders dangling from the stays. 'Step into the ankle boots,' she commanded, and when Cheryl obeyed, she hooked the loops over the shiny round buttons, then ran a hand up the inside of Cheryl's thighs and touched her between them. 'You're getting nice and wet,' she observed.

Laura was getting wet too. Since Bronwen had awakened her to the desirability of women, she had thought about it often. And watching Cheryl being attired in that daring little black number was making her horny. It was making Luke horny too. She could see the erection straining the front of his jeans and remembered the outlandish size of it, wanting to share the experience with Cheryl. He was unusually big. She had seen him flogging Bronwen and felt an answering shiver of need for his blows. He had thrust his finger into Bronwen's arse and later she had witnessed him sodomising her. There were so many things Laura hadn't yet tried with him and she was scared, yet she wanted to finger-fuck herself desperately as his bulge swelled and he unzipped to release it from confinement.

Cheryl gasped as she saw it. Luke grinned and eased down low on his spine, leaning against the window arch, his genitals pushed forwards. He eased his fingers up his shaft, pulled back the foreskin and lightly spread pre-come over the purple knob. Meanwhile, Bronwen dropped the petticoats over Cheryl's head and tied them at the waist, then added the black skirt and velvet blouse. Cheryl was transformed into Edouard Manet's barmaid at the Folie-Bergère, or the proud owner of a high-class bordello where only the choicest morsels were on sale.

It suited her. She stood differently, bosom thrust out, hands on hips that were rounded by the corset. There was a challenging look in her eyes, a brassy come-and-get-it look. A warning glint too. No one would seriously consider welshing on the bill.

'How do I look, Laura?' she asked, and sashayed across the room.

'The part,' she replied, and her fears about Bronwen and Luke being rejected faded away.

'I can get hold of anything. I've friends who are costumiers and dress-makers, besides all the sweat-shops that manufacture sexy gear,' Bronwen continued, sitting back on her hunkers and admiring her work. 'Let your

105

skirt ride up. That's the way. Let the customer get a glimpse of your pussy hair, then whisk those petticoats down again. I know a troupe of cancan dancers who'll come along. All those high kicks and splits and they never wear drawers. That's how it was done in Paris in the old days.'

'But we don't only want that scenario,' Cheryl stammered, her concentration diverted by Luke jerking off. His tool burgeoned like the stamen of some exotic plant, huge and heavy in his hand. His palm could barely close round it, and his balls rested on the seat between his legs, two large fruits in a dark hairy net.

'We'll have anything we like. Alroy will come up with wacky ideas. He'll use colour and fabrics in the rooms and turn the cellars into punishment areas. Don't worry about a thing. He'll supply the implements, the racks, crosspieces and pillories. All you'll have to do is run your sedate hotel, and leave the underbelly to us.'

'Come over here,' Luke whispered seductively, and flaunted his prick at Cheryl. 'What about a sample of things to come, eh?'

As if hypnotised by the massive tool he offered, Cheryl moved across to him, hoisted her skirts, straddled his legs and lowered herself on to it, inch by slow inch. Her back was straight, her neck arched, and she moaned as he penetrated her fully.

Luke smiled at Laura and Bronwen and said huskily, 'Don't be jealous, darlings.' He spread his arms out and wriggled his fingers. 'I've got plenty for you.'

Mesmerised, Laura found herself standing beside Cheryl. Luke's left hand cruised up her leg and wormed into her knickers. She was vaguely conscious that he was doing the same to Bronwen on Cheryl's other side. It was easier, perhaps, as the redhead wasn't wearing panties. In front of Laura lay the window, with its view of the grounds and hills beyond. And Cheryl was so close, jouncing up and down on Luke's cock, hands at its base as she rubbed her clit frantically. A quick glance at her

106

face told Laura that she was utterly absorbed in the pursuit of pleasure.

True to his word, Luke did not lose sight of the needs of the others. His finger worked magic on Laura. Nothing rushed or uncouth, just a delicious side-to-side movement over the swollen nubbin, a firm massage of the whole area and, while she was almost screaming for his touch on its head, the granting of this bliss. His finger slid up and down from vulva to clit. She couldn't help wriggling her pelvis, wanting more. He gave it to her in generous measure. She came, gasping and writhing, opened her eyes and saw Bronwen stiffen, then thresh as she climaxed on his other hand.

They beat Cheryl. She lagged behind them, but only by a second. Luke was the last to reach his apogee, barking as he shot his load into the rubber sheath that lay between his skin and Cheryl's.

While Felan and his merry men hammered and plumbed, replaced obsolete electric wiring, took down walls and put up others, turned the great main kitchen into something worthy of a TV celebrity chef, stripped and painted and performed the hundred and one essentials in order to transform the dingy college into a five-star hotel, Cheryl and Laura busied themselves with furnishings, hard and soft, and engaged staff.

Outraged by a letter she had received from Dempsey Enterprises with an offer to buy St Jude's for a handsome sum far exceeding that which she and Laura had paid for it, Cheryl consulted with her and then wrote them a brisk refusal and doubled her intention to open within a month.

'I remember John Dempsey from old,' she explained to her friend. 'He's a leading light in the sailing club and has gone on to higher things, gaining a reputation as an entrepreneur, with his fingers in innumerable pies. I never appreciated his brand of male chauvinism and arrogance. I gave him a tongue-lashing at a Regatta Ball once. He'd put his hand up my skirt, fully expecting me to be bowled over by the honour. Since then our feelings towards one another have been those of mutual dislike bordering on detestation. He must be gutted that I got St Jude's first, but I'd rather sell it to Old Nick than to him.'

'Could he be a dangerous enemy?' Laura demurred.

'I guess. He's on the town council, so it's as well that Bronwen talked us into setting up a club, not a brothel. I don't see how he can harm us now.'

'How about offering a sweetener and inviting him to the grand opening? Other fat cats too. St Jude's is looking stunning, very stately and conventional. The local papers are printing a piece about it; we've been given airtime on Westcombe Radio and the bookings are coming along nicely. Bronwen and Luke will make themselves scarce and we'll leave the catering and arrangements in the capable hands of Thomas and Ursula.'

They had seen several applicants for the posts of cook and housekeeper respectively, and had decided on a stout, genial chef with impressive qualifications, and a fifty-year-old lady with glowing references who had a serene nature and a sense of humour. Other staff members had been selected, mostly from among local people.

Bronwen had brought Alroy into the fold. Once Felan was out of the towers, the designer had taken over. A sinuous, tall and beautiful black man, he was a sharp dresser, favouring blue suits, striped shirts and hand-crafted shoes from Milan, which he wore without socks. He breathed out the scent of sandalwood from his long ebony locks.

He was wonderfully camp, stalking the bare rooms and saying, 'I'm thinking images and roles. These towers! They're so *here*! They're so *you*!'

Encouraged by the expertise and flair that underscored his affectations, Laura and Cheryl left him to it. He wouldn't let them as much as peep till the work was complete, but when they did cross the threshold the decor exceeded their wildest dreams. He was ecstatic because they approved and demanded that they make him the guest of honour when the club opened, and give him life membership, free.

'I fancy him rotten,' Cheryl confessed.

'So do I,' sighed Laura, 'but he swings both pipes.'

Chapter Six

'That cheeky mare has had the bottle to invite me to the opening of her bloody hotel,' John bellowed above the rush of the waves and the creaking of ropes. 'Ready about! Lee-o!' he commanded, giving Ashley no chance to reply. 'Good God, man! What the hell's the matter? Put your back into it. Grab the jib! Jesus Christ, we'll be round the wrong side of the buoy in a minute! Bloody plonker! I wish I'd asked one of the girls to crew for me. She'd have done a bloody sight better, and I'd have got a stiffie looking at her tits!'

They were manning John's dinghy and taking part in a Saturday morning race, an event of little consequence, but one he was determined to win. Second or third place was never good enough for him. He'd received Cheryl's gilt, fluted-edged card with the post, and this had put him in such a towering rage that nothing would satisfy him but having her ex-husband as his crew.

Serve the bugger right! John thought. He should have kept her in line, the bitch! Crewing was a thankless task, especially when, like today, it was lashing down with rain. The ropes were wet and rough, blistering the toughest palm, and the wind was changeable, forcing them to tack from side to side. The boat was small, nothing like the size of John's yacht, but it required skill to steer her,

110

and gave him the chance to show off, especially to rookie mariners new to the club.

'She hasn't asked me,' Ashley hollered, barking his shin, hair dripping from under his sou'wester, face streaming, spray and rain running in rivulets down his yellow oilskins.

'What? Oh, she hasn't? Then why me? And why Councillor Pringle and his missus, and the Chief Constable? Who is she trying to impress? Goddamit! Look out! Jesus, that idiot to starboard missed us by a sparrow's fart.' John grabbed a rope and swung on it like some latter-day Captain Hook, hurling insults at his rival helmsman, 'Fucking hell! Call yourself a sailor! You're more like a bloody shirt-lifting pansy! You scraped my prow, you stupid sod!'

A gust caught the canvas. The dinghy leaped forward and, 'Brace the mainsail! Stop the spinnaker flapping. Look out, or she'll capsize!' John wrenched at the rudder and narrowly averted disaster.

They tore round the buoy and hurtled into the final lap. John could almost feel the trophy in his red-knuckled fist. Modest though it might be, it was another to add to his collection, a further symbol of one-upmanship for Emily to polish, but his annoyance with Cheryl continued to rankle. As he squelched into the men's locker room at the clubhouse, he harangued Ashley who stood there shivering as he unbuttoned his jacket, struggled with a soggy pullover, and then dropped his shorts and jockeys. He unlaced his oozing deck shoes and stepped towards the shower.

John barred his way, subjecting him to a scathing glance concentrated on the genital area. The cold had reduced Ashley's penis to the size of a cocktail sausage, while his balls had retreated, fleeing to the safety and warmth of pre-pubescence.

'That's the trouble . . . that thing there,' John snarled, pointing rudely. 'You were never man enough for Cheryl. I can't for the life of me understand what the commodore's hot-arsed harlot sees in you.'

111

This was too much, even for Ashley whose livelihood depended in part on keeping this objectionable bully sweet. 'Leave Yvonne out of it,' he muttered through chattering teeth.

'Ha! I left her long ago,' John sneered, snug inside the wetsuit that covered him from neck to ankle. Then he altered his tactics, letting Ashley make it to the shower, following and adding, 'I don't want to fall out with you, old lad, but you must admit your ex is a sodding infuriating cow. I'll do my damnedest to pull the plug on her, just you see if I don't. I'm not without influence around here, you know. She's not going to get the better of me.'

He unzipped the neoprene suit in which he always felt supremely comfortable, the spongy inner surface enfolding his nakedness in a way that was infantile yet sexual. He liked to feel it clasping his cock and testicles like a tight, velvet-covered fist. It was almost like wearing a spaceman's outfit. He thrilled at the idea that he could urinate in it if caught short at sea. He had done so this morning, feeling the damp warmth spreading round his bottom and down his legs, like a baby wetting its nappy. His pee simply soaked away, washed by the buffeting waves. Later he'd hand the all-in-one to Emily to clean and dry out, ready for next time.

His mature, muscular body appeared as he peeled the synthetic rubber away. He wore nothing under it, flesh dewed with a light patina of sweat, greying chest and pubic hair curling damply. His clenched buttocks, sturdy thighs and calves were those of a sportsman, competitive in the field and in every other aspect of life. It galled him to think a woman had bested him. He caught a glimpse of himself in the washroom mirror, and his gaze lingered on the lumpy appendages dangling between his legs. He'd always been proud of his tackle, his crown jewels, and he never hesitated to display them in front of other men, confident that they were up to standard. No one could say that John Dempsey lacked balls, in any respect.

He switched on the spray in the next stall. Ashley was rubbing himself vigorously, his skin turning pink, the hot

112

water cascading over his head and hitting his chest, then running down to drench his thighs, legs and feet. John saw that Ashley's cock had enlarged under the stimulation and, oddly, his own started to lift and thicken. He told himself that this was perfectly natural, a purely physical response to the heat, the slippery shower gel he was applying all over, the sense of well-being that now flooded through him. It was beyond all reason that it could be anything to do with standing naked in a shower with another man. Perish the thought!

Others were tramping in, each with a nautical tale of the morning's exploits. Bluff, hearty, they shouted out to John, congratulating him on his success. He dried off and put on clean boxers, a pair of grey slacks, a dark-blue jersey and navy blazer. Drinks would be served while the race underwent a post-mortem. They looked on him as their spokesman and leader, and he basked in their admiration. Men were so much more understanding than women. Logical, reasonable beings. They knew what was what. But as he headed out of the changing room and made for the bar, his cock stirred as he wondered if Peggy, that blonde bimbo of a waitress, was on duty. He was in the mood to give her one.

Cheryl extended an arm from beneath the duvet and picked up the phone trilling on the bedside table. She was half-asleep, disoriented till she clicked on to waking in her beautiful apartment.

'Sorry to disturb you,' said her mother. 'I wanted to catch you before you disappeared out or something. Thanks for the invite. Yes, Deven and I would love to attend your opening. Can we bring along a friend or two?'

'Bring the whole gang if you want,' Cheryl answered, stretching and admiring the pagodas and bridges and quaint little Oriental figures on the chinoiserie wallpaper she had chosen instead of stripes.

'How about you coming over this evening?' Joanna went on. 'You looked tired, last time I saw you. I've

113

planned a little surprise . . . something that will help you to relax.'

'Aromatherapy? Meditation?' Cheryl asked cautiously, wondering what particular aspect of holistic medicine she·was to undergo.

'Perhaps. You never gave any of it a whirl when you were staying here. Maybe now is the moment to clear your chakras.'

'I'm terribly busy . . .' Cheryl wanted to add 'Mummy', but remembered in time. 'The opening is on Friday. You can imagine what has to be done by then.'

'Give yourself a break. Leave Laura to cope, and you've a housekeeper, haven't you?'

'And a new manager . . . Simon Bell. We needed to take him on, but heaven knows, the hotel has to start paying for itself soon or there'll be a serious cash-flow problem.'

'Over-reaching yourselves?'

'Probably. Everything is so fiercely expensive. We didn't realise quite how much the furnishings and fittings would cost. And I had to buy furniture for the flat. Nothing from the old house was suitable, and besides, Ashley took most of it. I wanted so much to do it right. Had to find the proper antiques. Wait till you see it. I'm sure you'll agree that it looks great.'

'So? Will you come?'

'All right. But I can't stay long.'

When she had hung up, Cheryl cursed herself for giving in. She hated denying her mother anything and, having moved from Fell Tor almost a month ago, it seemed churlish not to indulge her this once.

She knew she was stressed. It had been a strain juggling with the builders, the prospective staff and the suppliers who specialised in hotel requirements from beds down to the smallest teaspoon. Everything had to be in keeping, spanking new and spotless. It was just as well that Laura had lately received a bequest from an elderly aunt, which had amounted to forty thousand pounds. This had proved manna from heaven, enabling them to complete St Jude's without adding to their already hefty bank loan.

It wasn't only the endless work and worry, she concluded, sitting at the dressing table and examining her face in the cheval mirror. Her sex life was proving complicated and she had almost decided to give up men for good, leading a chaste existence. Mark was acting decidedly proprietorial, making too free with the word 'we' in reference to themselves. As far as she was concerned there was no 'we' about it. There was he, Mark Warfield, and she, Cheryl Barden. Two separate entities, and she was happy to leave it that way.

He had helped her, and she was grateful. He was a reliable friend, and she cherished that. As a lover he earned a gold star, though Felan had been much more exciting, and Luke knew exactly how to make her come. She'd found herself making excuses to avoid meeting Mark alone, and they weren't entirely lies – she was too busy, too tired, too preoccupied.

Working in close proximity to Felan had been an endurance test. It was inevitable that they cross paths and she had thrown up barriers a mile high. One slip, one hint of weakness and he'd be in there, telling her what to do, imposing his ideas on her, robbing her of her hard-won independence.

She leaned her elbows on the dressing table's surface and studied her reflection. Tiny lines, sharp as incisors, creased the outer corners of her eyes. She dipped her little finger in a pot of moisturiser. According to the advertising blurb it should knock years off her appearance. She applied it carefully to the eye area, wondering why she was bothering. Hadn't she lately decided that men took up too much time, emotional issues were exhausting, and she'd far rather masturbate than actually shag?

She was not looking forward to meeting Felan in her office at ten o'clock. She had a shrewd idea what he wanted to see her about. His nose had been put out of joint when she ousted him from the towers and put

Alroy in charge. True, the groundwork had been done, but he had taken umbrage when she called in such a glamorous person to complete the decor. This angered Cheryl. Once again Felan was expecting her to account for her actions when it was none of his concern. Nosy about the purpose of the towers? She'd have to fob him off somehow.

As she planned her strategy, she applied cleanser to her skin, then a neutral base, the warm tones of her sun-kissed skin glowing. Mascara, eyeliner and lip-gloss, and she was ready to face him. She twisted up her hair and secured it with a tortoiseshell clip, then dressed infor-mally in shorts, a T-shirt and trainers. The weather was forecast as hot. There had been a spell of sunshine, except on the day of the sailing club race, and she had chuckled with wicked glee to imagine John Dempsey and Ashley looking like drowned rats. She had always despised her ex-husband for kow-towing to that aggressive loud-mouth. The devil had made her send him an invitation to the opening. Gleefully, she looked forward to seeing his expression when he stepped into the restored glory of St Jude's. He'd be gutted!

It had seemed natural for the erstwhile headmaster's study on the ground floor to become the office. Laura and Cheryl shared it and their partnership was proving to be harmonious. They kept to their own space, each with an apartment, yet they often ate together out of choice and spent the evenings in one or other of their sitting rooms, watching television or listening to music. Cheryl still hadn't confided in her regarding Felan, and she knew Laura was puzzled by her coldness towards him. Ursula was already installed in the housekeeper's quarters; Thomas had taken up residence in the kitchen location; parlour-maids, menservants and a porter were giving everything a final polish; the barman was practis-ing with the cocktail shaker, and Simon Bell was doing his stuff in reception – answering calls and taking book-ings. Cheryl smiled to observe how often Laura made an excuse to go into a huddle with him, presumably on

116

hotel business, but when she reappeared, she was always bright-eyed and bushy-tailed.

A pattern was emerging. Two weeks of hectic activity were planned, during which their conventional guests would test the accommodation, then a weekend set aside for the first 'business conference', booked to take place mainly in the East Tower. No more than three dozen people were coming, all fully paid-up members of the club. This was a number that could be managed easily and she had left the details to Bronwen and Luke, who had hired their own assistants, entertainers, bartenders and caterers.

Bronwen had confessed to missing the pace and dynamism of living and working in London. She had kept on her flat there and was still employed part-time by Don't be Shy. So was Luke. This gave them plenty of opportunity to contact the right clients for St Jude's exclusive country club. They advertised by word of mouth and their enthusiasm and 'in' with the scene quickly won them a host of people eager to join. Everything was falling smoothly into place.

The only fly in the ointment was Felan and his awkward questions.

Cheryl barely had time to settle in her chair behind the imposing desk when he knocked for admittance.

'Come in,' she said, and pretended to be busy on the computer.

She felt him, smelled him, her every nerve responding to him before she raised her eyes to look at him. He was wearing cut-offs and a singlet and he was even more deeply tanned, presumably all over, for she couldn't see any white bits. Sport sandals protected his shapely feet and long, straight toes. His hair was unbound, straggling round his face, betraying the swashbuckler within him.

'Good morning, ma'am,' he said, smiling mockingly.

'You wanted to see me?' she replied, clicking Save, though there was nothing important on the monitor.

'I did. The towers,' he began, and her heart plummeted.

'What about them?'

'This Alroy character.'

'Was highly recommended. He's *au fait* with the very latest in design technology.'

'And this includes all the gear he's moved into the cellars?'

She turned defence into attack, demanding, 'How do you know about that?'

'I needed to go down and check the wiring. It was easy to get from one to the other, via the underground passage. Why, Mrs Barden? Wasn't I supposed to see the dungeon scenery and equipment? What are you trying to hide?'

Cheryl couldn't stop the flush that was spreading from her breasts to her brow. 'Nothing,' she shouted, a shade too quickly. 'You shouldn't have been there without permission.'

'I was doing my job. You wouldn't have liked the power to fail at an inconvenient moment, would you?' He looked at her, his face expressionless. There was no hint of approval or disapproval, of interest or affection or even desire in his eyes.

She did rapid mental calculations. He must have realised what the rack, the whipping-post, the pillory, the chains, ropes and sadomasochistic paraphernalia were all about. It was inconceivable that he didn't, though it had come as a shock to her when Alroy had shown her, elucidating on the use of this implement or that. Laura had been struck dumb, she recalled, her eyes round as saucers.

There seemed to be a lump lodged in Cheryl's throat. She swallowed and called Felan's bluff. 'If the lights failed anywhere in St Jude's it would be a minor blip,' she said calmly. 'You know we have a generator for emergencies.'

'Ah, yes, and the cellars have plenty of candles and braziers. I'll bet they give a realistic atmosphere, what with the black walls and scarlet drapes. Regular medieval torture chambers, if a trifle old-hat. Couldn't your pet designer have come up with something more original?'

She was right. He *did* know about it. This rocked her. It gave him an even greater advantage. She had pigeon-holed him as a strictly heterosexual male, straight down the line and no frills. Had she been wrong? Was he, in fact, conversant with kinky activities? It appeared that he wanted to dominate her mentally. What about physically? A sharp spasm of lust stabbed her at the idea. This spread, took a hold, inexorable as fate as he came round the desk and stopped behind her.

Cheryl was rooted to the chair, a wet spot staining her panty crotch.

His bare arm came over her shoulder; his hand touched the keyboard and he said dryly, 'I wouldn't have thought you had time for Solitaire.'

She realised that, in her haste to look extremely pre-occupied and busy, she had logged on to Games. 'It's a great way of learning mouse control,' she stammered.

He didn't move and his skin seemed fused with hers, his arm to her shoulder, his hand hovering. One small gesture and it would enclose her left breast. He didn't touch it, but she could feel her nipple rising like the hopeful nose of a household pet.

'What are you really up to, Mrs Barden?' he asked, bending over her, a strand of his hair caressing her forehead. 'Those tower rooms, never mind the cellars. D'you know what they remind me of?'

'No,' she muttered, achingly conscious of his naked thighs and the prominent bulge in those immodestly short shorts.

'A high-class knocking-shop.'

'I wouldn't know. I've never been in one.'

'Touché!' He chuckled.

She leaned forward, trying to get away from him. His hands descended on her shoulders, strong fingers curved like talons. Her heart was pounding, her sex prickling. She fought to be controlled, to talk, to argue – anything but grab him and have him fuck her with swift, brute force.

'You had the gall to go over the towers?' she blurted out.

'I felt responsible. It was up to me to see that Alroy had left everything secure.'

Cheryl stood, pushing back her operator's chair so that he had to move to one side. 'I have absolute faith in him. He's a professional through and through. I'm delighted with what he's done there.'

'And they'll be used for . . .?'

'Conferences. Private parties. All manner of functions. We're even thinking of amateur dramatics. There's a stage in what used to be the assembly hall.'

'I see,' he said dubiously, and his lips took on an ironic slant between the thin line of black moustache and the closely clipped beard. Then he said, 'Take off your shorts and panties, presuming you're wearing any.'

'What? Here? Someone may come in.' That's a stupid thing to say, whispered her demon. Shouldn't you have refused outright? Told him to piss off? Threatened to cry rape? You didn't. That means you want to.

'Here. Now. We've farted around too long.'

She could see there might be danger in objecting as she looked into his vivid blue eyes. She wanted to fight, but her will was as nothing compared to his tenacity of purpose. He robbed her of confidence. She was no longer the successful divorcee about to launch her own hotel. He reduced her to a wilting damsel with no more guts than the soppy heroine of a Victorian novel. She hooked her thumbs in the waist of her shorts and slipped them over her hips. Her thong followed and she was naked from the waist down, apart from her trainers.

He studied her without comment. It was as if he owned her. Then he pressed his hand between her legs. Her brown bush was saturated. It isn't too late to get away, she told herself, but he took her wrists and held them behind her back. Her lips formed into the word 'please', but she didn't know what she meant by it. Please stop, or please go on. She leaned against his arm and he slipped two fingers into her. He wriggled them around, moved them in and out, and frigged her clit with his thumb. Her breasts jiggled to his movements. She closed her eyes and pretended she was anywhere but in her own office, so vulnerable to interruption. The sun was warm on her face, the rays filtering between the shutters. The room was filled with the smell of their mutual arousal.

He released her arms and she fumbled for his cock, hearing the zip slide down, taking him out and beginning to jack him off. She wondered if he'd want her to suck him as he'd done before, and anticipated the taste of come on her lips. But, after withdrawing from her clasp and leaving her swollen, on-the-brink clit, he picked her up and sat her on the desk, her legs dangling. He pushed her back a little and she was easily accessible. He lifted her so that her knees were bent and her heels on his shoulders. A glance down told her that he was protected. He drove into her in one swift lunge. The force of his powerful hard-on made her squirm, taking every last inch of him, her body quivering. He held her under the buttocks, raising her to him, and she could not come that way, so she inserted her fingers between her clit and his cock base and rubbed herself vigorously.

Orgasm claimed her. Not in waves and peaks, but in one mighty thunderclap. He felt her come and rocked wildly against her, thrusting and thrusting in the last throes of climax. He pulled out of her. The office righted itself. Cheryl lowered her legs and sat up. She reached for the box of tissues in the desk drawer, then retrieved her panties and shorts. Felan's expression was calm and he tucked his cock inside his cut-offs, fastened up and brushed back his hair.

Then, 'Kiss me,' he said, and hauled her against him.

She thought it odd that this should happen now. The sequence of events was back to front. Didn't the kissing come before the fucking? She remembered the taste of him from that one kiss they had shared on the day they met. Now she trembled, as shy as a virgin. They had just performed a deeply intimate act, but kissing meant more. She had read somewhere that prostitutes never kissed their clients on the lips. This was a tender salute reserved for friends, children, husbands and close relatives, people they loved.

She believed this, for she'd not wanted to kiss Ashley for years.

Felan loomed over her. She felt so small in his presence, and she was nervous of revealing too much about herself as his lips lingered on hers. They moved tenderly, using slight pressure to part hers, his tongue dipping inside and her own meeting it. She melted like pink blancmange and was terrified. She didn't want to feel like this. It was too revealing, too close, something beyond those interludes of lust they'd shared.

The kiss froze the moment; an image that would be forever imprinted into the framework of her memory. It was so strong that she couldn't imagine recalling it without a wealth of emotion rising too. She wondered if he felt it as well, though his heart was a closed book to her. She might be nothing more than a quick poke, or more precious to him than all the riches of the world.

He took his mouth from hers and, about to leave, said, 'That's pretty much it, then. If you don't want me in the towers again, I'll concentrate on the stables, Mrs Barden. You're going to need one hell of a lot of garage space. Where are your rich clients going to stash their posh cars?'

'All right,' she agreed, too confused to argue. Anyway, he was talking sense.

'I'll do my best not to make too much racket and disturb your guests,' he went on, pausing as he reached the door. 'We don't want them complaining, like people who've booked package holidays in Spanish resorts and found themselves living on a building site.'

'No, I suppose not,' she replied vaguely, still bemused by his kiss. It could have meant nothing, or everything.

'Are you inviting me to the Friday bash?' he asked, subjecting her to the full force of his smile.

'If you want,' she said, and remained standing there, staring at his after-image when he was long gone.

'I haven't ridden a bike for ages,' Laura exclaimed, wheeling her machine beneath overhanging branches. 'Lucky to find a couple in the outbuildings.'

'And lucky for me that you're kind enough to cycle round, introducing me to the beauty spots,' answered Simon, his cheeks flushed with heat and exertion, his hair flopping over his forehead in that untidy way she found so appealing.

Showing him the countryside? Laura smiled to herself. OK. Let him say that, if he wanted, but they both knew they were looking for a place to have their first fuck. At one time, not so long ago, she would have thrown up all sorts of smoke screens, in complete denial of her own motives. Bronwen had put her straight. She had learned more from that outspoken woman than from Cheryl, close as they were. No, it was Bronwen and Luke who had taught her that it was all right to have strong sexual feelings and indulge them too.

There's little more evocative than aromas, she thought, turning off the road into a wood where the path was uneven and the trees and bushes enclosed her in a secret kingdom of her own. I'll never breathe in scents of wildflowers and undergrowth without remembering this magical time of my life. *The Emancipation of Laura Tilford*, she thought, and wondered if she could alter the name and use this as a book title. Not that she was keen. Her excursions into literature had ground to a halt. There were too many distractions. She had a lot of living to catch up on.

When Simon had arrived for an interview in answer to an advert in a trade paper, she had thought him uninteresting, at first. He didn't have Luke's flamboyant, rock idol looks; wasn't big and butch like Felan, or even openly lecherous like the workmen. But their eyes had met, and that smiling interchange as he introduced himself had seemed a good and pleasant thing.

Since then he had grown on her. Cheryl had given his appointment her seal of approval, but it was Laura who liaised between Ursula and the rest of the staff. Laura who sorted out problems concerning laundry and cash-and-carry purchases, and all the hundred and one problems that came up when catering for the needs of people who were willing to give St Jude's a try. Critical people. People who could make or break its reputation, to say nothing of the journalistic gourmets who wrote for tomes like *The Comprehensive Guide to British Hotels* and awarded stars from one to five.

And all I really wanted was to become a brothel-keeper, she thought. And even that has been thwarted, lest Cheryl and me get hauled before the magistrate and charged with keeping a disorderly house. Now it's a club, and this doesn't have the same thrilling and disreputable ring.

She looked back to see if Simon was following. He trudged along the path, pushing his bike. His was wiry, and not a lot taller than her, with a lean face and light-brown hair. His brows were a shade darker, and his hazel eyes were hedged by sandy lashes and creased with laughter lines. His jaw was strong and had a dimple dead centre. This gave him a determined aspect. She had seen him in action with dishonest suppliers, and it had been formidable. They didn't try to con him a second time. He was always kind and courteous to her, but remembering the ring of his crisp voice as he dealt with them sent shivers down her spine.

The sun struck hot on her bare shoulders and she was thankful that she had packed a bottle of screening lotion in her bag. The wayward thought sprang unbidden in her mind: she'd ask Simon to put it on for her. So far he had never touched her, never kissed her, and she wondered why. He wasn't married or living with anyone. He didn't even have a girlfriend, as far as she could ascertain. The horrible notion that he might be gay had tormented her, but instinct told her this wasn't so. She could tell by the way he looked at her sometimes, a measuring, dare-I-chance-my-arm look. After all, she was one of the bosses and he didn't want to risk making a move and offending her, did he?

'How much further?' he called out, and she heard the eager note in his voice.

'Not far,' she shouted back and turned down to where a stream ran through the narrow valley to the ford. Springy turf, the odour of wild garlic, the sound of water and birdsong and the amorous cooing of wood pigeons. Who could ask for a better love nest?

The bluebells were over, but the bank was starred with buttercups. She leaned her bike against the bole of a tree and sat down close to the water's edge, taking off her sandals and dabbling her feet in the icy coolness. She was wearing a gypsy skirt in floral patchwork intermingled with velvet squares. Her pink crop top was revealing, upheld by two thin straps, and she was glad that it was de rigueur to show one's bra this season. At one time it would have been the height of sluttery. Now she happily flaunted her white underpinning, her breasts upheld, pushed high, cradled in half cups, the satin straps on display alongside the top's spaghetti ones.

Simon walked towards her, then laid his bicycle on its side on the ground. He flopped down beside her, his arms clasped under his head, staring up into the vast green spread of an oak tree. The glade was hot, the sun hanging over it like a great molten disc. Laura let the rays dry her feet and rolled on to her back, stretching provocatively. She felt like a pagan. Simon and herself alone in this Eden. There was nothing else to do, surely, but celebrate male and female flesh.

You're being far too lyrical, she teased herself, while she lifted her hands to her breasts and caressed them lightly, watching Simon's reaction. He propped himself up on one elbow, facing her, and stared at her busy fingers. His shirt was unbuttoned at the neck, the sleeves rolled back, and it had worked out from the waist of his beige trousers. He had a slim, agile body, she had already noted and, as he observed her, so the long baton of his cock swelled and tented his fly.

She'd caressed herself openly in front of Bronwen and Luke. Even Cheryl had seen her disporting wantonly, but this was different. Never, in all the years she'd been married to Stuart, had she lain in the open air like this. There was nowhere to hide. Her body, though still sexy, was that of a mature women, with all the small imperfections brought about by time. It would be easier to pretend in the half-light, candles perhaps, or a full moon. Not this unrelenting glare. But Simon had an erection, just by looking at her, and this was flattering. Her hand progressed from her nipples to her pubic mound. She pressed it and pleasure jolted through her. Unable to resist temptation, she pulled up her skirt with slow deliberation. Her knees came into view, then her thighs and she spread them, the hem now resting on the white triangle that concealed her fork.

Simon gasped and leaned over her, cupping her cheek with his hand, stroking her lips with his thumb. Then he sat up abruptly, saying, 'I'm sorry. Please don't be angry. It's just that you look so beautiful lying there.'

She was inordinately pleased by the compliment, but said, laughing, 'What a chat-up line!'

'I mean it,' he said earnestly, and rested his arms on his humped knees. 'I'm not used to chatting up women. It's not my style. I got out of practice, you see, married to my wife for all those years, and I haven't felt like it much since she died.'

Oh dear, why couldn't he have brought out these revelations earlier on? she thought. When we were having a cup of tea together, for example. Not now, when I'm randy as a Siamese cat on heat.

'It's all right, Simon. Really, it is,' she said, wanting to comfort him. Poor man. She hadn't realised he was a widower.

'I wanted to tell you before, but there never seemed to be the right moment,' he went on. 'If you read my CV, you'll have seen that I was butler to Lord Rossley for many years. My wife was housekeeper. We'd always been in service together. Never had any children. It was just her and me.'

'You must miss her dreadfully.'

'I do. Her company and, mostly, sex,' he said, surprisingly. 'I've not had many women, but I've studied it from books. Tessa, that's my late wife, taught me too. We experimented together. She said that with all I knew about the clit, I could rate as the world's greatest lover. It has nothing to do with looks or the size of one's tool. According to their portraits, Casanova wasn't much to write home about and neither was Don Juan. They must have adored the clit and made love to women's minds too, realising that thought is a powerful aphrodisiac.'

Laura didn't know what to say. His frankness inspired her body with passion, while her heart rejoiced that he understood. She was starting to realise that many men were ignorant when it came to women's most sensitive organ. They assumed that because they found the penis in vagina to be the acme of bliss, their female partner felt the same. Luke was an exception, of course, but even he made love with ulterior motives.

Actions speak louder than words, Laura decided, and took off her top. 'My back is burning,' she said, and fished out the sun-oil. 'Would you put some of this on for me?'

'You're not angry?' he said, but didn't hesitate to pour a puddle of lotion into his palm and apply it to her shoulders.

'Of course not, Simon,' she said, while he kneeled behind her, his touch as smooth as silk, the exotically perfumed oil reminiscent of tropical beaches and azure sea. We could go away on holiday, Simon and me, she thought dreamily. I've got the wherewithal, or shall have once St Jude's starts going into profit.

He moved closer, till she could feel the rigid shaft of his cock nudging her, centre back. His hands trembled slightly as he worked the oil into her receptive skin. She didn't want him to stop – not ever – going into a kind of trance, almost purring with contentment. He pushed the bra straps down, and his slippery hands went further, over her shoulders and across the upper swell of her breasts. She leaned back into him, gyrating her hips a little so that she brought pressure to bear on his cock. His trouser closure felt hot and damp.

He removed his hands, screwed on the lid and set the bottle on the grass by her handbag. She turned towards him and he kissed her. They were still on their knees but he pressed the length of his body against hers. It was an experienced kiss, and, for a second, she envied Tessa who had been young with him once, learning about sex and how to get the most out of it. Lucky Tessa, who hadn't married a closet gay secretly hankering after those of his own gender.

Mouth pressed to open mouth, they kissed for some time, and she went weak all over, sliding her legs from under her and relaxing on the grass. He unhooked her bra effortlessly and the cups fell away. He stopped kissing her then, his hands gentle as they feathered over her breasts, rolling and roiling the swollen nipples, then bending to lick them. She started to unbutton his shirt.

Everything seemed to be in slow motion. She unbuckled his belt and opened his trousers. He undid the cord that fastened her skirt and she wriggled out of it. He took off his shirt and dropped his pants. This revealed a posing pouch made of fake tiger-skin. Good Lord, Laura thought, while thought was at all possible. Who knows what's worn under perfectly ordinary-looking garments?

The material was stretched to the limit by the bulky packet behind it. He kicked off his loafers and slowly, like a stripteasing Chippendale, pulled down one side of the pouch, then the other, showing a tangle of pubes but never quite revealing his cock.

'You take off yours, and I'll take off mine,' he murmured, standing above her, legs astraddle, the pouch partly rolled down.

His body was firmly made, lithe and agile. He was an

active person, never idle. He didn't have a beer belly and didn't smoke. While not a faddy eater, he followed a sensible diet. These facts floated somewhere in her brain, but she was focusing on how he intended to pleasure her.

I did it for Bronwen, so I can do it for him, she decided, and her knickers were down and off before she gave herself time to think about it. The grass was lush and the feel of it against her bare bottom highly arousing. She felt incredibly sinful, and loved it. Naked in a wood, not too far from the road. Other seekers of the Great Outdoors might come along that way at any moment. Simon dropped his pouch and looked down at her, and the desire in his eyes was so exciting that she wanted to reach out and touch him. His cock curved upwards, pale-skinned, rising from a thicket of brownish hair. He was circumcised because it had been fashionable at the time of his birth to rob baby boys of their foreskins, something to do with hygiene, not religion. Laura hadn't tried a cut male before. She stared at the very red, very wet and very exposed cock.

She salivated. Would it taste as juicy as it looked?

He guessed that she was about to reach out and caress it, and he stopped her, saying, 'No. Not yet. Lie there and let me arouse you.'

And he did. She had never been made love to so thoroughly. Simon didn't follow that male script of how to achieve orgasm as quickly and efficiently as possible. No, sex with him became a garden of desire to be explored at leisure. Even Luke could take a leaf from his book, she thought, moaning in appreciation as he stroked her lightly from toes to ankles to knees and thighs. He didn't proceed to her obvious pleasure zones till he'd sensitised the whole of her body. And when he did finally flick over her nipples with his tongue, she fizzed like champagne. He let her touch him then, and she made her hand into a firm tube, encasing his cock, rubbing it firmly and lingering on the mushroom-shaped helm. He was adept at self-control, his climax of secondary importance.

He spread her open, no fold or cranny hidden from his exploration, and she forgot to be embarrassed in case she didn't come up to his expectations. He smiled as he gazed down at her cleft, parting the lips and finding the core. He dipped a finger into the liquid centre and laved the delta and the excited clit. It was as if she was doing it to herself; he knew precisely where to touch and when, how hard to rub, or gently. When her agitated breathing betrayed the onset of orgasm, he stopped for a second, letting the feeling die back, so that he could wind it up again.

'I can't wait . . . I want it . . . now!' she begged at last, writhing against his fingers.

'Hush, darling. There, there . . . you shall have it. Trust me,' he answered, his voice unsteady.

He touched her once more and she cried out as her orgasm broke with awesome intensity. He held her briefly, cupping her pubis, then rolled on a condom and entered her. Her inner muscles clenched round his cock, the pleasure intensified as she felt him thrusting, gaining momentum. The control he had so far exerted gave way to a fierce hunger, and she closed her eyes and clawed at his back and urged him to go faster, harder, till he groaned and climaxed and lay still on top of her.

Laura held him fast, a happy smile on her face. A smug smile, she was sure. She hadn't been merely fucked. Simon had made love to her in every sense of the word. He made her feel special.

After a while, he rolled on to his side, but still kept one arm under her neck. He hugged her and said, 'I hope you're not going to wish you hadn't done that.'

'No, I shan't. It was my choice, Simon. Lord knows, I'm old enough to know my own mind.'

Was this his way of letting her down lightly? Was he the one who was already regretting it?

He kissed her gently, his expression wistful, then murmured, 'I'm glad you're not sorry. I should be gutted if you were. But I wondered, you being who you are, and me an employee.'

She linked her fingers with his, deciding to believe him. She couldn't go on avoiding commitment simply because Stuart had let her down. In one of the self-help books she'd been devouring lately, she had read that it was unrealistic to have expectations. Disappointment was of one's own making. One had no right to expect a person to behave in a certain way, simply because one wanted them to.

It was a hard philosophy to put into practice, but she was getting there slowly and by degrees. She hoped so much that one day she would be able to trust again, put all her eggs in one basket and fall in love, irrevocably, madly and with every particle of herself, holding nothing back.

She smiled up at Simon and said, 'I'm hotel-sitting tonight. Cheryl's going over to see her mother, and the skeleton staff are off duty too. We'll have the place to ourselves. Let's take it from there, shall we?'

Chapter Seven

*T*he purple silk slithered sensuously against her bare flesh, and Joanna stood without moving as Deven wound the sari round her. It was spangled with sequins and she admired her glittering self in the mirror. She was preparing for an important event in the pagan calendar, due to take place that evening, attempting to transform her mind into a calm, contemplative pool.

Deven appeared in the mirror behind her, a distracting presence. His brown fingers adjusted a fold of semi-transparent material over one shoulder. Beneath it she wore nothing but a brief, gold lamé bodice with short sleeves. Her thonged sandals were gold, so were her pendant earrings and the wide bracelets that banded her upper arms.

Her hair was still thick, and she hennaed it a vibrant auburn and added to the length with extensions. She wore it loose, though her costume was from India where traditionally a woman of her maturity and station would have parted it in the middle, drawn it back into a bun and modestly hidden it under a veil. Joanna was a woman of eclectic taste, taking aspects of differing cultures and using them to suit herself, ignoring conventions. Non-judgemental and open-minded, she had spent her life questing for answers to the meaning of existence, the universe and the mystery of creation.

The resurgence of interest in these fundamental issues had reached a peak in the 1960s and had never really gone away, recently invigorated by the dawning of the new millennium. Fell Tor was more popular than ever, a stream of disciples clamouring for knowledge. It had become a centre for crystal healing, astrology, tarot and runic readings, music and dance, regression, retreats and environmental workshops. Joanna gave students the opportunity to develop their spirituality, and encouraged the uninhibited exploration of the senses as a road to greater understanding.

'It's a here today, gone tomorrow world out there,' Deven remarked, his hands gentle as a woman's as he placed a wreath of stargazer lilies on Joanna's head. 'We can offer self-awareness.'

'I wish my daughter would accept our teachings,' Joanna answered with a sigh. The strong smell of the flowers was intoxicating, as was his touch, and she sank to her knees before him and unlooped the tiny ball buttons that held the front of his djellabah together.

'Tonight may be an awakening for her,' he said, his head up, staring into the middle distance as if lost in realms of his own.

'I pray so,' she whispered, admiring his muscular legs, and the splendid cock that reared towards her. It was a column of smooth, dark flesh interwoven with blue veins, the bulbous end enticing, already pearled by a single drop of pre-come.

She prayed for something else too. *Whatever gods are out there, please don't let Deven be the one who initiates Cheryl into Fell Tor's ways of love.*

The thought was impure and petty, but she was unable to share him with her daughter. Others, maybe. She had already witnessed him copulating with acolytes of either gender, had indeed taken part herself when he had suggested that group sex would be beneficial, but she drew the line at Cheryl. She couldn't tell him. He would be angry. Sometimes her cynical self took over and she doubted his sainthood. He was a man, first and foremost, with a man's lusts, ambitions and weaknesses.

She had made up her mind that he shouldn't have Cheryl, even if she had to knock him unconscious. To hell with denying selfishness, possessiveness and jealousy. She experienced them in full measure and rejoiced that she could still tingle with such powerful, even destructive emotions.

'Suck me,' he said abruptly, his finely chiselled face impassive.

She bent forward a little, took his cock in her hands and guided it into her mouth. Its unique smell drifted into her nostrils. He was always bathing, constantly anointing himself with essential oils, yet the pungent odour of raunchy male couldn't be masked. She tasted the tip he pushed between her lips, quickly followed by the thick shaft. No time tonight for the slow build-up towards a spiritual as well as physical union that might take hours. He was eager, behaving like a human, not a holy man.

He thrust into her throat and she felt him throb. Another drop of dew salted her taste buds. He grunted and drew away a little. She stuck out her tongue, teasing the helm and the underside. Reaching up, she found his nut-brown nipples, tweaking and pinching them. He shuddered and put one hand on her head to hold her steady, and the crushed petals bled perfume. She expected him to come over her face, but then noticed that his breathing was slow and deep. A long-time master, he was even now delaying his orgasm, controlling and directing it, while fanning Kundalini's smouldering fires. She pictured it in her mind's eye, that powerful, latent energy depicted as a coiled serpent, residing at the base of the spine.

'Slow down,' he said, signalling that she lower her hands and rise to her feet. 'Are you wet, Joanna?'

'Yes, Deven,' she whispered.

'Show me,' he ordered.

She lifted the bright sari and exposed her legs. They were youthful, smooth and tanned, with no saggy flesh or unsightly veins. Her bush was neatly trimmed and dyed to match her hair. It was matted with juice, and her lips were enlarged, the inner pair protruding round the plump clit. Deven stroked her, then raised his hand and sniffed the essence that clung to his fingers. His erect cock bobbed. He closed his eyes, exerting mind control. The engorged organ became still. Joanna recognised the power within him, and her pussy ached with wanting.

'Over there,' he said quietly, indicating the divan near the open patio windows.

They slept there sometimes, not always, needing their own space. When the mood took her, she liked to pretend that he was her husband. Her lord, to be obeyed and served. She dismissed this as play-acting. She was far too much her own woman to take on the yoke again, wasn't she? Yet there were moments when she needed to relinquish her matriarchal role, to become his chattel, his devotee, the object of his will. Maybe she would marry him, one day.

The couch was like a colourful island set in a sea of polished boards. She put her garland aside, pulled the sari up out of harm's way, and stretched on the scarlet velvet throw, sinuous as a cat. Deven arranged her so that her face, breasts and belly were buried in the sumptuous, richly hued cushions. He slipped an arm under her and raised her hips, keeping them in place with a bolster. Its gilded embroidery scratched her groin.

'The Rear Gateway to paradise,' he said, and she felt him against her, hairy legs rough on the backs of her thighs, his cock prodding into her bottom crack.

He was about to arse-fuck her, and Joanna liked it when he did, though she could never climax by anus alone, any more than through vaginal penetration. He knew this and wouldn't disappoint her. He discarded his robe, and she couldn't see his beautiful body from that position, but could feel it, her mind filling up with images. Milk chocolate skin, raven hair and lustrous eyes,

135

he was a marvel of co-ordination; muscles, nerves and sinews all combined into this perfectly proportioned entity.

Hell, but I'm lucky, she thought, as she felt him pulsing against her anal opening. I can't afford to let this one slip away, even if I do have to share my kingdom with him and become legally bound.

He slid a hand between her legs and dabbled his fingers in the soft folds, wetting them with her juice. She heard the slurpy sound it made as he lubricated her, and she pressed herself into his palm, moaning, urging him to go on. He indulged her and caught one of her breasts and teased the nipple through the gold fabric. She hitched her bottom higher, letting him know that she was on the brink of orgasm. His hands left her. The divan sagged as he sat up. She heard a packet ripping and the little rustle of latex.

She whimpered like a child deprived of a sweet, and he resumed, spreading her wetness around her arsehole, inserting two fingers to ensure it was slippery, then rubbing her clit from behind. She rocked against him, and he took his cock in hand and guided it further into her. It felt huge and she flinched, wanting to protect her small, forbidden orifice from his invasion, but only for a second. She had lost this second cherry years ago and used Ben Wa Balls on a regular basis, and vibrators and a lingam, keeping the tight passage flexible.

Deven was easing himself in, and she relaxed her muscles, concentrating on the sensations mounting in her as he poked and stroked her. He pushed harder and the whole of his helm disappeared. Another firm thrust and his cock was embedded, his groin welded to her rear, his glossy pubic hair brushing against her fissure as he moved, slowly at first, then faster. It wasn't exactly pleasure she felt, nor yet pain, but a sensation of being stuffed to capacity as he rode her fiercely, his fingers rubbing.

'Remember to keep your tongue touching the roof of your mouth,' he gasped, pistoning in and out. 'Remember your third eye. Pull the energy upwards, up the spine, through all the chakras to the top of your head. Oh . . . *oh*! Are you coming?'

'Yes! Yes!' she cried, as her orgasm broke and she was borne aloft, unsure whether she was expanding her consciousness, or just enjoying a bloody good screw.

Deven had no doubts, it seemed. She clenched her sphincter round his cock as he gave a final jerk and ejaculated. She lay still, his body quiet on hers, his hands in her hair. He never, ever treated her in a cavalier manner, turning away from her and snoring, or simply getting up and leaving as if, having shot his load, she was of no further interest to him.

He held her and caressed her, his fingers moving over her tenderly. Then he became still and she wondered if he slept, listening to his breathing. She raised one of his hands and kissed it, and he smiled and stroked her hair, giving it little, affectionate tugs. She took time out to savour this moment. It was precious and she didn't want to waste it.

The evening was warm and the setting sun cast swathes of colour over the sky, mauve and green, shot across by flame, holding the night clouds at bay. Cheryl drove her car from the stables-cum-garage and round to the front of St Jude's, pausing to admire the twin towers. Once they might have been part of the courtyard, helping to form a protective square, with walkways for bowmen. There were still arrow slits, sharp as punctuation marks, in parts of the ivy-hung walls, but many changes had been made, mostly during Queen Victoria's reign. The area had been roofed in and contained a communal hall, with rooms leading off, and passages connecting with the kitchen, the laundry and the backstairs that allowed the cleaners access to the guestrooms. Even so, St Jude's remained impressively Gothic.

In a couple of days it would come alive, as those invited to the party enjoyed its hospitality. She couldn't wait, an almost orgasmic frisson rising from the base of her spine to her cortex. She pressed her bottom into the leather seat, flimsy skirt caught between her buttocks. She'd changed into clean panties after her shower, but the crotch was already damp.

Damn Felan Boynton, she thought. I hope his balls drop off.

It galled her to realise why she was hanging around instead of heading off towards Fell Tor. The view had something to do with it, but that wasn't the whole story. Felan had started work on the outbuildings. He could have done overtime to get the job finished, but there was no sign of him, and she told herself that she was glad. Since that moment of lunacy in her office, he'd not so much as spoken to her. Who did he think he was? God's gift to women? Cheeky sod!

She revved up angrily and the car responded. It was brand, spanking new, an olive-green Range Rover in which she felt terribly important. Practical, of course, for they were a little off the beaten track. Who knew what winter might bring, the weather turning nasty, with floods and frost and snow? It might be up to her to keep the home fires burning. Laura had her own runabout, but this sleek, military-looking beast was insured for her to drive, and Simon and Ursula too, though it was unlikely that the housekeeper would dare, unless a state of national emergency was declared.

I should be wearing combats and a khaki jacket with numerous pockets for things like Swiss Army knives, maps and compasses, a torch, matches, and a first aid kit. Oh, and not forgetting the chocolate bar and glucose tablets. Her mind slipped notches and she was off in a daydream.

Up on the moors and the night was a dirty one, least ways that's how she'd planned it and she didn't mean weather-wise. But no, even though the man of her choice was there and the circumstances peachy, it was howling a gale and bucketing down with rain. She was in charge of half a dozen volunteers, all handpicked by the BBC for this latest in television entertainment, a cross between *Big*

Brother and *Castaway*. She had only been given need-to-know details and couldn't think why she'd applied. The important thing was that she was there, and so was Felan. By George, with her extensive SAS training, she'd soon show him a thing or two about surviving in the wilds!

They came to a hut and she gave brusque orders. They were to shelter there till daybreak. It was used by the mountain rescue team and fully equipped. Soon a log fire sent shadows dancing over the wooden walls. Supplies were found and her exhausted group ate, then rolled themselves in sleeping bags and crashed, dead to the world. She sat by the fire with Felan, planning tomorrow's route. His eyes were shining with admiration and he kissed her almost reverently, then made her comfortable on the hearthrug. She lay back and felt his hands moving all over her, fingers finding their way through her clothing to her nipples, then down to her clit.

'You're a marvellous woman,' he whispered. 'A born leader. I want to fuck you legless.'

The scenario was unwinding in her head. She had got to the bit where he was bringing on her climax and about to enter her, when the lane twisted sharply and the FWD nearly mounted the rear end of a tractor. This brought Cheryl down to earth with a jolt. The driver turned, grinned and gave her the stiff finger. He was big and beefy, with attitude. He thought himself cock of this particular dung-heap.

'Clod! Prat! Bumpkin!' she raged angrily as she swept past him. 'D'you need the whole road? Can't you keep that beast under control?'

She rounded the next bend and jammed on the brakes. Sheep, baaing stupidly, blocked the lane. There's nothing quite as idiotic looking as a shorn sheep, she decided, honking her horn at the guy who ambled along, herding this collection of animal cretins. If one stopped, they all stopped. If one decided to nibble at the bank, sure enough there they were, nudging up behind and tucking in.

'Jesus, what daft things! They look as if they were put together by a committee. Get them out of the way,' she shouted, but the shepherd merely stared at her, ruminated on the piece of straw protruding from his teeth, and shook his had.

'You can't hurry nature, missus,' he observed.

She didn't stop to argue, disconcerted by the way he was looking at her. She was seated too high for him to see, but she knew that her knees were exposed. She made no response, yanked her skirt into place, kept her legs together and eased the car forward, and the sheep had no choice but to break ranks and let her through. Matters like this are going to be managed a little differently now I'm in the area, she thought, but foresaw problems. She and Laura were regarded as strangers. This much had been made obvious by those they were employing from the village. It might take twenty years before they began to be accepted, and even then with reservations. Foreigners. Townies. That's what they were.

She reached Fell Tor without further mishap and was met by Joanna, who took her hands and kissed her on both cheeks, then said, 'You're overdoing it. Nothing shouts stress more than a woman's skin and the bags under her eyes.'

'Thanks a bunch for reminding me that I'm getting on. It's all I need,' Cheryl replied acidly.

'You look radiant,' said Deven, standing close and kissing her brow, his hair waving about his shoulders, a bright red caste-mark placed just above the centre of his arched black brows. 'Come to the garden. The others are waiting for you.'

Divine guru, she thought, you smell like spices borne on the trade winds from an exotic island. You look at me in that wise, deep way that makes me feel as if only we two exist, but Mother's eyeballing me and, regretfully, I must give you a miss. Yours is one cock that it wouldn't be prudent to sample.

In fine weather the garden was used as an extension of the common room where meals were served and debates

140

held. A marquee had been put up and, not far away, people were chanting and dancing round a huge bonfire. Young, not so young, it was a curious assembly. Beads and feathers, body-paint and complete or semi-nudity, this in itself gave them a uniformity. The reflected flames set the nearby lake ablaze, bathers frolicking in this natural watering hole.

'There are faint echoes of "love-and-peace", I'll admit,' Joanna said, smiling indulgently at her followers and linking her arm with Cheryl's. 'That was long ago and far away. It's a grimmer world entirely now, and you could say that these are refugees from self-centred materialism. The majority of people don't give a toss about global warming or endangered species or their fellow beings, just as long as they get rich quick and grab all the consumer goods the media tell them are vital to their existence.'

'And aren't they? Is it wrong to aim for a better standard of living?' Cheryl didn't want to spend the evening arguing with her mother. They never agreed on these issues. She had avoided contact with the denizens of Fell Tor as much as possible. They were harmless enough, but she couldn't go along with their ideas, though envying them a little. It must be wonderful to have faith in something, to believe in every reported phenomenon from flying saucers to fairies at the bottom of the garden.

She was of the opinion that Joanna and Deven were doing rather well. She didn't see them starving or sleeping rough, and there never seemed to be any shortage of money. Materialism? Who was kidding whom?

'You're prickly as a porcupine,' Joanna said, slipping an arm round her waist and smiling. 'As I said ... all work and no play makes Jill a very dull girl.'

The marquee was like the Tardis; it expanded when one got inside. Cheryl had seen it several times before when it had been hauled out of store and erected by some of Fell Tor's finest, but with her dogged determination to avoid being drawn into solstices and other festivals, she had never entered its hallowed precincts.

It was like another world, a pleasure dome lit by perfumed candles standing in wrought-iron girandoles, and with velvet and silk swags draped from the ceiling. Incense swirled up from the snarling mouths of bronze serpents. Prayer mats added their colour to the walls. The thick posts upholding the canvas were garlanded with vines, trailing plants and banners, the wooden floor softened by carpets.

Cheryl's ear was seduced by dreamy, celestial music relayed through speakers. A large TV screen was showing underwater images – calling whales and basking sharks, the playful, intelligent dolphin, rainbow fish flitting in and out of grottoes. Naked girls and personable youths, graceful as merfolk, swam around touching each other's bodies, fondling pert breasts, lightly furred pussies and strapping cocks. Some rose to the surface, treading water, linked by mouths and at the genitals.

Cheryl watched and wondered and lusted, her nipples peaking under her strapless cerise top, her wrap-around, rose-patterned skirt clinging to her hips, and her panties working into her damp crack. The decor of the marquee had been cunningly contrived to appeal to the senses. It could have been modelled on a Turkish potentate's summer palace where, cares of rulership set aside, he idled with his odalisques.

There were low tables spread with piquant dishes of mushrooms and pulses, pasta and garlic sauce, home-baked bread, fruit from the orchard, butter and cheese produced in Fell Tor's dairy, wine pressed from grapes grown in the vineyards. Carafes of cider and firkins of ale were there for the taking, and bowls of potpourri and perfumed unguents that could be enjoyed by anyone.

The couches and deep armchairs formed a rough circle, and Joanna led Cheryl over to where a bounteously endowed, linten-haired woman stood, saying, 'Norma, you've already met Cheryl, but this is her first experience of one of our gatherings.'

142

'We want you to be her guide,' Deven said, his clear voice carrying. Heads turned in his direction. He smiled and seated himself in a thronelike chair, and Joanna occupied a stool at his feet, holding herself like a queen, or a prima ballerina.

'As you wish,' Norma said, her accent Australian, her round face as guileless as a child's. 'There's a new moon tonight, Cheryl,' she continued. 'So, in its honour, we're celebrating goddesses and sacred harlots. They can be Egyptian, Greek or Roman, from the planet Zogg or any place. Let your imagination soar,' and she pointed to a huge pile of clothing in all shapes and sizes in the middle of the floor.

Most of the women present were already wearing versions of the goddess theme ranging from the Botticelli *Venus* to Isis, with a bewildering variety of female deities lobbed in for good measure. The men favoured white tunics to the knee and laurel wreaths, going for the Grecian look. One of them caught Cheryl's eye. He had an impudent face, cropped bleached hair and wore a ring in one eyebrow and a stud in his nose. He was exceptionally good looking, healthily tanned, on the young side. In fact, he couldn't have been much older than her son. This made her squirm. Tim was coming to the party at St Jude's, and Daisy had promised to be there too. How could she even think of coupling with such a youthful Adonis?

'His name is Aiden,' said Norma, catching on, then added, 'Have a drink,' and after a couple of glasses, Cheryl found that the idea of bonking him didn't seem so preposterous.

'I hope he's not into hugging trees. I can't hack that,' she burbled: the wine was astonishingly potent.

'Oh, no. He's a new kid on the block. Came along for the ride, I guess. You want I should introduce you?'

'Not yet. Let me get acclimatised.'

'What you need, kiddo, is a massage. First off, pick out a costume.'

Spoilt for choice, Cheryl held up this one and then that

from the pile. They were all gorgeous, even those made of leather that might have been more suitable for a dominatrix. She dithered between a bacchante tunic with a leopard-skin pashmina and a diaphanous chiton in radiant white that reeked Aphrodite. Norma nodded in approval of the latter, and Cheryl draped the robe over her arm and followed her to a curtained-off portion of the tent.

There the atmosphere shifted again. Everything about the alcove was warm, friendly and feminine. Two massage couches were already in use, the occupants being attended by scantily clad women. Cheryl was suddenly embarrassed. Did she really have to bare all? She could decline, of course, but that was chicken. Besides, there was Aiden, and the wine had put her sensible self on hold.

'Let me help you,' Norma said, and undid the knot that held Cheryl's sarong-style skirt in place. It dropped away and one of the girls hung it on a hook. The little top came next, and her breasts were exposed, nipples crimping in the draught. Only her panties remained. Cheryl unlaced the ribbon ties and wriggled out of them, then shed her sandals.

Her nudity was accepted without comment. Several of the women were so absorbed in each other that they hadn't even noticed her come in. They lay on cushions, their naked bodies and limbs entwined, hands busy caressing the full or conical shapes of breasts, their pelvises thrust forward, sensitive parts touching. Cheryl could see the folds of their sex parting as they pressed closer, their pussies kissing in a way that must have been intensely satisfying. Nothing was neglected, fingers and mouths seeking swollen nipples and clits, but slowly, sensuously, without haste, the experience one to be savoured. She could not turn away, admiring the roundness of their thighs, the polished sheen of their knees and the delicate curves of their ankles.

They were excited, emitting little moans that made her wet. She wanted to join in, but Norma had her spread herself, facedown, on a padded bench. She relaxed, engulfed in sybaritic luxury, her ears attuned to the soft, fluttering cries of the women taking their pleasure of one another, and the music reaching the alcove via back-up speakers. Bells tinkled, flutes trilled with every note embellished, while stringed instruments produced weird cadences. These sounds added to her trancelike state.

Now she could feel hands working on her, soothing away every ache. 'We'll use talcum powder, not oil,' she heard Norma explain. 'It allows a feather-light touch.'

Cheryl felt as if she was being sprinkled with raindrops that made her skin silky. The hands glided over her, now delicate, now strong, across her shoulder blades, down her spine, dipping between the relaxed crease of her buttocks and fingering the taut mouth of her anus. Cheryl felt it open and she gasped. An exploring digit probed it, and she wasn't at all sure about this, though an exciting, aching, raw sensation welled up inside her.

'There, there, honey. Take it easy,' Norma whispered, and Cheryl realised that the hands belonged to her. 'Now, over you go, and let me get at those awful tight knots screwing you up.'

More talc was dusted over her, and Cheryl floated in space as Norma's strong hands resumed their magic. They were joined by others and she couldn't be bothered to lift her heavy eyelids and take a peek. Starting at her feet, they massaged each toe, and the sensation was akin to having her clit stimulated, but this time it was ten little organs of pleasure, not one. Other hands cruised up her body, circling her navel, under her armpits and round her breasts, alighting on her hard and hungry nipples, then gliding away. Cheryl imagined that she was being massaged by the four-armed Hindu goddess Kali, one hand caressing her temples, another fondling her belly, and the others lightly manipulating the insides of her elbows and thighs and the backs of her knees.

Bliss hovered, just beyond reach, and she moaned and twisted her head from side to side as those repeated sweeps around her breasts roused but did not satisfy.

She parted her legs and humped the air, then felt fingers combing through her bush and parting her sex. She held her breath, afraid to move in case they ignored the tip of her clit.

'That's enough,' Norma said, and every hand was removed, leaving Cheryl trembling, the ache within her resembling pain.

'No. Please,' she heard herself whimpering, her voice high-pitched and strange. 'I was just about to come.'

'So you shall, honey,' Norma promised. 'But we want to dress you first. Your ma and Deven are already outside, preparing their invocation to the moon. We should be with them, worshipping our goddesses, reserving our sexual energy and coming at the height of the ritual.'

Rising reluctantly, Cheryl clung on to that thought: she would be allowed orgasm, but not yet.

Aching with frustration, love juice trickling down her inner thigh, Cheryl stood while the white chiton was dropped over her head and banded by a silver girdle that criss-crossed under her breasts and was then passed across her back and round her waist. It was a one-piece garment with long sleeves, slashed from shoulder to wrists, and drawn together with fancy clasps. The women clustered around her, brushing her hair and braiding it with ribbons. Excitement crackled in the air, each person there aroused by the promise of spiritual and physical ecstasy when the young moon trailed her mysteries across the indigo sky.

They were all beautiful in their own way, including the solidly built, 35-year-old Norma. Cheryl longed to make love to them, to feel their breasts in her hands before darting down to where their depilated or hairy mounds opened, like ripe figs 'dripping with luscious fluid. She remembered the experience she had shared with Bronwen, Laura and Luke; it seemed fate had decided that she should have more than one initiation.

A mirror, tilted on its mahogany stand, threw back her image in the candlelight. This was a dreamscape, surely?

146

She hardly recognised herself in this beautiful goddess, imperial, yet promiscuous. Her height added to the impression of regality. Her breasts, which she sometimes considered too large, seemed perfect. Her narrow waist and wide hips were those of a corn deity, Demeter perhaps, bringer of fertility and abundance.

I should be carrying a cornucopia, she thought, then lost it as she saw Norma leading someone forward. It was Aiden. He came close and touched the tip of Cheryl's tingling nipple. 'Are you up for this?' he asked.

Up and over and way beyond, she thought. If someone doesn't fuck me soon, I'll explode like Mount Vesuvius. Watch out Pompeii.

'Who gave you permission to touch me?' she snapped bossily.

He withdrew his hand as if scalded, muttering, 'Sorry.'

She didn't answer him, just smiled. Close up, she could see that not only his eyebrow was pierced. The small, wine-red nubs of his nipples were also ringed, and linked by a thin silver chain. She reached out and tugged firmly, making his flesh stretch.

'Have you any more?' she asked, recalling how Daisy had insisted that she wanted her belly-button done on her sixteenth birthday. That had nearly caused World War Three. Ashley had taken a stand and Cheryl had sided with their daughter. The argument had rumbled on for months, but eventually Daisy came home triumphant, flaunting a little gold sleeper in her dimpled navel.

'I have,' he murmured, and she sensed that he was rather shy under the bravura.

'Where?' she insisted, and his colour deepened. She had embarrassed him and this was refreshing after Felan's treatment. She was in charge. This encounter would be orchestrated by her.

'Where d'you think?' he asked, his eyes widening as he challenged her.

She glanced down to the front of his linen kilt and she saw his cock stirring. The fabric was thin and the outline of his burgeoning dick showed promise. Her breath hissed sharply as the sudden thought struck her. He couldn't mean he was pierced there? *Could he?*

She'd read an article in a magazine found hidden under Tim's bed, a top-shelf porno publication that had shocked yet aroused her as she flipped through it. Open-crotch shots of glamorous models with well-defined clits; men with extra-large dicks; couples at it, or pretending to be, and articles on tattooing, scarring, branding and ringing. There had been illustrations of cocks with quite thick rings passing through them. This had roused her to such a pitch that she had put her hand up under her skirt and touched herself, right there in her son's bedroom. Her curiosity had continued to niggle. What would such a ring feel like attached to a prick pushed deep in her? Would it add to the sensation? Clitoral piercing had been mentioned too. It made hers burn, just thinking about it.

'I'll bet you're shooting a line,' she said, her voice unsteady. 'What have you had done? Navel piercing? A bolt through your tongue? That's nothing unusual.'

'What about this then?' he replied, and lifted his kilt waist high.

Her eyes leaped to his crotch. It never ceased to amaze her how the attention was immediately riveted by a cock. Large or small, stiff or limp, the first thing one looked at when a man exposed himself was his organ. Aiden's was shapely, sticking out in front of him. He wasn't circumcised, his foreskin was attached, rolled back from a firm, fat, shiny wet head. But it was different from any she had seen before. A polished black ring passed through the head. Her fingers itched to turn it gently and test his reaction.

He did it for her, nimble fingers moving the onyx full circle, and a fresh drop of jism poised at the single eye, then trickled down to anoint the ring. He didn't stop looking at her, holding his cock higher and pumping it as if testing its readiness. The onyx turned easily, tempting her tongue to savour it, and her mouth to enjoy being gagged by his shaft.

'Doesn't it hurt?' she said, her own loins cringing.

148

'Not any more. It was sore when I had it done,' he replied, and took her hand and guided it to his crotch. 'Have a feel,' he encouraged.

She didn't hesitate, fingertips exploring him, running up the silky stem, encountering the ridge of foreskin and the cool, smooth surface of the ring. Her other hand slipped between his thighs, encountering the tautness of his balls. She weighed them in her palm, and her nails scratched over the sensitive scrotum. His breathing became shallow, betraying his rising excitement. She ventured to turn the ring a quarter-inch. His cock expanded further, the head an angry-looking purple.

'Why did you have this done?' She was fascinated, watching the effect her touch was having on him.

'You can see why, can't you?' he muttered. 'It makes it all the more sensitive, and you'll enjoy it too, when I stick it in you.'

'You think I'll let you do that?' she asked, toying with his emotions as she was toying with his bejewelled prick.

'I want you,' he said, and the arrogance had left him. He was nothing more than a young man less experienced with women than he liked to portray. 'You're lovely. I noticed you as soon as you walked in. Are you going to let me fuck you?'

'Yes,' she whispered, and couldn't believe she'd just said that.

'It's nearly time,' Norma cried, as she herded her flock outside.

Cheryl had forgotten all about her, forgotten the impending ritual, forgotten everything except this youth who had aimed his beauty like an arrow straight at her heart, or rather straight at her pussy that quivered in response.

He let his kilt drop and linked his fingers with hers. 'Come on,' he urged. 'Don't want to miss the climax.'

Damn right! she thought. I've already missed it once tonight!

The bonfire's flames roared up, raining sparks, and the worshippers were holding hands and swaying, their eyes

149

fixed on Deven, who dominated the scene from a knoll. Many were in the pool, as if believing that the water would wash away their sins. And the pale sickle moon was gradually appearing, starting her progress across the heavens, attended by a retinue of stars.

Deven was declaiming, his arms lifted to the skies, presumably invoking the deity, though it was impossible to catch his words from where Cheryl and Aiden stood.

'Let's go in,' he said, daring her, and before she realised what she was doing, she found herself waist deep in cold water.

Her robe lifted and floated around her, the ripples penetrating her heated parts like icy, impudent fingers. The feeling on her bare skin was wonderful. Her feet sank ankle deep in the silt, and she waded out further, till the pool shelved and she found herself swimming. She wasn't alone. Heads were bobbing everywhere, faces upturned to the moon. Her robe was inhibiting and she wanted to take it off, finding the shallows again and struggling with the girdle.

'Here, let me,' said Aiden, surfacing close by. She felt his hands on her breasts, thumbs rolling the chill-hardened nipples. As he pressed urgently against her, she could feel the solid bough of his cock, no way deflated by the cold.

Somehow, the girdle was unknotted and she was free. She seemed to be weightless as Aiden lifted her. She clasped her hands at the back of his neck, spreading her legs so that he could lower her on to his erection. Then she closed them round his hips and wriggled into position, her channel filled up with him, certain that she could feel the ring chafing against her inner ridges, even though he had rubbered up. Aiden moved her up and down and the water sloshed around them and she could hear ecstatic cries rising from the throats of the crowd as the ritual reached its peak. Couples were shagging in the water, on the grass, by the bonfire, under the trees. Men with women, women with women, men with men: some-times they were so entangled that it was impossible to

150

see who was doing what to whom, like erotic carvings on the façades of Indian temples.

Aiden kissed her, then slipped out of her and carried her effortlessly from the pool and round to the back of the marquee. He laid her on the grass and stretched out beside her, as wet and naked as she was. In the faint glow through the tent walls, she saw him smiling at her, then he went down on her, licking her, sucking her; then he rubbed her clit against the latex-covered cock-ring till she cried out with the force of the climax that shuddered through her. Then he mounted her, pumping hard into her convulsing body until he, too, came with a loud, triumphant shout.

Cheryl flung back her head and stared at the virgin moon, a chaste, pale goddess whose worshippers were adoring in time-honoured fashion. She had sworn never to get involved in Fell Tor's rites, but she and Aiden had also poured out their libation, whether they believed in it or not.

As Cheryl prepared to drive home at dawn, she slid a disc into the player. It was a recording of Giacomo Puccini's masterpiece, the Chinese fairytale opera *Turandot*. She flicked to the track halfway through Act 1. This was a choral hymn to the moon sung by the populace of old Peking while they waited to witness the execution of a young prince. Despite the harshness and brutality of the opera's beginning, the music had now changed, with a melody delicately floating in the air above a wistful boys' chorus. It seemed appropriate for the experience she had just gone through. She was light-headed with fatigue, but exhilarated, fingers tingling with the exhaustion of a sleepless night.

Aiden had insisted on seeing her again, and she'd given her permission for him to accompany Joanna and Deven to the bash at St Jude's. She wasn't quite sure about this. Tim and Daisy would be present and she was worried enough about how they would take her change of appearance, to say nothing of a man half her age dancing attendance.

The moon theme ended and she switched off. She rarely used classical music as a background, only occasionally, like that reunion screw with Mark. She accorded it respect and liked to concentrate on it one hundred per cent. It relaxed her body and allowed her soul to expand. It acted on her like a sort of oxygen, or the very gentlest of balms. It dissipated fears and melancholy, and solaced loneliness and brought comfort. It was sexual too, those clear-toned violins and wonderful operatic voices that made the hairs on her skin move. It opened up the secret places of her heart, made a thousand longings surge from the hidden centre of her being, a thousand colours, a thousand visions and forms.

Oh, it was all right to bowl along the road to salsa or other Latino tunes, but *real* music was sacrosanct.

The roads were deserted, except for a milk float and a postman on his bike and Cheryl was deep in thought. She hadn't said goodbye to her mother. In fact, she'd seen very little of her, absorbed as she was in helping Deven perform the rituals. Cheryl had the distinct feeling that she was avoiding letting him have much contact with her. She shouldn't worry, she thought. I don't want him, not really – not enough to risk the shit hitting the fan.

As she recognised landmarks that told her she was nearing St Jude's, so the apparition of Felan returned to haunt her. She had successfully pushed it away for hours. Aiden was so thorough a lover, caring, considerate and eager to please, that she had almost forgotten that dark-visaged bully. A barnyard rooster was crowing somewhere in the village when she drove through and she reached the house without encountering anyone. The stables and outbuildings were deserted and she put the car away and scuttled inside, her heart thumping with the dread of an encounter with him.

She was tired and vulnerable and had a million things to do that day. The last thing she needed was to be tormented by him. She headed for her bedroom and a bath. Lakes were all very well, but there was nothing like a long, sensual soak in perfumed water. She promised herself this treat, where she could lie there undisturbed, reliving the events of the evening and then perhaps snatch a couple of hours' sleep.

Chapter Eight

'*B*ow tie? Of course it's a bloody bow-tie do. Can't let that bitch think we don't know how to dress,' John snarled at his wife over the breakfast table. 'Have you something halfway decent to wear? Or are you planning to arrive looking like a scarecrow, as usual.'

Emily Dempsey glanced down at the knife by her plate, wondering if she had the courage to stick it into his thick, bullfrog throat. She could picture his face turning ashen as the blood gushed from his jugular. He'd try to staunch it with his napkin, rising, clutching the back of the chair, choking in his own gore as he struggled to order her to call an ambulance. She'd delay, standing staring at him, and then shouting all those things she'd wanted to say for years, calling him bully, adulterer, liar, swindler – the man who had married her and made her life a living hell.

'Has my evening suit come back from the cleaners?' John queried from behind the newspaper. 'You didn't forget to take it in, did you?'

'It's ready. Hanging in your wardrobe,' Emily said, visualising hacking it to shreds.

She'd read about a policeman's wife who had done just that to her husband's uniform when she found out he'd been unfaithful. The force had sued her for wilful

154

damage to its property. She'd lost, but how satisfying it must have been to slash away with the scissors, the cloth a substitute for his penis.

Emily was worried about her own attire for the party. She hadn't bought a new dress for ages. John didn't like to spend money on her, though she was certain he was generous to his tarts, but maybe not. Would he be as mean-spirited and tight-fisted with them as he was with her? He'd never admitted to having other women, and no one had told her, his cronies tight as clams, but she was sure of it, smelling their smell on his underclothes sometimes when she took them from the laundry basket and stuffed them in the washing machine.

Selfish, selfish bastard! Emily knew it was un-Christian, but she hated him. Every time he took the boat out, she prayed that it would sink and he'd drown.

You could leave him, a voice inside her whispered, but it had done this from the time the wedding ceremony was over and they'd gone on their honeymoon. She had never left, hoping against all hope that things would improve. At the start she had been infatuated with him, swept away by his looks, his arrogance and his big talk. A virgin when they married, she had blamed herself because she didn't enjoy going to bed with him. It had never occurred to her till much later that this might be his fault.

Her children had become her be all and end all. John was as harsh a father as he was a husband, and she shielded them, particularly the boy, Rupert. John wanted him to go into the family business, but Rupert, now nineteen and the eldest, had declared his intention of studying the performing arts. He wanted to be an actor. Emily had money of her own, but was afraid to defy John and support Rupert through a course at drama college, if he was lucky enough to audition successfully.

The girls, Ruth and Eva, were more malleable, in the fifth and sixth form at the private school they attended. Plain girls, spoiled and far too plump. They were Daddy's pets, and there was no doubt that he favoured them. He would, of course, Emily concluded dourly. They are females and his daughters and, as such, constitute no threat. He thinks I'm no threat, either. One day he may be in for a shock. She was so tired of being his dogsbody. She was nearly forty, and rapidly sinking into middle age with no incentive to drag herself out of it. John had succeeded in destroying any enthusiasm she might once have had.

When he met her, she had the potential to be a concert pianist. No chance once the ring was on her finger. He soon put a stop to that. He had filled her life with his own ambitions and her belly with his babies, but had magnanimously allowed her to install the grand piano from her family home in their own house near Westcombe. This was a new property, expensive, security checked, solidly built to resemble a nineteenth-century mansion, though it stood among many others that had sprung up like mushrooms where once there had been a wartime aerodrome.

'I don't mind you practising, my dear,' he had said. 'Keep your hand in, so long as it doesn't take up too much of your time. You can play for our guests when we entertain.'

He liked her to perform then, drawing the limelight to himself.

Oh, those horrible parties! And oh, the boring videos of yachting events featuring himself and his mates which he insisted on showing, every would-be sailor there wanking their ego, and John most of all. He was always the life and soul, of course, a regular Jekyll and Hyde. They thought him a wonderful man. What a star!

The more they drank, the coarser they became, usually demanding brash 80s pop tunes, throwing themselves about in a theatrical manner and touching each other up.

Apart from this one concession to Emily's skill, when they were alone John sneered at her love of the theatre, was offhand when she wanted to visit art galleries, and told her she was turning Rupert into a sissy should she book seats for them at the ballet.

156

Now she refilled his teacup and then her own. He grunted and went on reading *The Times*. If only he'd take a different paper, she thought, observing him without appearing to do so. How refreshing it would be to see a daily rag by his plate. I'm sure he'd prefer it, drooling over page three girls with bare, silicon-enlarged tits. He's not only a bully, he's a hypocrite. How can I possibly endure it if he's elected mayor? It was wonderful when he was in America. I didn't miss him at all. I'm going to have to leave him, and soon. I've had it up to here with the sailing club and his circle of toadies. Each one of them is insincere, dancing to his tune, brown-nosing because they fear him.

But the idea of living on her own and running her life was terrifying. She'd never paid a single household bill and didn't know how much John had in his bank account. He controlled all financial matters, gave her an allowance for food and household items and to pay the cleaner. She was as helpless and dependent on him as one of his office workers. And he made certain that it remained that way.

But you wouldn't be on your own, insisted the inner voice. You'd be with Rupert. Hasn't he already said that you could buy a small house in London and he would live there with you while he attended theatre school?

'You've got the money to do it, Mater. It only needs the guts,' he had said. 'You might even consider having piano lessons again.'

Something had to give, and soon. Rupert would storm out for good if he and his father had yet another blistering row. But what about Ruth and Eva? her cowardly self protested. It was the one that had been her gaoler for a seemingly endless sentence, the one that whinged on about keeping the home together for the children's sake – you can't split them up – they need a father and a mother – and so on and so forth.

They can come and stay with me, often, she assured herself. They're happy with John and he can play on their sympathy by acting the deserted husband. He can get a housekeeper. That's all I am anyway – a glorified chief cook and bottle washer, with the occasional fuck thrown in, if he can't find another orifice.

Oh God, my language! she thought, appalled by her vulgarity. But it's frustration that's doing it to me. Cynicism has corroded my once bright optimism. I need love so badly that my heart feels as if it will break sometimes. Human kindness, sexual fulfilment. I've never had this, not with a man, not with John, or with a woman. I satisfy myself when the pressure builds up too high to resist, but I'm so ashamed of masturbating. Supposing someone found out? Supposing John caught me at it? I'd die of shame.

A lot of feminist propaganda had passed her by and left her standing, but she'd devoured articles by forthright ladies who had declared that it was natural for a woman to enjoy her own body. Men had always jerked off. That's how they'd learned the quickest and most efficient way to reach an orgasm – their own, of course. But even when given the green light and being told that it was normal, Emily was still guilt ridden, taught by her mother that 'nice little girls don't touch themselves down there'.

She and John had never discussed the matter of her climax. He assumed that (a) she didn't experience desire, or (b) she came when he did.

Her eyes glazed over and she no longer saw John, the toast-rack, the butter-dish and marmalade. Instead a tall, broad-shouldered man with high, chiselled cheekbones came into view. He dismounted from his ebony stallion and strode towards her. He was wearing a triple-caped greatcoat over a velvet jacket. His frilled cravat contrasted with his swarthy skin and, as he doffed his high-crowned hat and bowed, his black curls brushed his collar. But it was his form-hugging buckskin breeches that fascinated her. They outlined the shape of his cock, lying against his inner left thigh. Emily wanted to unbutton him and take out that serpent. It would uncoil in the warmth of her hand, and probably spit at her.

158

They were standing on the seashore, and she was a Jane Austen-kind of genteel young miss who wouldn't entertain such wayward fantasies. Oh dear, Emily thought, and the picture vanished. I've been watching too many TV ads for holidays abroad. There's one running at the moment that has a similar storyline.

'Right, I'm off,' John said, slapping down the newspaper and pushing back his chair. 'Where are the girls?'

'They've gone to school.'

'Who is looking after them tonight? Rupert?'

'No, he's going out.'

'Useless boy. It's time he stopped all this nonsense and either went to uni or came into the firm. I intend to have another go at him.'

'The girls are staying with Ruth's friend. Her mother has kindly offered,' Emily answered, refusing to take the bait.

'I'll be back in plenty of time to get ready. Don't hold me up, will you, Emily? No dithering at the last moment.'

She didn't say anything, didn't move as he bent and dropped a kiss on her head in passing. That was about as much as she got from him these days, and she was relieved. Why should he use her when it suited him? He was simply getting rid of his spunk. Like any other bodily function, it seemed to mean no more to him than taking a piss.

When he had gone, she carried the crockery into the kitchen and loaded it into the dishwasher. Mrs Macdonald would be in shortly, the lady who 'did'. There were a couple of phone calls she should make a little later. Yvonne Harper, the commodore's wife, was holding a meeting of the Westcombe Ladies Charity Organisation, and would expect Emily to be there, taking the minutes.

Rebellion surged up. She disliked Yvonne intensely, that blowsy, snobbish cow! She took that back. Cows were gentle, soft-eyed creatures. It was an insult to them. Harpy might be a better description. Trollop even more apt. And the way John fawned over her at the sailing club dinner-dances was nothing short of sickening. I shan't phone her, Emily decided. If she wants me, she knows where to come. In fact, I might resign from her damn charity. She doesn't do it to help the needy, none of them do – it's a way to pass the time and make themselves feel that they're important.

She remembered Cheryl Barden, the only one in the club with whom she had anything in common, but she'd been too shy to forward the acquaintance. Anyway, Cheryl hadn't gone there often, seeming to be as uninterested in it as herself. So, she'd struck out on her own, had she? She'd bought a hotel and, from what Emily gathered by his griping and grumbling, it had been a property that John had set his sights on. Bully for her! Inspired by this, she went upstairs and rooted through her wardrobe, searching desperately for something even vaguely suitable to wear to the party.

Felan bent at the knees and ducked his head to see in the bathroom mirror. That was the trouble with his cottage; the ceilings were so low that he was forever striking his head on beams or lintels.

He combed his hair, then tossed it back and clamped a hand round his ponytail, tethering it with an elastic band covered by a narrow black ribbon. It threw his strong features into relief. He'd shaved carefully, reducing his beard to a strip outlining his jaw, while his moustache was pencil thin. It suited him, gave him a devil-may-care look. And was he? Not exactly. He took his work seriously and the business was flourishing under his command. As for his personal life?

He shrugged his shoulders into a night-dark velvet jacket worn over a black T-shirt and tight black jeans. He was partially conceding to the formal dress that Cheryl and Laura would expect, having bigwigs on the guest-list, but couldn't bring himself to go the whole hog. Penguin suits had never been his style. Black leather cowboy boots with Cuban heels and square toes worn under the straight-legged jeans gave him a swaggering look.

160

He had got used to living alone, once Rebecca had gone. He was left with her debts and the thank-God feeling that they'd never had children. It was easy to slip back into bachelordom, eating and sleeping when he liked, working till he dropped or idling on a river bank with his fishing rods. And he could take his pick of women, when he felt inclined which, once bitten twice shy, was seldom these days. He'd gone back to self-relief, a practice he'd never really given up, even while shafting Rebecca frequently when they were newly-weds and madly in love.

His blue eyes narrowed and, instead of himself in the mirror, he saw the face of his boss – not the rather sweet, good-natured Laura, but Cheryl, that aggravating, argumentative termagant. His mouth hardened and he was uncomfortably aware that his cock was thickening in his close-fitting jeans. Sure, she was the sexiest thing he'd seen in ages, but that didn't mitigate the fact that he wanted to slap her.

This was an unfortunate turn of phrase, considering the agitation taking place in his loins. It brought up startling visions of her bent across his knee while he administered six of the best to her bare backside. Lust burned in him like an insatiable thirst. His palm almost tingled with the force of that imaginary contact. What would she do? What would she say? He grinned as he thought of her fury. She'd absolutely hate being mastered. Or would she? Maybe she'd secretly like it, getting hot and wet between the legs as he walloped her, pressing down against his lap, trying to find something to rub herself on.

'Sod it!' he muttered aloud, obsessed by the need to come.

It would be no use arriving at St Jude's with a hard-on. He found it difficult enough at the best of times, walking around with a semi-permanent erection whenever he was likely to bump into her. That was one reason why he had been avoiding her. The other was because she needed a lesson, in his opinion. He wasn't going to dance to her tune. Let her stew, perhaps wondering why he was giving her the cold shoulder. It was all a matter of self-preservation. He couldn't afford the emotional upheaval of another relationship that was likely to fail. He'd wasted five years of his life on Rebecca and didn't intend to repeat it.

What to do about his rampant cock? The more he tried to restrain it, the more it surged. Fluid seeped from the slit, dampening the inside of his jeans. He wasn't wearing boxer shorts and relished the delicious feel of the denim rubbing against him – cotton chafing engorged flesh.

Give it a rest! he lectured himself. Just pick up your car keys and get going. And lay yourself open to her snide remarks and veiled insults? No way. Like Samson being robbed of his strength by Delilah, so his unsatisfied desire would make him vulnerable.

He went into the bathroom, placed a toilet roll handy and undid his fly. The mirror over the pedestal basin showed his cock as it burst from its confinement. This trebled his excitement, the sight of that thick, angry-looking organ making the blood rush into his groin. He touched it, stroking the length of the swollen stem till it throbbed. Rough with impatience, he unbuckled his belt, pushed his jeans down and slid a hand into the aperture between his legs, cupping the full, heavy testicles. He wanted Cheryl's lips there and imagined her drawing one of them into the round O of her mouth. He started to shake, the force of desire making his mouth dry, his slippery cock wetting his fingers.

He was now blind to anything except rushing towards completion. He used Cheryl's image to bring this about – the sight of her breasts swaying as she moved, the stone-hard tips of her nipples, her mouth beneath his, her agile tongue, those little, tempting shorts she insisted on wearing. He remembered the smell of her, the wetness of her pussy, her gasps when she climaxed, and his fingers worked up and down his cock, the strokes getting faster and more frenzied.

Cheryl disappeared. Only white heat remained, gathering in his balls, shooting into his cock, spewing out in a thick, pearly jet. It hit the basin, followed by another, and another.

'Jesus God!' Felan whispered, his knees shaking, the final spasms of orgasm leaving him weak.

His cock was so tender that he removed his hand, bracing his arms on the porcelain and resting there. Then he spun the tap and washed, removing every trace of come. He was calm again, all passion spent and, when he'd dried and tucked himself away in his jeans, he could hardly remember why the urge to climax had been so strong.

And isn't this always the way of it? he pondered, clicking off the light and returning to his bedroom. It's just the same when you've fucked a women, no matter how desirable you found her. Once you've had it, you could throw your hat at it.

'Wicked,' Daisy pronounced, as she swept into the hall dramatically. Not for nothing was she a fashion designer, albeit an embryonic one.

'You like?' Cheryl said, wanting to hug her.

'You can say that again,' Daisy enthused, gorgeous and extreme, the colours clashing in her spiky hair, her make-up garish, her tie-dyed top skimming the little bolt in her navel, baggy trousers and stack-soled mules completing this frenetic, anything-goes look.

'What on earth have I spawned?' Cheryl said, forgetting and speaking aloud. Sometimes, when faced with her creation, she could empathise with Baron Frankenstein.

Daisy didn't notice, rushing on. 'Can I hold a show here? That staircase! Yummy. Imagine models floating down it, displaying my latest. Have I told you about my new range? I'm mixing cotton with Chinese silk. PVC with lace. There's a Punk comeback. Fleeces are out. Everything's more creative. I don't know – more like rubber and canvas.'

'Sackcloth and ashes?' Tim cut in, tousle-headed,

laconic and rangy, managing to look the archetypal undergraduate. He was tall and loose-limbed, a sportsman as well as an academic, and Cheryl had to be very firm with herself to stop doting on him.

Now her heart swelled with pride to see them both, even though he was baiting Daisy. This was par for the course. They were talented and intelligent and had always sparred, sibling rivals who instantly banded together should anyone outside the family threaten.

'Shut up!' Daisy retorted, dumping a holdall on the floor, her arms filled with plastic-covered coat-hangers from which dangled a variety of outfits. She never travelled light.

'The rag trade's the last refuge of the terminally untalented,' he quipped.

'Mum . . . tell him!' Daisy screeched.

'Fashion's a luxury. It's human nature to show off,' Cheryl the mediator said, then changed the subject. 'I've so much to show you. Get your bags upstairs and I'll take you on a Grand Tour.'

She was more pleased to see them than she let on, even to herself. This was the final touch, and she was sorry for Laura. Harry had emailed from Katmandu and Vicky had phoned last night. Both wished her luck for the opening, but it could not possibly be the same as actually being with, talking to, putting her arms round her children, grown-up though they were.

There was one fly in the ointment. Wasn't there always? Cheryl's first instinct was to take Daisy and Tim all over St Jude's, proudly showing them every nook and cranny of this unique old building. But what about the towers? How was she to explain the exotic trappings above and the sensational cellars below? And if she didn't unlock the doors, wouldn't they think it strange? Tim was already displaying a caring attitude towards her that was heart-warming, though a tad patronising. He had gone into a huddle with Mark on arrival, wanting to know the ins and outs of his mother's investment, presumably vigilant in case the old girl was being ripped off.

She had managed to keep Mark in the dark concerning the club. It had been easier to do once she had put a curb on their relationship. He hadn't liked it, but that was tough. Sulk though he might, she wasn't prepared to offer more than friendship and the occasional fuck.

Tim scented something, saying as they finished up in her apartment, 'What's with the towers?'

'Eh, well, nothing much at present,' Cheryl lied. 'We're toying with the idea of hiring them out as conference centres. You know, where firms can send their young executives, having them stay under one roof for the weekend and thrash out policies.'

This seemed to satisfy him for the time being, and within minutes Daisy had spread herself from the guest-room allotted to her. Soon a trail of feathers and sequins, a shoe here, a scarf there, cluttered the sitting room.

'Do I really have to share the bathroom with her?' Tim moaned, then brightened. 'This is a great place. What a bargain! And you've got the flat looking super. Is there anything to eat? I'm famished.'

'Is Dad coming tonight?' Daisy asked, examining her face critically in the gilt-framed mirror hanging over the marble fireplace.

'No.'

'I suppose I'd better make the effort to see him now I'm here,' Daisy went on, and her heavily made-up eyes were rebellious. She'd never forgiven Ashley for the belly-button-piercing débâcle.

'It's up to you,' Cheryl said diplomatically.

Daisy heaved a sigh and flopped down on the couch. 'I was hoping I wouldn't have to visit the old sod, but the vacation's started and I'm not coming home again. I've the chance to go to Italy and work with Alessandro.'

She breathed this name with the reverence she might have accorded a saint. Cheryl racked her brains but nothing happened. Alessandro was obviously someone famous in the fashion industry, but she couldn't for the life of her remember who.

'Alessandro?' she ventured, steering Tim in the direction of the kitchen that she had stocked with him in mind.

'Oh, you're hopeless. Surely you've heard of him. He has this fabulous atelier in Milan, and wins all the major awards. I met him in Paris and he was absolutely wonderful. Asked me then if I'd care to work with him.'

Cheryl had a flash of a lecherous middle-aged Lothario intent on seducing her daughter. Italian, to boot! With a silken tongue. He'd be short and overweight, but a sharp dresser, with greying hair, melting black eyes and an adoring entourage. In no time at all Daisy would be swept off her feet and flat on her back with his Mediterranean prick lodged inside her.

Daisy rummaged in her bag and brought out a magazine. It was already open at the relevant page. 'Here he is. That's Alessandro,' she said and thrust it under Cheryl's nose.

This was even worse. Alessandro wasn't short, he was tall, but she had been right about him being dark and dressing as if affiliated to the Cosa Nostra. She felt her libido kickstart. The man was a menace, his rock-idol looks and sizzling charisma appealing to women young and old, and probably men too.

'Who is paying for the trip?' she asked crisply, handing back the magazine.

'The college is offering financial aid, and I thought perhaps you or Dad might cough up the rest,' Daisy answered, sticking her tongue out at Tim who had returned with a cheese and tomato doorstep in one hand, and was grimacing at her.

'Look, I'm pretty busy right this minute, but we'll talk about it later,' Cheryl said, already feeling frazzled, and they hadn't been home five minutes.

There were three bedrooms in her apartment and all were large, but she could feel claustrophobia settling in. She doubted that she'd be able to invite a man back later

166

with them in close proximity. Not that her private life was any of their business, but she wouldn't be able to relax, no matter what handsome hunk waggled his prick at her and wanted to make love. She sighed, her body tense, her nerves jangling. Tonight could be make or break time. The press would be there, and local notables, so she must be on her best behaviour. It would have been nice to let her hair down once it was over, but there was little chance of that, even though Aiden was due to arrive. She didn't foresee getting into his knickers with Daisy and Tim on guard like a pair of Rottweilers.

Laura couldn't resist taking one last look round before the first guests arrived. The hotel was opening its doors at noon. There were twenty bookings already, consisting of twelve double rooms and eight singles. It wasn't bad for a beginning. More were expected tomorrow. Not everyone could get away by Friday and the phone had been ringing with enquiries non-stop.

She had seen Daisy and Tim and was rather glad that her own offspring could not make it. She was simply too busy to bother with them at this stage. It was all extremely exciting and her stomach was home to fluttering butterflies as she whisked through the upper floors, checking on every last detail, her passkey making each room available for inspection. It was with a heady feeling of pride that she admired the decor, tweaked imaginary creases from the bedspreads, inspected the en suite bathrooms and opened the little refrigerators to make sure they were well supplied. The ambience was of a more gracious age, but with all modern facilities: power-showers, TV, landline phones, everything to ensure the latest in technology amidst a gracious setting of chintz and lace, mahogany and gilt.

Laura experienced the same buzz as she had done as a small girl with her first doll's house. It was all so fresh, so new, so perfect in every detail.

Then she thought about the towers and this added another dimension, a dark skein of lust knotting deep inside her. Bronwen and Luke were expected soon for the inaugural meeting of the club. Slowly, slowly, to begin with, but by the close of the summer season when the hectic flood of ordinary clientele would settle down to a trickle, then it would come into its own. Laura couldn't wait. The sight of the dungeons created from cellars by an inspired Alroy had turned her cold, then hot, an adrenaline rush of terror and a hot bolt of desire shooting through her.

Those gloomy realms of pain and pleasure had been oddly familiar, like the settings that haunted her dreams. She had recognised the implements of bondage and punishment as clearly as if they had been part of a nightmare or something she had experienced in a former life. The impressions were tantalisingly vague but had the same connotations as the set of the tango movie – blood-red and black, with a dominating male figure. She had a perverse longing to throw herself at his feet and have him use and abuse her. Yet, when it came down to it, who used whom? Did he subjugate her, or was she in control?

She had the sensation of not really knowing who she was. Maybe if I find out about the dungeons, I'll learn about myself, she thought.

She walked along one of the corridors and met Simon coming the other way. They were quite alone, their footsteps muffled by the wall-to-wall Wilton. He stopped. So did she. His strong hand gripped her by the wrist, and with the other he unlocked the linen cupboard door and pushed her inside.

'Simon! What are you doing?' she protested.

'I'm about to make you come,' he said, and eased her back against the shelves that lined the walls, piled high with monogrammed towels, table napkins, sheets, pillowcases and duvet covers.

'You can't. Not here,' she murmured, putting up a token struggle. 'Someone might find us.'

'I've locked the door,' he assured her.

Laura stopped fighting him. He was too attractive, and

168

the setting added an extra piquancy to the situation. It was like being back in the womb, enclosed and warm. Lit by a small window, it had always been a storage place for household linen, and Ursula had kept it that way, though it had been repainted, equipped with more shelves and fitted with radiators.

Had anyone ever been fucked there before? Laura wondered. It was likely. There must have been a butler who enticed the maidservants inside, or a housekeeper with an eye on lads with tight-muscled bums and easily aroused cocks. It seemed as if her own excitement was augmented by the passions of long-dead lovers.

Simon wasn't wasting any time. He had her skirt lifted and her panties pushed to one side, slipping a finger deep into her. She leaned back, legs pressed together to take her weight, trapping his wrist between her thighs. He worked her inner core till it yielded up its moisture, then made her crack slick wet, reaching the rapidly engorging folds of her lips. Her clit became erect. Simon located the sensitive head and caressed it. She moaned, closed her eyes and enjoyed her climax.

'Good girl,' he whispered, and she heard the whine as he unzipped. Still riven with orgasmic convulsions, she felt his cock edging its way into her. Unable to help herself, she parted her legs to make it easier for him. Up and up it went, grazing her G-spot, and she stood on tiptoe, glad that he was just the right height for a knee-trembler.

A sweet smell of Spring Dawn fabric softener rose from the linen behind her, released by the heat of her body. She could smell herself, too, that pungent post-come odour of her juices, coupled with the taint of rubber from the condom he wore. She wished they didn't have to bother with it, longing to have his fluids mingle with her own, but this wasn't the way of things in this era. Perhaps later, if they were both tested and pronounced clean and if they cleaved to one another and didn't stray, maybe then they could make love properly, skin to skin, semen mixing with female essences.

But this was better then nothing. Oh, God, yes! And she squeezed his cock within herself, squeezed and relaxed, then tightened again. Simon pumped with his hips, his trousers wrinkling down, and she pushed up his shirt and dug her nails into his bare bottom, urging him on. Her clit was stirring again, stimulated by the savage butting of his cock root, but it wasn't sufficient to bring her off. She tried hard, concentrating on the feeling, her frustration growing, but the pressure was wrong. Simon came to the rescue. Even in his own extremity he managed to slide a hand between them and massaged her clit, matching the strokes to his thrusts.

Their frantic movements made the shelves shake and she had a moment's bourgeois panic in case anyone passing might hear them, or Ursula walk in, checking bedding. It was wonderful and embarrassing all at the same time. Something dropped on her head, smothering her face just as she came in another glorious rush. She gasped, shook off the avalanche of pillowcases, and heard Simon yelp as he finished in a succession of jerks.

He sighed, paused, then started to laugh. He pulled out of her, and Laura's feet touched ground again. 'Shit,' she whispered, appalled at the mayhem they had created from Ursula's linen husbandry. 'What the hell do we do now?'

'Don't worry,' he soothed. 'Leave it to me.'

Laura was hot and sweaty, but did the best she could to tidy herself before opening the door a crack and peering out. A cleaning lady was hoovering far down the corridor and didn't hear her as she walked out and sauntered off, trying to look casual. Inside, she was in pieces, thinking, I'm not cut out for this. But, catching a glimpse of herself in one of the several mirrors that alternated with landscapes on the walls, she saw that her eyes were sparkling, her cheeks were flushed and she wore the unmistakable look of a woman who has just been thoroughly fucked by a man she really likes.

* * *

A success or what? Cheryl thought to herself as she took a break from circulating among the guests. She wished she *had* invited Ashley, if it was only to rub his nose in it. She escaped into the hall, followed closely by Aiden.

'Don't do this,' she said, rounding on him like a tigress.

'But, Cheryl . . .' He put his hand on her bottom, cupping the underside of one cheek.

She removed it, saying sternly, 'No buts. I told you to lay off. The mayor's here, to say nothing of my son and daughter.'

Aiden looked like a fallen angel, with his bleached hair and white, Indian-style suit. His facial piercings glinted, and she dropped her eyes to his crotch, but his jacket was too long for her to see, though memory painted a clear picture of the onyx adorning his cock.

The sight of him went to her head like strong drink, but she clung steadfastly to her resolution to preserve a squeaky-clean image. Everyone invited seemed to have accepted, driven, no doubt, by prurient curiosity. Cheryl could almost hear the gossip. 'Two women without husbands owning a smart hotel. There must be more to it than meets the eye. They are probably no better than they should be.'

The leading lights of the local branch of the WI were there in full force, and the group who ran the village hall and organised fund-raising functions: sometimes the same stalwarts doubled up on both.

'You look different,' Aiden continued, utterly without shame as he ran a hand up her back and twanged the elastic of her bra. 'You weren't wearing one of these last time.'

'I don't want to think about that . . . not now,' she reproved, though her nipples responded to the chafing of the underwired cups, and she couldn't stop staring at his mouth and remembering his face buried in her bush, his tongue bringing on her orgasm. 'I'd better go back before I do something I'll regret,' she added in a stilted voice.

'I like your dress,' he commented, leaning his shoulders against the wall.

171

His lean legs were crossed in those slim cotton trousers, his sun-browned feet in thonged sandals; not the Jesus type worn over socks by old men, but sexy, *Arabian Night's Entertainment* ones that spoke of the desert and a Bedouin tent and an imperious, hawk-faced sheikh who had kidnapped her and was about to bend her to his will.

'I like it too,' she managed to bring out. It had been expensive, but she doubted that she would ever wear it again. Made of midnight blue devoré, it had three-quarter-length sleeves, a draped bodice and swirling flimsy skirt that reached her ankles. Her only concession to high fashion was a pair of court shoes in blue mock-crocodile leather.

The outfit had been chosen to make a statement. It said, 'I'm rich. I'm successful and I'm here to stay, so you may as well get used to the idea and court my favour.'

Several people had already got the message. Councillor Pringle had been charm itself, his wife too, while the Chief Constable, disappointingly evening-suited instead of uniformed, had beamed at her genially and suggested they hold the next policeman's ball under St Jude's august roof. She'd left John Dempsey to Laura's tender mercies once she had greeted him. He had been as smarmy as she recalled and she'd felt instant pity for his wife, the downtrodden Emily. Reed-slim and five foot eight, she stooped as if trying to shrink into herself. She had short hair that needed styling, beautiful eyes with long lashes, an English rose complexion and slender artistic hands.

'She used to play the piano. Still does on occasion. Would you like her to play tonight?' John had asked, daring Cheryl to refuse.

'I think that's rather down to Emily, don't you?' she had replied cuttingly and walked away.

Now Aiden said, 'I came especially to be with you. Where's your bedroom?'

'It doesn't matter. We're not fucking, and that's that.'

His lower lip rolled out. 'Why not? I sacrificed time for

you. I should have been at the shaman class, finding my totem animal.'

'Oh, give me a break!' Cheryl had had enough of self-centred young adults for one day. 'Come back tomorrow. Can't you see I'm up to my eyes? Joanna may think me mercenary, but this is important. Goodbye.'

She turned to go but he detained her, his fingers on her arm, light but steely. 'When can I see you again?'

'Call me tomorrow.' He let her go, looking so dejected that she was smitten with guilt. She reached up and kissed him on the lips, adding, 'Look, I'm sorry, but you can see how it is. I want us to be together again, I really do. It's just bad timing. Ring me. OK?'

'OK, if that's the deal,' he said petulantly.

As she went to leave him, she turned and met Felan head on. He was dressed in black and had appeared with the suddenness of a pantomime villain popping up from a stage trapdoor. All he needed was a cloud of dry ice.

'Good evening, Mrs Barden,' he said, subjecting her to his sardonic smile. 'Having fun, are we?' And he nodded to where Aiden stood, eyeing him. 'I'd never have put you down as a cradle-snatcher, but I see that I was wrong.'

Chapter Nine

'Whew! Thank Christ that's over,' Cheryl exclaimed, swivelling in the chair in matron's office.

It was one of her favourite places, with its shower stall, examination couch and medicine cabinet, now empty of all save the innocuous Red Cross box containing bandages, sticking plasters and aspirins. She could picture it in the days when a martinet reigned supreme, respected by pupils and staff alike. There must have been many times when the cane had played a merry tattoo on bare, quivering bums. There were one or two male persons Cheryl would like to see bent over with their trousers down.

Now she lifted her feet and rested them on the desk, skirt draped demurely on either side. She was about to kick her shoes off, setting her toes free, when a hand came across and clasped her ankle.

'No,' Felan said. 'Keep on your heels. I've something to show you.'

She frowned, too tired to get into an altercation with him. Everyone else had gone, except this rude individual. Her mother had gathered up her groupies and ferried them back to Fell Tor, including a sullen-faced Aiden. Mark had taken his reluctant leave, after angling to share Cheryl's bed. She had used the children as an excuse to put him off. John Dempsey had insisted on kissing her hand when departing, and the back still felt gummy from contact with his slack wet lips.

'Come and see me, any time,' she had whispered to Emily, and been rewarded by a shy, hesitant smile, though the pale-blue eyes had been awash with tears.

Dear God, she's a stranger to kindness. I must do something for her, she had resolved, ignoring both John's obvious dislike of herself and the way in which he had been flirting with Laura and anything else that dragged a skirt, including an unimpressed Daisy.

She and Tim, though behaving impeccably throughout, had now announced that they were off clubbing, familiar with the hot-spots of Westcombe. Cheryl had given them a key, warned about getting too drunk, though knowing it would fall on deaf ears, and advised on the most reliable taxi service. Laura had vanished. Cheryl had noticed that she and Simon kept disappearing during the evening, heading in the direction of the linen cupboard. Each to his own, she concluded.

The resident guests had pronounced themselves delighted with both the party and the accommodation. Simon had given a short talk, advising them on walks across the moors and trips to the Standing Stones or Westcombe Bay. The canapés had been excellent, the wine of acceptable vintage, the service impeccable. Now the staff had cleared up and retired. All that remained was for her to get rid of her *bête noire*, Felan.

'And what is this you want to show me?' she asked, adding caustically, 'I thought I'd already seen everything you had on offer.'

'Not quite,' he said, and gave her an arch wink. 'There's much, much more.'

She couldn't make up her mind which she disliked most – when he was being argumentative or, as now, roguish.

'Oh? And why d'you think I'm interested?'

'Call it a hunch. I don't believe you've ever plumbed the depths of sensuality,' he said, bending over her, his arms braced each side of her chair. 'You're not the sort of woman who's satisfied with ten minutes of concentrated fucking. You like it long and slow.'

'I've had that recently. You'll have to invent something more exciting.'

'With the boy in the white suit? Tut, tut, Mrs Barden.'

He stared down, his face only inches from hers. She reluctantly approved of the way his beard had been clipped, emphasising the strong line of his jaw. He was far and away the most desirable man she had ever seen. He was also an infuriating bastard.

She moved, made to rise, saying, 'I'm knackered. Time to sleep. Can you let yourself out?'

'In due course,' he replied calmly, and straightened, though still boxing her in.

He was watching her with a slow, considering smile. She stood up, but couldn't step past him. This irritated her all the more. 'I told you, I'm bushed. Get out of the way,' she said angrily.

'You disappoint me, Mrs Barden. Have you lost your nerve?' he mocked.

'I don't know what you mean.'

'Chickening out of coming with me.'

'Where?'

'You'll see.'

'Oh, very well. Have it your own way. Best to get it over with, I suppose, then I can dive under my duvet.'

You've capitulated a mite quickly, haven't you? sneered her demon. Hoping to satisfy the churning, pussy-lubricating arousal that you've been suppressing all evening? There are some itches it's better not to scratch.

This worked in reverse. Damn it! No one was going to tell her what to do, not even a schizoid part of herself.

She squared her shoulders and said to Felan, 'All right. Get on with it, whatever it is you're so determined to show me.'

His eyebrows lifted and his quirky smile deepened. She battled with paranoia as he cupped her elbow in one hand and marched her in the direction of the arched door that led to the West Tower. Her heart was pounding, fit to burst out of her chest, but indignation took over as he produced a key and inserted it in the lock.

'I thought you were told to hand in all the keys,' she hissed angrily.

'I did, but had a spare set cut. You never know when I might need to get in fast,' he said urbanely. 'Fire, for instance. Leaky pipes. There are a dozen incidents when you might have to ring for me.'

'Bloody liar!' she blazed, fingers unconsciously spread into claws, ready to rend and tear.

'Dear me, we are in a wax, aren't we? I was simply acting in your interests, and that of St Jude's.'

'I think what you've done is illegal. I shall ask Mark if I can sue you,' she threatened.

'You do that, but not now,' he retaliated, maddeningly calm.

She took a deep breath and went in. That damp, dank atmosphere that had once reigned in the towers had been replaced by the smell of paint and paste and freshly sanded wood, mingled with the warmth generated by the extended central heating system. The lighting was subtle, originating from overhead spots, and wall brackets that were reminiscent of gas-lamps. The passage floor was bare stone, but the rooms were carpeted, and Cheryl expected Felan to take her to one of them, or even accompany her upstairs where decadently perverse decor awaited the visitor.

He did neither and a chill clutched at the pit of her stomach when he guided her towards the shadowed aperture below the stairwell. This led to the dungeon. A blast of cool air hit her as he opened the door. He switched on the light. A single, naked bulb lit the twisting stone steps with unmitigated harshness. These could have been leading anywhere – the back alley of a seedy bar or one of those interminable staircases stinking of piss that connect the levels of multi-storey car parks, or maybe the primrose pathway to the netherworld of strip joints. She had to remind herself that it was none of these, simply a route to a fun-place designed to amuse the members of her club.

The steps spiralled down. A black curtain hung at the bottom. Felan lifted it and stood back. Cheryl walked into Alroy's weird torture chamber set. The lights glowed red; so did a brazier heaped with mock coals. The cross-piece loomed, empty and waiting, its dark wood polished, chains and manacles gleaming.

'Nice little touch, those seats. Add a few round tables with candles in bottles, olives and breadsticks and wine and you've got yourself a new spectator sport,' Felan commented. 'That's what I'd do if it were mine.'

'Well, it's not yours, so butt out,' she said, her voice quavering.

His face hardened, and his eyes were as cold as the Arctic Ocean. He reached for a rope dangling from a pulley fastened to the vaulted ceiling, then snarled, 'Give me your hands.'

She obeyed him, too astonished to speak. He snapped a metal cuff round one wrist, then spun her and unzipped the back of her dress. 'What the hell . . .?' she began, but the devoré acquired a will of its own, the bodice slithering to her waist and slipping from her arms, then progressing to the flagstones where it lay like an indigo puddle surrounding her blue shoes.

Was this really her, this woman she saw in the mirror on the opposite wall? Lean as a hunter, with breasts jacked high by a black brassière, the dim light playing over her flat stomach, the dark pubic hair puffing above the minuscule black tanga – long thighs, long legs ending in high-heeled courts, a handcuff on her wrist. She flushed from head to toe as she imagined Tim or Daisy coming in and finding her like this. But another side of her throbbed and burned with an entirely different heat. She lifted an arm and freed her hair from the pins and combs that had held it in a demure coiffeur, and it uncoiled round her face and shoulders. She gave her head a shake, and the woman in the mirror smiled slyly.

Felan's stern expression did not change. He forced her arms above her head and snapped another cuff round her free wrist. He attached an iron clip to the chain linking her manacles and attached it to the rope, then hauled on it, lifting her so that her arms were stretched taut and her feet barely touched the ground.

Only the top layer of Cheryl's mind was working properly, the rest a quagmire of fear, disgust and rage at his high-handed behaviour and shameful, gusset-wetting lust. Her arms were aching, her wrists rubbed by the metal bands, and her bladder was sending out urgent signals. She regretted that last cup of coffee.

Felan paced around her, saying thoughtfully, 'You can't deny what you feel, Cheryl. You need me.'

He appeared in front of her. 'You think?' she said, and spat at him.

Calmly wiping the saliva from his chin, he moved a pace closer, his fierce eyes and his attitude stirring her, despite herself. 'That wasn't a very nice thing to do,' he chided softly. 'Time you were taught a few manners.'

His fingers reached to the back of her and clicked the bra clasp. The delicate garment left her breasts, hanging loose like two lacy baskets. He pushed them up so that they banded her chest, then took both nipples between his thumbs and forefingers, rolling them till she wanted to scream with frustration. He lowered his head and bit one, teeth gnawing painfully.

'Ouch!' she cried, but didn't want him to stop, desire flooding her from tits to clit.

'Hush,' he admonished, raising his head. 'You know you want this. I'm giving you the chance to have it, while keeping up the pretence that I'm forcing you. That's what it's all about ... the dungeons ... the restraints ... the pain. I'm your master now. I shall hurt you and show you how much pleasure you'll get from submission.'

'So you *do* know about this place, have known its purpose all along. Where ... when ... how did you learn about perversions?'

'It's not important,' he said, and his hand was at her

crotch, rubbing her through the black satin. 'I can do anything I want with you.'

His voice was low but infused with power, and the words turned her on as much as his touch. He slapped her pubis, making her body jerk. Her sphincter almost let go. She regained control just in time. Then she was back, leaning against him as his fingers wormed into the tanga, combing her bush and opening her swollen folds. She could feel his cock like an iron bar under his jeans, and she pressed her thigh against it. It grew larger, hot and humid. He chuckled and the dungeon resounded as he brought his hand down across her bottom with a force that shocked her.

He stepped back and went to a rack that bristled with all manner of instruments devoted to chastisement, returning with a paddle covered in white leather. He flexed it between his hands, then let the flat end go with a little twang. Cheryl shuddered, then tried to convince herself that he was testing her. He gave a sinister smile and paced round her. She twisted her head as far as she could, trying to follow his progress, still half-convinced that he was out to frighten, not hurt her.

He came to rest where she could see him, and he tugged at her panties, working them down past her hips and thighs till they joined the dress on the floor. The feel of air on her skin added fuel to her already blazing fire. He stared at her mound, then traced all round it with his finger. She knew she was wet, but couldn't help it, mortified when he caressed the pink, juicy surface. Her body was a traitor that needed to be punished. He rubbed her clit and she was on the point of coming when he stopped.

'You're a horny bitch,' he purred, lifting his finger to her lips and putting it inside. She could taste her salty essence and smell her heavy perfume. 'Look how up for it you are,' and he turned her to face the mirror again.

The reflection was beautiful. She admired her naked self; the raunchy sight of the bra like a bondage strap above her breasts, the heavy flesh hanging below, the nipples standing out like cobnuts. Then there was the man in black behind her, holding her with an arm round her waist, his palm resting on her belly, fingertips buried in her pubic floss. She ground her hips against his cock, hot as a branding iron as it pressed into the crack of her buttocks. The tiny mouth of her anus pursed in anticipation of his invasion.

'Unchain me,' she begged, using the enticement of her bottom to persuade him. 'I want to suck you.'

He gave her an angry shake. 'Did I tell you to speak, slave?' he shouted.

'N-no,' she faltered.

'Then don't.'

'But I need to –' Here she stopped, unwilling to say that she was finding it hard not to wet herself.

'Be silent!'

He slapped her across the breasts, belly and thighs, very nearly precipitating disaster. The pain was excruciating and she clenched her thighs together, only a few drops of water escaping. He was lost to sight. She could hear, sense and feel him behind her. The pause stretched out like a yawn in the ether, while her skin burned from the slapping, her bladder throbbed and her sex yearned.

Suddenly he was fingering her again from behind, toying with her inner lips. It's as if he has a map, she thought. He had located the stem of her clit where it rooted far back near her pubic bone, then gently circled it and rubbed the fat little button. She felt an orgasm rising, then dying back as he changed position. She moaned her need, but he ignored her. He was so quiet that she wondered if he had left the dungeon, abandoning her there for hours, till he chose to return and release her.

I'll report the crazy sod to the police, she vowed inwardly. He can't treat me like this!

But she knew that there was nothing she could do. No breath of scandal must besmirch St Jude's. She had too much at stake. For what seemed an eternity she hung there, her arm muscles cramped, her spanked skin on fire, the heat echoed by her needy clit, and her bladder demanding relief. She wriggled fruitlessly, feeding her imagination with lewd pictures calculated to help her come off, imprisoning her aroused clit between her tightly clenched thighs, hoping this would bring about a climax. All it did was increase her need to pass water.

A swish and a sudden draught behind her gave scant warning. Then agony bit deep as the paddle connected with her bare rump, powered by the full force of Felan's muscular arm. She yelped. The animal instinct to empty the body and run when danger loomed proved too much for her will-power. As the stinging pain swamped her, so her muscles loosened. She felt the warm urine trickling down her inner legs and joining the midnight dark pool of her dress. The paddle landed again, lower this time, catching the crown of her hindquarters, making her bottom quiver. She screamed, and tears welled up and flowed over. No one had ever treated her like this before. How could he do it? The cruel, arrogant bastard.

He went on thrashing her and now her feelings changed to ones of strange acceptance. There was nothing she could do. Felan would have his way with her, no matter what. She had entered the eye of the hurricane, a peaceful place to escape into as he lowered his arm and beat the backs of her thighs. A glow filled her, blood-red with passion. It spread from her stripes to her cunt. Now her awareness centred on every sensation – the soreness of her buttocks, the wetness soaking her legs, the core of her that convulsed hungrily. She wanted this peculiar union between herself and her master to go on forever. When he stopped, as abruptly as he had begun, she felt like an abandoned orphan.

His probing fingers found her entrance and she writhed on them as he inserted three and worked them in and out and around. His thumb kept up rotation on her bud till she yelled, nearly blacking out with the force of the mightiest orgasm she'd ever had. Felan lowered the rope, freed her arms, massaged her sore wrists, then found a long black hooded cape and wrapped her in it. She came to herself, frowning, puzzled.

'What about you?' she managed to say.

He picked up her wet dress and her panties and handed them to her. 'This was for you, not me,' he said, still poker-faced and apparently deadly serious. 'Part of your education. If you intend to run a fetish club, then you should at least have a smattering of what it entails.'

'How very altruistic of you,' she said, feeling as if her body and probably her inner-self would never be entirely her own again. He had put his mark on her, physically and spiritually. She wished it had been anyone else but him.

He'd seen her at her weakest. She'd wept, peed and come in front of him. She hated him for this. Where was her dignity now? How could she ever face him in broad daylight again? But he had also given her the power to express her deepest, most secret desires, to hand her will over to him, and with it the responsibility for her actions. It didn't matter that the floor below where she'd hung needed swabbing or that her new dress would never be the same. She'd let him use her, but not for his own pleasure, it seemed, although he still had a massive erection. What he'd gained from the encounter was something entirely divorced from a simple climax.

She was piqued, too. Why didn't he want her to give him head, or have full intercourse? A girl could take this as an insult, thinking that she wasn't sexy enough. He was trouble with a capital T and she'd sussed it from the first time they'd met.

He escorted her from the dungeon and said goodbye in the hall, as formal as a judge. Then he let himself out. She felt as if she'd just been through a learning curve, but wasn't sure how or why.

'Wake up, you lazy tyke. This is the big one,' Bronwen said, bouncing on the bed and then kneeling astride Luke's chest, pushing her pubis close to his face.

'Oh hell, babes, just another five minutes,' he groaned

sleepily, trying to escape and burrow deeper into the pillow.

'No. Now,' she insisted. 'Today's the day.'

'What's the time?' he grumbled, but was beginning to wake, smiling at her and stretching out his tongue in an attempt to lick her russet bush.

'Six o'clock, and I'm picking up the minibus at seven-thirty.'

'Time for a shag then,' he said, pulled her down under the duvet and rolled over on her.

Bronwen cuffed him playfully about the head, then stilled as his mouth came down on hers. His tongue plunged between her teeth and his hands seized both her wrists and held them. Capitulating entirely, she lifted her legs, placed her feet against his chest, then opened herself wide; cunt, breasts, the whole of her surrendering to the pleasure of lovemaking. He went down on her, lips moving into her crack, then past her perineum to her anus. She had a moment's panic. Was she clean there? She hadn't yet showered or done anything except make a cup of tea. Luke didn't seem aware, happily burrowing away.

It was lovely and she scratched her nipples, pulled and rolled them, those rose-red teats darkening as they swelled. Luke tongued her clit, then he sucked it, drew it between his lips, gave it no quarter, and the feeling gathered from each part of her, inside and out, or so it seemed. She didn't move, her legs bowed, his face buried in her soaking wet bush, and the sensation grew, reaching a plateau from which the only way out was orgasm.

'Luke, go on ... go on!' she implored, leaving her breasts and burying her hands in his hair, grabbing his ears to use as levers to make him work faster.

She arched her spine, then lifted her hips off the mattress, desperate for more, and at the point when the orgasm was unstoppable, he sank his fingers inside her, her muscles convulsing round them as he aped the back and forth motions of intercourse. The sensations were fierce, a series of short, sharp shocks that vibrated from

184

her toes to her brain. Luke let her down gently, kissing her pulsating clit; then he rose and kneeled between her legs, guiding his cock into her. His own need took over and he thrust deeply, filling her with that out-sized weapon, the end ramming against her cervix and the width stimulating her G-spot.

Now she was made conscious of his strength, submitting as she did when he spanked her with his hand or used his belt on her naked rump, or tied her up and gagged her, playing those sex games they both enjoyed so much. He gripped her bottom in both hands for greater purchase and rammed and plunged till she shook. She looked up, and his head was back, the cords of his neck straining, an expression of near agony or extreme ecstasy on his face. Then he gasped, and she felt him coming. He jerked madly several times, and then settled back on his heels, still linked with her but empty of passion and drained of spunk. When he finally withdrew and removed the condom, its teat was heavy with his fluid.

Bronwen cast an anxious eye at her watch. Six twenty-five. She leaped into the bathroom and showered. She could hear Luke in the kitchen brewing more tea. Wrapped in a fluffy pink towel, she gave herself a moment's respite, staring out of the window of their top-floor flat. This gave access to a south-facing roof where she and Luke sunbathed. The apartment was large and old and the rent cheap by today's standards, under five hundred pounds a month, but she wasn't happy about having her son, Gavin, stay during the school vacations. The loft space above them was a squat for dozens of marauding pigeons with their accompanying filth.

She didn't think it good enough for Gavin, and he spent most of his holidays in Cardiff with her mother. She was particularly keen to do well at St Jude's. If the club flourished, and she saw no reason why it shouldn't, then maybe she could have him visit there sometimes. This coming weekend, the club's baptism of fire, was therefore doubly important to her.

185

As far as she could see, everything had been planned down to the last detail. Bronwen wasn't stupid and didn't imagine for one moment that just because she and Luke had pleasured Laura and Cheryl they wouldn't expect the highest performance from her and her helpers. She was in charge, with him as second-in-command, and she sweated a little with anxiety as she climbed into a black thong and bra, jeans and a T-shirt, then applied make-up and screwed her flaming locks into a bunch at her crown.

Laura had assured her that the housekeeper, Ursula, wouldn't interfere in any way. So far, that cheerful, rotund person had given her no grief, as helpful as you please, and hadn't as much as entered the towers, told they were Bronwen's province. And Bronwen had Thomas, that tyrannical kitchen despot, eating out of her hand. Though there might be an overspill into the bedrooms of the hotel proper, he and his minions would supply food, consisting mainly of buffet snacks and a cold collation which would be laid out in the towers' bars. Both would be in use, linked as they were by a covered-in bridge, as well as the below-ground passage that connected the dungeons. If any club member needed to pass through the hotel foyer where he or she might bump into staff or conventional guests, then they had been advised to dress discreetly. Otherwise, they parked their cars at the back and entered through one of the towers' frowning portals.

Bronwen was never happier than when her nimble mind was ferreting away at problems. If she had been born in different circumstances, she could have been a high-flying businesswoman. Organisation was her forte, especially when it concerned the great and burning drive of her life – fornication.

'Ready, Luke!' she carolled cheerfully, grabbing up her bags, packed last night and containing vital equipment.

'Ready, babes,' he shouted, and she paused to admire him. He had that natural talent for clothes which gave him a fashion model look. It didn't much matter if they were a touch scruffy. He'd ensure they were designer labels and wear them with an air.

Filled with a bubbling sense of well-being, she locked the flat and tripped down three flights of stairs, out into the London street where the traffic roared non-stop. The air was fume-filled, the drivers grim-faced and prone to road-rage, and Bronwen hurried to where her car was parked, flung the bags into the back and edged her vehicle into the honking stream. A couple of miles away was a garage and there, waiting for her, was the green mini-bus that she had hired as transport for herself and her gang, including Alroy, who had been promised star-dom for the night.

'I'm so nervous I want to puke,' Cheryl confessed to Laura, putting the finishing touches to her costume in her bedroom.

Laura had helped her into her brothel madam's dress, drawing the stay lacing so tightly that she could hardly breathe. This added to the feeling that she was about to throw up. Her square-cut bodice was so low that her nipples kept poking out over the edge. No matter how she tried, she couldn't keep them in. Her petticoats frothed round her legs, the thick black stockings were upheld by garters so restrictive that she feared she might wind up with varicose veins, and she was terribly conscious of her bare pussy and bottom. Bronwen had dared her to leave off her knickers, and the air tickled her slit and excited her always alert and sensitive bud. The little black ankle boots were tight too, high heeled and laced up the front.

'You look the part,' Laura said, herself transformed into Boudicca, wonderful tousled, waist-length wig and all. She too was knickerless, and Cheryl couldn't help noticing that she had shaved her quim.

'Did you do that, or did someone help you?' she asked, and Laura tugged at the hem of her no-more-than-a-lampshade skirt.

She had the grace to blush. 'I had help,' she confessed.

187

'Bronwen?' Cheryl couldn't see when she could have fitted in a shaving session, for she had been rushed off her feet since arriving there at noon, the mini-bus disgorging a bevy of lovely girls and strapping hunks, to say nothing of Alroy in a gleaming white satin suit.

'As a matter of fact, no,' Laura admitted, abandoning the fight with her hem and pirouetting in front of the mirror on her stilt heels. 'It was Simon. He's an expert at that sort of thing. He really, truly loves women, their clothes, their cosmetics, their naughty bits. He helped me dress, after he'd shaved me.'

'You told him about the towers?' Cheryl flashed, suddenly apprehensive. The last thing they needed was a horde of vice squad heavies disrupting their première.

'Well, yes, sort of,' Laura admitted, and it was odd to see a warrior queen looking so embarrassed. 'Don't worry. It's cool ... *he's* cool. He knows such a lot about everything to do with sex, and is totally broad-minded.'

'He'll blab to Ursula.' Cheryl was really furious with her. It was all very well being cock struck, but common sense should have prevailed.

'No, he won't. I promise. It'll be useful to have him on our side, as it were. He can help cover up,' Laura insisted earnestly. 'He said he'd like to join in.'

'Did he, indeed?' Cheryl wasn't convinced. 'I hope he's not expecting a freebie.'

'I wouldn't have done anything to jeopardise the club, you know that, Cheryl,' Laura went on. 'I'm sure he'll be of benefit.'

'He made a fine job of your pussy,' Cheryl had to agree. 'But I don't want him putting Bronwen's back up, nor Luke's either. Is he your latest lover?'

'Yes, and we get on awfully well. Speaking of which, am I mistaken, or is there something going on between you and Felan Boynton?'

'What makes you think that?' It was Cheryl's turn to flush. Brazen it out, she thought. Sweet Jesus, you're supposed to be a bawd, goddamit! Stop blushing like a silly schoolgirl.

'I've felt it for some time. One can tell when there's chemistry between two people, and the electricity crackles where you and Felan are together.' Laura had recovered her equilibrium, turning the tables on Cheryl. 'Is it serious?'

'Laura, don't go there.'

'I mean, do you like him?'

Cheryl let the question hang in the air for a moment, then, 'Like?' she said. 'Like? No. Lust after? Oh, yes.'

'And have you done it?' Laura asked.

'I don't think that has anything to do with you,' Cheryl said, cutting her off and feeling mean, but the very last person she wanted to be reminded of on this most important occasion was Felan. She had a job to do, and intended to carry it out to the best of her abilities.

She found this easier than she expected. Bronwen was waiting to introduce her when she entered the East Tower. She was surprised at the ease with which she slipped into her role. Like an actress she came in on cue: she was no longer Cheryl Barden, but the confident owner of a Temple of Joy where anything was acceptable between consenting adults.

The tower was already humming, the background music Latino, the bar doing a roaring trade and Thomas's carefully prepared snacks going down a treat in the reception room. This was filling up with figures in black leather, red leather, purple and blue. Women in basques, catsuits or nuns' wimples; men in monks' habits, Roman togas, cardinals' robes, and a few business suits. Some wore masks, but those whose faces were exposed showed expressions ranging from sober, anxious and preoccupied, to warm, festive and lustful. A few stood around talking; Cheryl picked up on city jargon concerning mortgage rates and stocks and shares.

There were tempting racks of clothing that Bronwen had acquired should anyone wish to change into another costume. In a way, it reminded Cheryl of the night she had spent at Fell Tor, only this time it was for sluts, not goddesses. Baskets of dildoes and vibrators were to hand,

and others containing condoms in all colours, shapes and sizes. Bronwen had thought of everything.

A huge bull of a man, his pate tonsured, his friar's cassock open over a massive belly and jutting cock, was holding court on a dais. Several women in the flimsiest of nightgowns were waiting their turn to be put over his broad knee and spanked. Those who had already been accorded this singular honour were proudly displaying bottoms that glowed through the silk chiffon, red as those of baboons.

There was a strong smell of leather everywhere. The waiters, bearing trays of caviar, rollmop herrings, smoked salmon in brown bread parcels and prawn vol-au-vents, were attired as fitted their positions as underlings. Studded collars with lethal-looking spikes spanned their muscular necks. From these stretched chains and thongs that girded their torsos. Their tanned, splendidly developed chests were naked, and gold rings glinted in their pierced nipples and navels. The briefs that fitted like gloves were cut in such a way that their stiff cocks were exposed, lifted high by chain bindings, and their rumps were bare, with the narrowest of gussets passing between their buttocks.

The waitresses also wore collars, but some were dressed in close-fitting, wench-type velvet bodices with their breasts projecting through cut-outs, and tiny shorts hoisted high, making the crotch dig into their cracks, plump labial wings exposed on either side. A substantial portion of fleshy bottoms showed, some with telltale stripes left by the lash. Others were naked to the waist, their breasts encircled with chain mesh that emphasised these plump attributes, and starched tutus that dipped and swayed, exposing depilated or luxuriantly furred mounds.

'What d'you think?' Bronwen asked, attired in full dominatrix kit: thigh boots, mesh stockings, long gloves, a black rubber bustier and an apology for a skirt, the rich hue of her magnificent bush drawing the eye.

'You've done a fine job,' Cheryl said.

'And there's more. Wait till you see the theme rooms, and the dungeons, and I've brought down dancers of both sexes. There's something for everyone tonight.'

'Ah, my darling bosses,' said Alroy in honeyed tones, mincing towards them, rendered almost seven-foot tall by the exaggerated heels of his size-twelve stilettos.

'You look magnificent,' Cheryl said, shaking her head in wonder as she gazed at his emerald-green lurex dress that fitted without a wrinkle to the knees, where it flared out into a fishtail.

'Thank you, love. You're too kind, but I had to make an effort, didn't I? I've never been a guest of honour before.'

He did indeed look wonderful, a bizarre, high-camp transvestite, his shiny brown skin offset by the sparkling fabric, his dreadlocks teased into a crown of bead-encrusted braids. Green gloves to above the elbow covered his arms, and his neck was adorned with strings of paste gems that matched those in his pendant earrings. He could have looked garish, but he didn't. He looked like an exotic empress from some faraway time before mighty civilisations were swept away by a cataclysm, a meteor hit perhaps, that had tilted the earth on its axis and changed the face of the globe.

'Have you been introduced to everyone?' Cheryl asked.

'I stood at the doorway with Bronwen and welcomed them as they came in,' he said, with a proud tilt of his chin. Then his heavily painted eyes turned predatory as he scanned the crowd. They fastened on a muscle-packed pugilist wearing the accoutrements of a gladiator. 'Pardon me, ladies, but I've just seen the man I want to fuck me brainless tonight,' he added, and rustled off, wafting a cloud of perfume with an underlying patchouli base.

Luke appeared centre-stage, the master-of-ceremonies, in a navy chalk-stripe double-breasted suit, his hair slicked back, a wide-brimmed hat at a rakish tilt.

'He looks like a gangster, or a tango dancer,' Laura breathed, close to Cheryl's ear.

'A gigolo's more the ticket,' she answered pithily, though aware of his louche appeal.

'D'you think he'll dance with me?' Laura asked wistfully. 'I've had lessons.'

'In Westcombe?' Cheryl couldn't quite see those who ran the tea-dances in the Winter Gardens encouraging a demonstration of this hymn to passionate, sensual male dominance during the rather tepid afternoon sessions.

'Of course not, silly. I found a teacher in Bath. I'm not bad at it now. I'd love to dance with Luke.'

'That'll set the world on fire, I'm sure. Boudicca and Rudolph Valentino strutting their funky stuff.' Cheryl couldn't help being acerbic. She was battling with the fear that Felan might materialise at any moment. It blighted her enjoyment.

'Ladies and gentlemen and those who aren't quite sure,' Luke began, amidst laughter. 'The slave auction is about to begin. Up the stairs and the first turning on the right. The Seraglio Room. Drinks will be served during the bidding.'

'This we have to see,' Cheryl said.

There was a rush for the staircase and she was borne along with it. She was curious to witness this first ever event held in the chamber that Alroy had rigged out in opulent Oriental style. Her body was becoming aroused, responding to the pressure of the wildly attired people all around her, the air positively quivering with testosterone and costly perfume and sexual excitement. She was being drawn into the hedonistic spirit of it. What would it be like to bid for a dishy male slave, and how would she feel if she herself were auctioned?

'These are the rules,' Luke said, mounting the slave block. 'Each of you will pay a hundred pounds, part of which we'll donate to charity, and in exchange we'll issue you with ten thousand dollars in mock money to use during the bidding. Liam here, and the buxom Celia, will come among you, take your money and issue you with the play cash. Meanwhile, the first slave will be displayed. There are forms to fill in should you want to put yourself up for sale, and each slave already on offer has given the auctioneer his or her details; experience, sexual preferences, and SM role preference – top, bottom or switch.'

Liam and Celia were a pair of flash operators, he wearing nothing but a black bow tie and a jock strap, and she in a leopard-print cache-sexe and jewelled nipple-clamps. Her breasts were huge, with teats like organ stops, and Liam had a most impressive bulge. Neither objected when punters wanted to fondle their attributes. The monetary exchange went like a bomb.

Cheryl wanted to join in. 'But I didn't bring any money,' she said to Bronwen.

'Neither did I,' wailed Laura. 'Though I don't think I'll ever dare bid.'

'Owe it,' Bronwen replied. 'I shall. Have you seen anything you fancy?'

'Yes. Just,' Cheryl said, as the first lot was brought to the block.

He was a handsome, well-proportioned slave, and the auctioneer read out his particulars. His name was given as Karl, and he was in his late twenties. He was American, a lecturer in literature taking part in an exchange scheme at Oxford University. He enjoyed every aspect of role-play. Apart from that, he was footloose and fancy-free. Courageous too, thought Cheryl, as he stood there bold as brass, wearing nothing but a collar and chain. His cock was erect, rising from a thicket of dark curls, his balls like ripe plums between his thighs. And he was circumcised. But then, Cheryl had heard that most American men were. She'd never had the chance to find out.

The slave-master permitted a woman to suck Karl. It cost her two thousand pounds in Monopoly money. She was allowed a minute, and no more. Karl stood there stoically, his cock immersed in the kneeling woman's mouth. Others clamoured to do the same, waving pretend bank notes at the auctioneer. They were refused. There was no way Karl would be encouraged to come till he was bought, his energy and spunk to be saved for his purchaser.

Cheryl jumped into the bidding and won. 'I'm gob-smacked!' she exclaimed to Laura, who was standing beside her, goggle-eyed. 'I never expected to get him. Now what do I do?'

At the same time, she was wishing Felan could be there to see her triumph and was especially charming when Karl strolled over, as casual and at ease bare-naked as he would have been in jeans and sweater. He had greenish eyes, long brown hair, a strong jaw and straight prominent nose.

'Hi there, ma'am,' he drawled, with a flash of perfect bridgework. 'I've been told to collect the amount and hand it over, then I'm yours to command.'

When he returned, she was still wondering if she dare have him. He was exceptionally good looking, with that smooth, boyish charm, and she'd spent most of her cash to get him. According to the rules, he was hers for the night. And why not? she counselled herself. You want him, don't you? You're curious to see what a circumcised dick feels like. Go for it.

She was discovering the singular thrill of a new man, unexplored territory, as it were. Mark had proved to be a gem, then there was Aiden, a trifle peevish now, but fine for a one-night stand. And what about Felan? her conscience or inner demon or higher-self questioned.

What about him? All he wanted to do was get the upper hand.

And you enjoyed. Went along with it. Wanted more. In spite of what you say. And 'the lady doth protest too much, methinks.' Don't you really long to be mastered by him?

Sick of arguing with herself, Cheryl grabbed Karl by the prick when he returned and said, 'Fancy a trip to the dungeon?'

194

'Ready when you are,' he replied with a dazzling smile, his cock expanding another inch in her hand.

The dungeon was similar to that in the West Tower, and Cheryl hoped that a visit there with another man would make her stop remembering her initiation into bondage by Felan. It was equally gloomy and scary. A woman brushed past her and she turned to see her leading a naked man by a leash attached to his genitals. A beautiful young woman wearing a snowy-white wedding dress was chained up in a corner, her bodice pulled down to show her nipples pierced by rings that supported small weights. Her partner had lifted her skirt to expose her hairless labia from which other weights were suspended. Her feet were apart, held in place by spreader bars.

This is for real, Cheryl kept reminding herself. This is their idea of entertainment. A dominatrix manifested a wry sense of humour by eating her supper off a paper plate through which her consort's cock protruded. Latex clad, he was lying on the floor, his arms and legs bound with straps.

'How about that?' Karl whispered, and Cheryl felt his hand come to rest at her waist. 'Would you eat your supper like that?'

'I'd rather feast off you,' she answered, and pressed back against him where they stood near the wall. The sights and sounds around her were stimulating. Everywhere she looked it was to see couples or threesomes engaged in some peculiar sexual ritual calculated to bring them to climax, later if not immediately.

Two naked women were bound together by chains and attached to a hook in the ceiling. A masked man in a cassock was flogging them, their skins blooming like roses under the multi-thonged tawse. A man was cuffed on to a rack, blindfolded, gagged and helpless as his male partner, tattooed, shaven and pierced, flicked at his scrotum with a riding crop. A woman, bare to the bone, was tied in a chair with a hole cut in the seat. Her legs were wide apart, and Cheryl could hear her moans as hands fondled her breasts and played with her wide-open entrance, rubbing her clit, poking fingers into her fully exposed cunt. Then her cries were stilled as a man stood over her and inserted his cock into her mouth.

Karl raised Cheryl's skirt and caressed her backside, then between her legs, slipping a finger inside her and moving it gently. Her eyes were riveted on the scene being enacted before her. Others had come down too, and were watching, finding it as arousing as she did, beginning to caress one another, not caring whom or of what sex.

Karl continued to massage her clit, and she reached round and found his cock. It was hard and heavy, the bare tip wet with pre-come. Her skirt and petticoats were proving a hindrance and she tugged at the ties. They gave and Karl helped her take off the restricting garments, laying them aside once she'd taken a condom from her pocket. St Jude's had provided them, and now she was going to take advantage of this. She was nude from the waist to the welts of her black stockings. She felt deliciously wanton and ground her buttocks against Karl's cock. A moment's resistance and then the length knifed into her, right up to the hilt.

'Like to watch, do you?' he murmured, and licked her ear. Cheryl shivered.

'I might learn something,' she said.

'I doubt it,' he grunted, pushing into her hard.

She bore down on it, and he slid his hands up to grasp her hips, pulling her even harder on to himself. She felt her bottom cheeks spreading slightly and he moved slowly and rhythmically, rotating his pelvis, his helm grinding against her cervix, his coarse pubic hair brushing against the skin between her parted buttocks. One of his hands came round across her belly and she squirmed with pleasure as his fingers found her clit. She moaned, and let him know that he was pressing the right button, and though his in-and-out movements were speeding up, he didn't stop rubbing her.

The twin sensation proved too much and she climaxed,

her whole body shuddering and flushing hot and cold. Karl reached his own completion, and while the intense, beautiful orgasmic spasms gradually subsided, he pulled out, turned her in his arms and kissed her. Then he lifted his head and she saw his eyes shining in the dim, reddish light.

'You're great, honey,' he said, and she knew that he meant every word. 'Will you be my date for the whole night? I'm your slave and you haven't whipped me yet.'

'We'll see,' she said, and picked up her skirt, throwing it over her arm. She might as well go on as she had started, bare arsed and willing. There seemed little point in dressing again.

Chapter Ten

*L*aura left the dungeon, her mind spinning. Those strange scenes of sex and sadism, with loads of masochism thrown in, had been the final straw, smashing her romantic illusions to smithereens. It had been hard enough struggling with ideas for a novel, and she'd put it on hold since being so deeply involved with St Jude's, but now it seemed that reality would make the project impossible.

The impetus had gone and she brooded on this as she wandered along the passage that led to the West Tower. People passed her, couples or singles or groups, each hurrying towards his or her fantasy goal, and she began to question the motives that had driven her to put pen to paper, or rather cursor to screen, with a mouse dancing attendance.

It had begun with loneliness, and dissatisfaction in marriage. She'd sought solace in books and hungry, physically and emotionally, had found comfort in fulsome best-sellers whose contents had become ever more explicit as the censorship laws relaxed. She had read them in bed and, if Stuart was out (and he usually was), it became a one-handed read as she pleasured herself. She began to think: I can write these, conjuring my own handsome hero and graphic love-scenes and creating a world of derring-do. I can live through the feisty, wilful heroine, and wind up in the arms of the bad-boy alpha male, who, of course, I shall reform.

Now, however, fantasy had become reality. She was no longer spurred by frustration. She'd had Luke and tried lesbianism with Bronwen and found a soulmate in Simon. All she had to do was trust him.

Where was he? She hurried now, needing him. He'd half-promised to be there, if he could get away without rousing suspicion. She glanced at her watch, not part of Boudicca's regalia but no matter. It was the witching-hour, and the reception desk in the foyer should be closed.

The West Tower was similarly laid out as its counter-part in the East. The dungeon was every bit as gloomy and popular. The ground floor served refreshments and there were female wrestlers pulverising one another in a ring, surrounded by those who were betting on the outcome, excited by muscular, nude women showing their parts as they grappled.

Laura headed upstairs and into her Mecca, a large room transformed into an over-the-top art deco dance hall. Almost immediately a man appeared, slight of build but dressed immaculately in an old-fashioned evening suit.

'I've been waiting for you,' he said, hazel eyes serious, his normally unruly hair brushed back, darkened and shiny with gel. It threw his cheekbones into prominence and gave him a raffish air.

'Oh, Simon, I'm so glad you're here,' she said, lighting up inside.

He took her hands and spread her arms wide, scrutin-ising her. 'I love the outfit, but change into something more suitable for dancing,' he said. 'I'll come with you and help choose.'

The music infiltrated her blood, nerves and guts – the orchestra, the piano, the accordion, and sometimes a voice singing in that moody way associated with Argen-tina, or Spain. Several tangoists had taken the floor. The men, and therefore the leaders, were dumpy but nifty of foot. The women were taller, wearing beaded Charleston dresses and following each move as if their legs were chained to their partner's. As they were manipulated and twirled, their skirts flared, displaying their bare thighs and bottoms, and a tantalising flash of something ruder.

Laura hung on to Simon's hand and they found a dressing room chock-a-block with costumes. Others were there, trying on plumed helmets and hats, vampire cloaks, chain-mail bodices, crotchless trousers, bondage trappings, and the highest of high-heeled footwear. Laura went to a rail that housed items from the Roaring Twenties.

'That's it,' Simon said decisively as she took down a frock made of tangerine silk. 'That's the very colour that's associated with tango.'

'And black,' she reminded, holding the costume up against her. It was preferable to that of a warrior queen, be she never so British.

There were no changing rooms so, with Simon's assistance, she got out of her gold leather bodysuit, her armbands and boots and stood completely naked while he shook out the dress. He looked at her and her nipples peaked. There was something in his hazel eyes that warmed her to the cockles of her heart, and beyond. She wanted him then and there, but he was calling the tune, and she knew he was right. It would be all the more exciting if their desires were whisked to a frenzy by tango.

The dress fitted, a straight little number with no sleeves and a V-neck that plunged to the waist. The hem was scalloped and fringed. 'Now then, stockings,' Simon said, and rummaged in a chest of drawers. He produced a flesh-coloured pair and she rolled them up mid-thigh, secured by elasticised garters.

'Shoes,' she murmured, and there were several on a rack nearby.

She sat on a stool and thrust her toes into black courts with Louis heels, flashy paste buckles and long ribbons that Simon wound round her ankles and criss-crossed up her calves like ballet pumps.

'Hair and make-up,' he said next, and had her move to the mirror and cosmetic table.

Soon her hair lay close to her head in a sleek bob, with side curls following the contours of her cheeks. He dusted her face with beige powder and added rouge, then thickened her lashes with mascara and outlined her eyes with kohl. A bright-red rosebud of a mouth completed the illusion. She was now a flapper of the post-Great War generation, flighty, cocktail drinking and dance crazy. He found her a jade cigarette holder and a jet-embroidered purse, then finished off with a headband sporting an osprey feather.

She went back to the dance hall on his arm. He selected a table and she left her bag on it, but they didn't sit down.

'I won cups for ballroom dancing not so long ago,' he said, then he seized her by the wrist and spun her into his arms. 'Now dance with me, dance as you've never danced before.'

The music beat in 4–4 time, and she stepped and gyrated and Simon guided her, made her bend like an aspen to his movements, his hand flat on her back, then sliding down to rest on the upper swell of her buttocks. He held her pressed close to his chest, her right arm bent and pulled in against him. She could feel his cock through his trousers and her flimsy dress. His leg passed between hers, feet placed correctly, strangely formal for so intimate a dance. Her own followed suit – the intricate steps, the long strides, the pauses, the passion, the male aggression and female submission.

He changed to tenderness, his smooth-shaven cheek pressed close to hers, cradling her as if she were made of spun glass. The music surged and her heart beat in time to it. She could feel her juices wetting her inner thighs, but didn't falter. He was so easy to follow, far, far easier than the portly aficionado she'd partnered at the classes held in a ground-floor flat in Bath's beautiful Royal

Crescent. He'd been elderly and smelled strongly of garlic.

It had helped though. She knew what Simon expected of her. She was haughty, yet pliable. Willing, but on her own terms. He bent her backwards over his arm as the music concluded, then pulled her upright again, holding her more tightly. They stood in the centre of the floor and no one gave them a second glance as he lowered his head and suckled at her breast through the silk.

His hand was between her legs, and there was nothing to prevent him from pushing a finger into her. She gasped and pressed down on it, forgetting they were in public. He looked at her and smiled, and her dress now bore the emblem of his mouth, a wet, dark patch lifted by her stiff nipple. He withdrew his finger and lowered her skirt, then fetched her bag and took her to a divan in an alcove. It was unoccupied, everyone else either dancing or copulating or simply sitting around and drinking. No one seemed in the least perturbed by anything that took place.

The divan was cushion heaped, and Simon and Laura sank into it. They were partly hidden from view but the idea that someone might be turned on by watching them excited Laura, and she flung her arms round him and ground her body into his. He was ready, if amused by her abandon, and he took off her headband and lifted her skirt till the fringes tickled her belly, then stretched her open so that he might look at her. She stared down the length of her body, seeing the bare hump of her pubis, the cleft sharply defined, and her honey-gold thighs meeting the pale tops of the stockings, banded by black garters. And then there were her dancing shoes, the ribbons crossing and re-crossing, and this half-undressed state was more arousing then if she had been stark naked.

Leaning back, she stared into Simon's eyes. 'Masturbate,' he said.

Embarrassment made her flush under the rouge. He wanted to see her performing this very private act. The idea was so arousing that she lowered her hand and started to rub herself with her middle finger, just as she did when alone. She played with it, moistening her finger pad with juice and rubbing each side, then round the top, varying the pressure, sometimes hard, sometimes light. She spread her legs wider and Simon leaned over, watching intently. This encouraged her and the need grew, making her ache inside. He unbuttoned his trousers and took out his cock, holding it in his hand and massaging it, and the novelty of its lack of foreskin intrigued her.

She felt herself all over, finding the pencil-like stem of her clit, fondling it for a second, then rolled the flesh away from its tip. She used both hands now, pressing the folds back, exposing it fully, making it stand out proud. Now she wanted it hard and wet, and scooped further juice from her pussy, smoothing it up and over her bud.

'Harder, darling. Come for me. Do it now,' Simon urged.

Her crisis was only seconds away and her hand responded to his order, rubbing vigorously. She felt his fingers in her, giving the added zest she needed. Her heart began to thud, her breathing quickened and her eyes no longer focused.

'Ah, yes. It's coming . . . it's *here*', she moaned.

Then Simon's hands were on her, turning her about and pushing into her from behind. It was just what she needed to round it off, those long, fast strokes from an ample erection. He opened her wide and plunged in deeply, a hand pushed under her to pinch her nipples. She arched her back and thrust out her chest to meet that delicious touch, halfway to a second orgasm.

'I'm sorry, darling. I'd give you another, but I can't hold back,' he grunted, and then came with a flourish, and kept on thrusting even after he'd finished.

Laura came down to earth to the sound of a light spattering of applause. She looked up, went into panic mode, and wriggled from under Simon. An interested ring of spectators surrounded the divan. All were

203

smiling, and several of the men were bringing themselves off, shooting jets of come into the air. The women were playing with their quims, or with those of their companions. There was the astonishing sight of Alroy, bent over from the waist, legs splayed, his green lurex skirt about his ears, and the gladiator's dick buried deep in his arsehole. Another man, older than him and wearing slave's manacles, kneeled between Alroy's legs and was moving his head up and down as he sucked the designer's cock.

Laura adjusted her dress, glad to observe that Simon's trousers were now respectable. She was fast becoming liberal-minded, but even so was relieved when he said, 'I'm hungry. What say we go and find some supper?'

Cheryl bumped into Emily in the supermarket. She'd dropped in there to pick up some shampoo. It was the only place in Westcombe that stocked her favourite brand. Gone were the days when she marched in with a shopping list a mile long. Now Laura and Ursula saw to all that, ordering through the Internet or making excursions to the nearest wholesaler. She didn't miss it one bit, bored to death with catering and managing and cooking for so many years of marriage.

Hurrah for divorce and St Jude's, she thought. All she had to do was keep the books and be charming to the guests. This gave her ample time for sunning herself in the altogether on her own private terrace and cooling off in the swimming pool. This was one of the advantages of living near the coast – in summer an almost tropical complexion could be acquired without the fuss of going abroad. Though the sun was lower now, and the land definitely thinking about mellowing into autumn, it was a hot day and she intended to get back to her lounger and tan-enhancing oil as soon as she could.

It was then that a soft, cultured voice spoke from the other side of Aisle Four, where the shelves were lined with lotions and potions, deodorants and toothpaste, and everything for personal hygiene, including lubricating jelly and Durex.

'Hello,' said Emily. 'I'm glad we've met. I wanted to thank you for the other evening. It was kind of you to invite us.'

'It was a pleasure to see you,' Cheryl answered, and meant it – not the nasty John, naturally, but she'd been genuinely glad to welcome her.

'I don't get out much,' Emily went on, and she seemed to be apologising for herself. 'John's the gadabout.'

I'll bet he is, Cheryl thought sourly, but said, 'Won't you come and see me again? You play, don't you? Music is one of my things. I'm sure we have a lot in common.'

She envied the way Emily blushed. It was very appealing, and she found that she wanted to awaken her to her body's potential, doubting very much that John had taken the trouble to do so. Emily wasn't so much slim as willowy, with long feet and artistic hands. Her hair was silvery gold, thick and springy but too controlled, and Cheryl wanted Bronwen to take a look at it and make suggestions. Her clothes needed re-routing too. They smacked of parties organised by friends who were into pyramid selling. That loose, cream jersey jacket, worn over leggings in the same material and the cowl-necked blouse beneath, was far too staid and lacking in imagination. No doubt they'd cost Emily a packet, but she might as well have gone to a high-street chain store.

Cheryl could imagine that she had been talked into ordering. She was a people-pleaser, frightened of her own shadow and terrified of giving offence. John Dempsey had done a very thorough job of destroying his wife's self-worth. Cheryl had come to that conclusion when she first met them at the sailing club. It had been her very last visit. She had gone under sufferance, and had kept her vow never to repeat it.

Sir Galahad was blowing his horn somewhere in the misty mountains of elf-land, and the stirring notes shivered through Cheryl, urging her to join the crusade. She would save Emily and open her eyes to all those wonderful experiences that were hers by right. She didn't have to live a life that was as unutterably stale, stilted and artificial as her own had once been.

'What are you doing tonight?' she asked, trawling through her mental diary. As far as she could remember she was free. She didn't see much of Laura lately. She and Simon were as if soldered together at the genitals. Even more so since the extremely successful party in the towers, which was to be repeated shortly.

'Nothing much. John's away and the girls have gone camping with the Guides and Rupert's visiting friends in Brighton. I was going to take the opportunity of watching an opera video. I can't when they're around. It's all pop. Not Rupert, of course. He loves the classics, but John's not keen. He likes sport.'

'You don't share many interests?' Cheryl enquired gently.

Emily shifted uncomfortably in her navy, rope-soled espadrilles. It was obvious that she did not want to be disloyal, but, 'Not a lot,' she confessed.

'Then why don't you have a TV and video recorder set up in another room?'

'He'd still object to what he calls "that bloody awful row". I'd have to have it on ever so quietly, and you can't do that with opera, can you?' Emily's eyes were smiling, as if she dared hope that she'd at last met someone who would understand.

'Quite right. I turn up the volume full blast. Look, I've lots of opera recordings and am gradually switching to DVD. Puccini's my favourite, but I've the movie version of Bizet's *Carmen*, with Placido Domingo and Julia Migenes. Filmed in Spain, it's the definitive work, in my opinion. We could watch it after dinner.'

'Really? I'd like that. What time?'

I've done it now, Cheryl thought. There's no turning back. Lady Emily of the Lake, this may well be your rite of passage. 'Why don't you come round this afternoon? D'you like the sun? I shall be on the terrace. Bring your bikini, and there's a pool as well. With any luck, the guests won't be using it and we can skinny-dip, if you like.'

'I don't know about that. I've never swam in the nude. But are you sure? I don't want to be in the way,' Emily said timorously.

Cheryl placed her hand on Emily's, where it gripped the shopping trolley handle. 'I shouldn't have suggested it if I didn't want you,' she assured her, very conscious of those smooth-skinned, ladylike knuckles beneath her capable, strong fist.

Images flashed on the screen of her brain, of Emily naked in the dreamboat of a sexy bed in her apartment. She'd only ever slept in it with Mark, and that some time ago. In her mind, Emily was writhing in the throes of orgasm, a state of grace brought about by Cheryl as she caressed those small breasts and licked the clit that poked out between the pink lips of Emily's neat little cleft. She'd put money on the flesh being thin, not plump and voluptuous like Bronwen's or delightfully shaven like Laura's.

Desire coiled like a tight spring inside her, and her own greedy sexuality awoke. In an instant the thong, which cupped her mound so closely, dampened where it pressed into her crotch. The afternoon promised more than simply soaking up the sun. Apart from the chance to educate Emily body-wise, and clear her head of nonsense implanted there by that dictator John, she anticipated the rare enjoyment of spending time with someone who shared her passion for opera. That in itself was enough.

They parted at the checkout and Cheryl put her carrier in the Range Rover. She'd bought more items than she had intended, but this was the way of the supermarket. There was an alley near by, part of the old town when Westcombe was no more than a fishing village. It now housed antique shops, and several devoted to charity. Unable to resist the lure of a possible bargain, she set off after a quick glance at the sky. It was all right. Not a cloud in sight. She could sacrifice half an hour's tanning time, as the weather looked set to be hot all day. She strolled up the alley, pausing to check the window of the first antique emporium she came to, squinting at brass and china, cut glass dressing-table sets and bedraggled teddy bears with moth-eaten fur and outrageous price tags.

The charity shops proved beneficial, and she came out of one carrying a large bag. 'What have you got there?' said Felan from the other side of the lane.

Her heart did a double flip. 'A pair of Gustav Klimt prints – *Women Friends* and *The Virgin* – reproductions but decently framed,' she answered, hating herself for so much as acknowledging him.

'Let me see.' He took the bag from her and part lifted one out.

'Don't drop it,' she warned, and her wayward body came out in goose bumps.

'Would I?' he admonished, smiling crookedly at her. 'These are nice. Did you pay much for them?'

'Sixteen pounds for both.'

'A steal,' he commented, still perusing the prints. 'I admire Klimt. He openly celebrates Eros, and uses woman as his inspiration, a vamp, a sex object, but ultimate fulfilment. You must be made up to have got them for that.'

'I am. Now give them back. It's time I wasn't here,' she said, almost too emphatically.

'Not yet.' He stuffed the pictures under one arm and frogmarched her next door.

It was a recherché teashop that rejoiced in the winsome name of The Settle. It was run by a pair of spinster ladies and specialised in homemade scones with strawberry jam and chocolate cake to die for. Had it been the height of the season, there would not have been any room, but visitors were thinning out now. A waitress bustled up.

'Table for two, sir?' she enquired, her West Country accent as thick as the clotted cream she served.

'In the smoking area. We'll have coffee.'

'Nothing to eat, sir? We shall be laying up for lunch

soon, sir, but you can sit over here,' and she led them to a table with high-backed wooden benches on each side.

'I don't want a coffee. I don't want to be here with you. I want to get home,' Cheryl hissed as she reluctantly sat down opposite him. 'And give me my pictures.'

He handed them over and she placed them carefully, upright on the floor by her feet. 'Are you wearing any knickers?' he asked.

This staggered her. 'What?' she gasped.

'Knickers. Are you wearing any?'

'You've got a colossal cheek. This is neither the time nor the place.'

He lit a cigarette, grinning across at her wolfishly. Then she felt something nudging her knees apart, sliding under her skirt and touching her. The chequered table-cloth hid it, but she guessed what it was. He had stretched his leg, slipped a foot out of his sandal and was frigging her with his big toe. Mark had once dared her to go public in the Yew Tree, but hadn't followed through. Felan was about to do so.

'You've got panties on after all. Spoilsport,' he accused, increasing the pressure.

She was afraid those at the other tables would smell her body heat and musk. She kept her eyes down as the waitress returned, placed the mugs before them and went on her way. Felan crushed out his butt in the ashtray and added cream to his coffee. His bare toe didn't cease its relentless frottage, working the thong up and up, driving it into her slit.

'Felan! For God's sake!' she whispered urgently, but it was too late. She came, riven by the sharpness of it and sweating with the effort to sit there unmoved, as if no torrent of feeling was cascading through her.

His eyebrow raised sardonically and he withdrew his toe. 'Wet,' he remarked, and rubbed it on the carpet, then wriggled his foot into his sandal again. 'My turn,' he went on.

'How d'you mean?' she asked suspiciously, as she coped with the contractions causing havoc inside her.

She wanted his cock to fill her, wanted to clasp it and grind on it, and finish off that way.

'You like novelty, don't you? Or have I been misled?' he answered, and it was as if he burrowed into her psyche and raided the storehouse of her sexual secrets.

'Do I?' She felt safer with this verbal fencing, and her cleft was quieting down.

'I believe so.'

'I don't know what I want any more,' she admitted, and added crossly, 'You've done things to me that I never dreamed I'd put up with.'

He chuckled, and said, 'Good, Mrs Barden. And you've been pleasured?'

'Yes,' she said, and couldn't meet his piercing blue eyes.

'And I've shocked you?'

'Yes.'

'And I'm about to shock you again.'

'So, what more can you do here that will shock me?' As soon as the words were out she regretted them.

'Get under the table and suck my cock,' he said.

The teacups clinked. There was polite chit-chat all around; the waitresses were busy, scribbling orders on their little pads; the gateaux and sponge cakes sat solid under the glass bells that protected them from thieving bluebottles; and Felan had just made this outrageous, crude and totally unacceptable suggestion.

'You're joking,' she said, trying out an unsuccessful laugh.

'Do it, or I'll stand up and tell everyone that you're running a scandalous club.'

'You wouldn't.'

'Wouldn't I?'

'You mean it, don't you?'

He didn't answer, and with a last look round the teashop, she went down on her knees, screened by the settle and the tablecloth. She crawled to his crotch. He was already unzipped and his cock was erect, protruding through the opening in his boxer shorts. She smelled the

210

animal odour of excited male. She reached up, pushing back the clothing and freeing him, dipping a hand into the aperture beneath and sliding her fingers over his balls. His cock bobbed against her face and she took it in her mouth. She heard him catch his breath and smiled round the thickness of his stem. That would teach the bugger! Let him try and keep his cool as she wanked him off.

It became a game, and she wanted to make him lose control. She moved her head as briskly as she could in that confined space and worked him with her hand while her tongue played with the foreskin and helm. She sensed that he was on the brink, hearing him groan and feeling his firm hands on her head. He started to come and she swallowed his juices, tasting his taste again, relishing the bitter sweetness.

He handed her down a serviette and she wiped her mouth on it, then emerged to hear him say to the waitress, 'My fiancée dropped her engagement ring. Have you got it, darling?'

'Yes, *darling*,' she replied, scowling at him, then darting a look round for signs of voyeurs.

'Well done. Very well done, indeed,' he said urbanely.

She couldn't find the words to answer this. He took the bill; the waitress retired and he was zipped up again and ready to leave. 'I always said you give great head. You'll see me again when you least expect it.' And with that he was at the pay desk and out of the door.

I won't go, Emily thought, as she unpacked the groceries, put some in the stripped-pine unit, some in the fridge and the rest in the chest-freezer. Cheryl was only being polite. She doesn't really want to see me. I'll ring up and say I'd double booked, make an excuse, spend the afternoon in the potting shed – anything.

She made a tomato salad for herself and ate at the kitchen table. The garden sweltered under the Indian summer heat, and the thought of swimming had never been more appealing. It was one o'clock. She stacked her plate in the dishwasher, then went upstairs and dug out her costume from the bottom of a drawer. A bikini? Hardly, and she was far too long in the tooth for such a thing. She'd wanted one, of course, stared at them longingly in the shops on the seafront, but never dared. It was all right for Cheryl with her youthful figure, but Ruth and Eva would laugh her to scorn. As for John's reaction? It didn't bear thinking about.

Her costume was newish, black, sleek and cut high at the sides. She'd bought it to take the girls swimming, though they'd quickly outgrown this. It was more fun with their friends, particularly if there were boys involved. Emily enjoyed the water but couldn't work up the enthusiasm to go alone. That was it, really. She was always by herself. The kids moving on, and John engaged in God only knew what.

She went to the airing cupboard and took a large beach-towel from the pile. She rolled her costume in it then, on impulse, rooted for a bottle of protective lotion in the bathroom. Factor fifteen. One that she insisted the children used if they were going to be outside for long. Not Rupert. He insisted on something much lower, with an exotic, coconut odour, smoothing it all over his exposed skin and turning a coppery brown within a short while. He often disappeared down to the sand dunes for hours on end, and she sometimes wondered what he did there, besides sun worship.

She fished out a beach-bag and stuffed both towel and costume in it, with oil and sunglasses in a side pocket. Feeling foolish and a bit of a fraud, she set the security alarm and let herself out of the house, carefully locking the door behind her.

As she drove along the coastal road in the direction of St Jude's, her mind wandered, and she kept visualising Cheryl. She'd looked like a gypsy in the supermarket, bronzed and bold and beautiful. Her skirt had been too short, her top too tight, her jewellery too big, but she'd been impressive, nonetheless. That thin, animated face, those shrewd green eyes, and her hair, long and shaggy and chestnut coloured, just the way Emily would have liked hers. She had always wanted to look like a Pre-Raphaelite model: tumbled locks, dreamy eyes and incredibly lovely velvet dresses in medieval style. You could never quite tell if they were saints or sinners, nuns or fallen women, and it didn't matter.

The village was in thrall to afternoon somnolence. Had it been set near Mediterranean shores instead of the Bristol Channel, the natives would have been comatose. As it was, a few were enjoying a siesta, but most soldiered on, unwilling to become party to sloppy Continental habits, mowing their lawns, taking their dogs for walks, and generally making themselves hot, sweaty and bad-tempered.

This was not the case at St Jude's. Emily covered the gravel drive and circled the pond with its statues of large-breasted mermaids sporting beneath the fountain, then parked up and, following her nose, went round to the back. She could hear distant noises from the dining room where some of the guests were partaking of lunch. The kitchen sounded busy too. A youth in tight Levi's and no shirt who, judging by the pruning shears at his side, should have been tending the rose bushes, leaped up guiltily when Emily appeared. He had been dozing in the shade of a cedar.

'Can I help you, miss?' he said, captivating her with his wide smile, short, spiky hair and rugged, attractive face. His bare torso gleamed, the muscles of his hairless chest well defined.

Oh, you could help me, beautiful young man, she thought. You, with your skin like velvet and your worn, stonewashed denims clasping your bulge. What sweet music we could make together, were I only ten years younger. She was startled by her feelings, lust gripping her, that yearning for adventure and danger, that reckless longing to risk all in order to have a personable male bringing her turbulent release. He was a gardener, a bit of rough trade, but she regretted that he would never know how close he had been to putting his cock in a lady.

He had canny blue eyes, obviously accustomed to taking advantage if he could get away with it, but treating her with respect because she was older and upper class. They stared at each other for a second, then he repeated, 'Can I help? Are you looking for the entrance? It's round the corner.'

'I know. I've left my car there. I've an appointment with Mrs Barden.' So much left unsaid, she reflected, so polite and restrained. In different circumstances, were we marooned on a desert island, for instance, we'd be rolling on the grass, tearing at each other's clothes, hands everywhere, caressing, kissing ... Oh, God, I must stop this. My panties are getting wet.

'She's out the back, sunbathing. It's kind of private, 'cos she likes to strip off,' he answered, an impudent, laddish grin taking over from the friendly smile.

'Thank you,' Emily said, and hurried off before she did something so incredibly foolish that she would rue it to the end of her days – possibly unbuttoning his fly and releasing the cock which she could have sworn was growing more prominent as they talked.

Like the children following the Pied Piper's flute, she was drawn by strains of music: Maurice Ravel's, if she wasn't mistaken. She walked between a maze of high bushes and came to a terrace. Cheryl was there, stretched full length on a sun-facing padded lounger, a parasol clipped to the head-end to shade her face.

She wore nothing but a black triangle that barely hid her mound. It couldn't be called a bikini, more a string, with narrow thongs that circled her hipbones and disappeared into her bottom crack. Her breasts glistened with oil, the nipples dark and prominent. Emily swallowed; this was almost too much, coming directly after her encounter with the gardener.

The music was issuing from a portable CD player. 'That's *Daphnis et Chloé*,' Emily exclaimed, glad of a distraction.

214

'Got it in one, and you didn't have to phone a friend,' Cheryl said, smiling. 'Clever of you to spot Ravel. Most people only associate him with the *Bolero* and ice-skaters. It's the full score of the ballet, with a wordless chorus.'

'Such atmosphere and magic,' said Emily, enchanted by the music, this secret nook and the unashamed sexual allure of her hostess. 'No other work of such sheer sensual beauty exists in the entire orchestral repertoire.'

'I very nearly agree, but there are so many I adore.' Cheryl lifted a lazy arm and gestured her to come closer. 'You'll have to forgive me, but I never move when I'm browning myself, only to follow the sun round. And woe betide anyone who forms a shadow between it and me.'

'I've brought my costume.'

'Goodie. See that door in the wall over there? That leads to my apartment. You can pop up and change, if you like. I've already prepared a lounger for you. We can roast for a while and then take a swim. Hopefully, the inmates won't have the same idea. There's nothing quite like having the pool to oneself.'

With Ravel's music still weaving a spell round her, Emily darted across the terrace and up the stairs. It was the back way to an apartment that was sumptuously decorated and furnished. Even a cursory glance gave a wealth of information about its owner. Flamboyant yet tasteful, broad in scope but harmonious, everywhere was evidence of a cultured woman with diverse interests. There were books, videos, a stereo player and paintings. Emily crossed the sitting room and nosed into the dining area and kitchen. She wondered where she should change and tried a couple of doors leading from a passage. One was a bathroom and the others too tidy to be other than guestrooms, now unoccupied, a study complete with computer, and then Cheryl's sanctum.

It was like a Master Bedchamber from a former time, with Regency overtones. Cheryl's personality was imprinted on the atmosphere as strongly as the perfume that Emily was beginning to associate with her. There it stood on the dressing table, a fuchsia-and-gold box labelled Shocking de Schiaparelli. Greatly daring, Emily took out the bottle that was shaped like a dressmaker's dummy and took a long, hard sniff. All the emotions she was feeling about Cheryl seemed to be encapsulated in that heady brew and she shivered, having a sudden premonition that her life was about to change beyond recognition.

She replaced the bottle and undressed quickly, laying her clothes on the bed, then wriggling into her costume. Self-conscious, and that hadn't changed, she shrugged the towel round her, picked up her bag and trotted back the way she had come.

Cheryl was in the same position. She opened one eye behind the dark glasses and said, 'My, my, you've a stunning body, Emily. You should flaunt it more frequently.'

'John doesn't like me showing off,' Emily replied quickly, hiding behind his name in order to assimilate Cheryl's compliment.

'John sounds like he's a pain in the arse,' Cheryl said, then waved a languid hand towards a tray standing on a round table under a sunshade. 'Pour me a glass of squash, please, and help yourself.'

Emily did so, then gingerly lowered herself on to the lounger set close to Cheryl's. It was thickly padded and comfortable. 'I've a recliner in the garden at home, but don't use it often. My conscience always pricks if I'm not gainfully employed,' she ventured.

Cheryl's glasses came off and Emily found herself coming under the scrutiny of scornful green eyes. 'Oh, snap out of it, for fuck's sake! You've really let that husband of yours get to you,' she stormed. 'Tell him to go swivel!'

'I can't,' Emily said, appalled to find her throat choked with tears.

'Why not?' It seemed that Cheryl wasn't about to let this one go.

'Because . . . because he knows best, usually.'

'Bollocks!'

'There are the children.'

'A lame excuse. How old are they?'

'Rupert's nineteen. Ruth's fifteen and Eva's two years younger.'

'Then it's high time you asserted yourself. You're a good-looking woman who deserves better. I want to help you achieve happiness. Will you let me?'

Emily could no longer keep back the tears. Like a dam bursting, she poured out all the disappointments, humiliations and downright petty tyranny of her life with John. Cheryl said nothing, simply handed over a box of tissues and waited till the angry sobs became an occasional hiccup.

Then she said, 'I'm not surprised. I guessed it was like that. I take it that you don't want to leave him?'

'Not him so much as my home and children.'

Cheryl got up and bent over Emily, then sat beside her and put her arms round her. Emily felt completely drained by her outburst. Cheryl's touch was immensely soothing and she wanted to cuddle up to her, like a child coming home, breathing in that delectable scent that penetrated the oily smell of sun-lotion and the faint hint of pussy wafting from her tanga.

'I understand. It took finding Yvonne Harper in my bed to give me the strength to ditch Ashley.'

The mention of the commodore's wife made Emily sit up straight. 'She's a nasty bitch. I'd like to see her get her comeuppance.'

'We'll work on it together. John has a vendetta against me because I gazumped him on St Jude's. I also told him to fuck off, when he wanted to put his hand on my pussy at a sailing club function. Oh, no, Emily, he's not whiter than white.'

'I think I'd already realised that. God knows what women see in him, for he's never once made me come.' Emily brought this out in a rush, unaccustomed to sharing such private matters. She could feel herself going hot all over, and it had nothing to do with the sun.

'That figures,' Cheryl said thoughtfully. 'He's probably

succeeded in convincing himself that you're not interested in sex.'

'I am! Oh, yes, I am! But not with him,' Emily cried,
eager to tell all now she'd started. 'Even that boy just
now . . . the one who was gardening . . .'

'Jason?'

'Is that his name? Well, I wanted to lie down on the
grass with him. Isn't that awful? He can't be more than
eighteen.'

'Seventeen, actually, and no shrinking violet, so I've
heard down the grapevine.'

'That's no excuse. I shouldn't be thinking that way.'

'Why not? Oh, Emily, stop torturing yourself.' Cheryl
drifted a hand lightly down Emily's spine, then picked
up a towel. 'Let's swim. Afterwards we can scorch for
another couple of hours.'

The pool was accessed from a neighbouring terrace
assigned to the guests. It was in a glass-roofed structure
with large sliding doors that could be opened or closed
according to the weather. Double glazed, it was ideal for
winter bathing, but now, south facing, it was filled with
the light and heat of the sun.

The water was lovely, holding Emily in a warm, liquid
embrace. As Cheryl had predicted, they had the pool to
themselves. 'That's great,' she said, and slipped off her
thong, leaving it lying on the tiled edge and gradually
lowering herself in, using the wide marble steps. 'Try it,
Emily. There's nothing like swimming in the nude.'

The sight of Cheryl's nakedness disconcerted Emily.
She'd undressed in the showers at boarding school, but
had always felt ashamed of her body, and now there was
this woman asking her to bare herself. She wasn't sure
that she could. The pool was shallow at that end. She
bottomed it while the wavelets lapped her breasts. She
wanted to feel them on her sex. Cheryl was floating on
her back, her red-brown nipples clearing the surface, the
dark swathe of pubic hair clearly visible. Then she rolled
over and commenced a length, her arms cleaving the
water effortlessly.

To hell with it, Emily thought, and hooked her thumbs under her shoulder straps and dragged the costume down to her waist. It was more difficult to manoeuvre it off under water. It was designed to cling and protect its wearer from exposure.

'Let me,' said Cheryl, rising up from under the surface, shaking back her hair and showering Emily with drops.

'Thank you,' Emily said, and was rewarded by fingers tugging off the restrictive garment. 'Oh, that feels so nice,' she chortled happily, as the water lapped around her, worming its way between her legs and into her intimate places. She struck out boldly, nudity adding an entirely new dimension to the pleasure of swimming.

'I wonder if John could be persuaded to have a pool dug,' she called out to Cheryl as they swam side by side. 'I don't mind paying for it.'

'You have that much money?' Cheryl sounded surprised.

'Yes. I was thinking of leaving him and buying a house in London and living there with Rupert.'

'*That* much. And still you let him bully you. Forget it for now. This is your time. I'll race you,' challenged Cheryl, and Emily forged ahead, resorting to a rapid, splashing crawl and reaching the steps ahead of her.

They collapsed into each other's arms, and Emily couldn't resist kissing the wet skin of Cheryl's shoulders. 'I knew we'd be good friends,' she whispered.

'That too,' Cheryl said, and Emily felt her hand on one of her breasts, skimming a pointed fingernail over the nipple that was erect with cold and excitement.

She couldn't repress a gasp, and Cheryl smiled as she caressed her face and her neck till Emily felt boneless, like a rag doll. Then Cheryl's other hand dipped down under the water and Emily felt soft fingers idling round her sex, parting the floating fronds of hair. She didn't move or resist, shy, confused, but wanting that touch to go on. It did. Cheryl began a soft, circular motion round Emily's clit, with a breathtaking awareness of what she needed. Emily had never experienced anything like it, and realised that the mewling sound echoing under the glass roof came from her own throat.

She closed her eyes, thought of John and her marriage vows, and then forgot everything, driven by the overwhelming desire for orgasm. She parted her thighs, lifted her pubis, felt the water adding to her own wetness and worked herself round that skilful finger. She didn't want gentleness now. Gasping, clinging to Cheryl's shoulders, she abandoned herself, coming in a frenzied rush. Then Cheryl's fingers plunged into her, taking the tight spasms as wave after wave of sensation rolled over Emily.

'Oh ... oh ... I didn't know ... didn't realise how it would be with a woman,' she murmured, crying again, but with relief this time.

Cheryl held her tenderly, giving her time to come down to earth. 'I've only just learned myself,' she said. 'And it doesn't mean that I don't want men any more. Far from it. It's kind of upped my appetite. There's so much I can show you, Emily. I want you to meet Bronwen. She works for St Jude's, but in a different capacity to the usual staff. Then there's her boyfriend, Luke. When you've spent time with them, you'll wonder why on earth you waited so long.'

There were noises from the hotel, voices and laughter coming closer. Cheryl rose from the pool, water streaming from her limbs. 'We're about to be invaded.' She chuckled, and as Emily hurried to join her, she wrapped them both in an enveloping towel.

They made their escape just as a jolly crowd of guests arrived, the men in trunks, the women in two-piece costumes or the conventional type. The men dived in at once, and the ladies lowered themselves gradually, with little excited shrieks. Cheryl looked back once, smiling to see them enjoying themselves. Then, still bemused and tingling from that shattering climax, Emily went upstairs with her.

Chapter Eleven

'**Y**ou'd better watch out. He's gunning for you and Cheryl,' Stuart said.

'Who?' Just for a second Laura couldn't think what her ex-husband was talking about. She didn't have any enemies, as far as she knew.

'John Dempsey,' Stuart went on, twiddling with the coaster on the knife-dented and deliberately distressed surface of the oak table. The Ship and Punchbowl was old, but not that old. Just done up to look as if it has stood there unaltered for centuries.

'Ah, yes. Cheryl did say he wanted to buy St Jude's and was spitting his dummy out all over the place because we got it. How do you know?'

'Ashley told me. He sees a fair bit of him, apparently, and Dempsey's out to ruin you, so that he can put in a bid for the property. Something to do with an American deal, from which he hopes to make mega bucks.'

'Thanks for the tip,' she said, and took a sip of scrumpy, that innocent-tasting but deceptively strong cider made from small, sweet apples and brewed in the West Country. Treated with respect, it was deliciously refreshing, and went with the surroundings of this public house on the quayside.

It was early evening and she had arranged to meet

Stuart there, finding it much easier to be in his company now that the dust had settled. They had parted amicably, if sorrowfully, and Stuart had wanted them to remain friends. She could not do this at the start, but had recently found it a comfort to occasionally get together with him and discuss mutual interests, mostly concerning Harry and Vicky.

He was looking well these days, had bought himself a bungalow and expanded the haulage business. She saw how he was attracting the attention of other women in the lounge bar. This was nothing new. Whenever he entered a room it was to have the females present gathering round him like moths to a flame. It was his stocky, dependable appearance, his mischievous smile, dark curly hair and sympathetic eyes. They felt they could trust him, and several had fancied their chances. And all the time they were ignorant of his predilection for members of his own sex.

'How is Terry?' she asked, aware that this relationship had developed, though Stuart hadn't yet come out.

'He's fine, thank you. We've only just come back from holidaying in Greece.'

'Lucky you. I wondered how you got that magnificent tan.'

He sobered and took a slurp at his pint of ale, then said, 'I'm thinking of selling up and going to live somewhere like that. Abroad, no one bothers if you're gay. Here, I have to keep it under wraps or it would affect the business.'

'And Terry would go with you?'

'Of course. We're an item.'

Laura was surprised at the hollow feeling inside her as she thought about being unable to contact him easily. Not that she did so often, but he was always there if she or either of their children needed help. She had been in love with him when they married, and though sex had quickly settled down into a routine couple of times a week, he had not been cruel, unjust or beastly, and had proved a caring father. She remembered him on Vicky's

222

wedding day, proud as a peacock when he walked her up the aisle. Had it not been for a rogue gene or two, Laura might have stayed married to him till they were parted by death.

'I shall miss you,' she said, and reached out and took his broad hand in hers.

'Me too, but you can come and stay. You and Simon or whoever. Is it still on with him?'

'So far so good.'

'He'd better treat you right or I'll punch him on the nose. And don't forget that I'm here for you if things go tits-up at St Jude's.'

'Why should they? Oh, you mean Dempsey. D'you seriously think he can damage us?'

She hadn't much liked the man when they met on the opening night, but failed to see what he could do. Talking with Emily had convinced her that he was a nasty piece of work, but even so . . .

'He's powerful in these parts and will soon be elected mayor,' Simon said. 'No doubt he'll run his campaign on the grounds of fighting crime and upholding morality. If he can prove that there's anything untoward going on at St Jude's, then he could prosecute and close you down. Is it all above board, Laura? Are your guests as white as driven snow? Or does St Jude's hide deep, dark and sinister secrets? If so, then I think it's rotten of you not to let me in on them.'

He was smiling at her in that warm, all-embracing way of his and she had another drink, then got a taxi home, leaving before she spilled the beans about the towers. She was ninety-nine per cent sure that Stuart would keep a still tongue in his head, but she daren't risk it.

'I hate to give any credence to ex-husbands, but, yes, Stuart's right,' Cheryl said, when Laura tapped on her door later that night.

'What are we going to do?' Laura followed her into the kitchen and watched while she dropped tea bags into mugs and added boiling water.

Cheryl, wearing a nightshirt with Winnie the Pooh on

the front, sat on the settee and curled her legs under her, tea in hand. 'Well,' she said slowly, 'I've a plan, and I'm sure Emily will help us. That way, she'll gain the whip hand, literally, over her horrible spouse, and we can stoop to unlawful, unscrupulous, but ever so useful blackmail. Here's an outline of my scheme.'

'You remember my mother, Joanna Newman?' Cheryl said, walking Emily towards the Range Rover in the courtyard. 'She was at St Jude's when we opened. She's got herself a gorgeous boyfriend. He looks like a maharaja. Anyhow, I'd like you to come over to her place. It's called Fell Tor, and they do all kinds of things there. I think you'd like it.'

'She was telling me about it. John dismissed it as tosh, behind her back, but I found it intriguing,' Emily replied, eager for fresh experience. So much had happened to her over the past few days that her mind was spinning, her pussy tingling and her nerves were stretched like bowstrings.

Cheryl had introduced her to sexual love between women, then she had met Laura and Simon, impressed by their sincerity. The resident beautician had brought her expertise into play, and Emily had been astonished by the result. A glamorous woman had stared back at her from the salon mirror; she had reminded Emily of Greta Garbo, with classical features and heavy-lidded eyes. Her hair had been layered, then flicked back from her forehead and ears in a style much favoured by female newscasters. It looked sophisticated yet sexy.

John had been in when she got home that night, but had not noticed her appearance, wholly absorbed in a re-run of highlights from the day's football matches. In one way this had been a relief, but it was also deeply insulting. She had returned to St Jude's whenever she could, needing her new friends with the ferocity of someone deprived of human contact for too long. Cheryl and Laura had shown her everything except the towers, and she had believed it when they said that these were reserved for special guests.

She continued to dress her hair as the beautician had advised, brazening it out should she happen to meet any of the sailing club wives. If John was oblivious to her new self, then they certainly weren't. Tongues were starting to wag. Emily revelled in her new-found notoriety and wondered how long it would be till it reached his ears. He was so self-obsessed that it probably wouldn't percolate for weeks.

All Ruth and Eva had said in passing was, 'What have you done to your hair, Mummy? Ugh! Gross!'

She had arrived at St Jude's midmorning and, having dumped her cream jersey outfit in the nearest charity shop, had opted for drab-olive shorts and a safari jacket. She couldn't help striding when she wore them, and was alert and lynx-eyed. It made her feel superbly confident, a member of Cheryl's elite sisterhood.

'Can I drive?' she asked, greatly daring. 'I'm insured.'

'Be my guest,' Cheryl said, and switched to the passenger seat.

Because Emily didn't know the way, Cheryl directed her to Fell Tor. 'It's so isolated,' she commented as they breasted a rise and saw the building set in a hollow, smoke weaving from one of its barley-sugar-twist chimney stacks.

'They like it that way. It might be better for us if St Jude's was more off the beaten track.'

'I love it,' Emily breathed, as the Range Rover jolted over the potholes in the tarmacked lane winding to the house. The day was overcast, but this did not detract from its picturesque charm.

Half a dozen people in jogging pants and sweaters were performing slow, meaningful movements on the grass. 'That t'ai chi,' Cheryl explained, 'a Chinese system of exercise and self-defence in which the best use is made of co-ordination and balance, with the minimum amount of effort.'

A further band of students sat by the lake listening to

225

a brown-skinned teacher with long black hair who Emily recognised as Deven, Joanna's friend and mentor.

They parked and Cheryl strolled into the house to find her mother. She was in the laundry room, overseeing the loading and unloading of several industrial machines. Some of the beginners, the humble end of the commune chain, were ironing. The large, stone-flagged room smelled pleasantly of damp warmth and washing powder. Joanna turned from instructing one of the young men on how to fold sheets correctly.

'Hello, Cheryl, and welcome, Emily,' she said, pushing back her sleeves. 'Lord, but it's amazing how much washing we get through here. But it's all part of the service. D'you find this at St Jude's?' She reached out and snatched the sheet from the young man's hand, nagging him, 'Good grief, Aiden. Didn't they teach you anything in the Boy Scouts? Give it here. Cheryl, take the other end, would you?'

They stretched the linen between them, then folded it once, twice, until it was reduced to a flat pancake. Cheryl picked up another. 'Can I help?' Emily asked nervously, sorry for the very good-looking person that Joanna had addressed as Aiden. She'd seen him before, at Cheryl's party, but only from a distance.

'No, don't worry, my dear,' Joanna said briskly. 'We'll leave them to it. Time for a glass of sherry, I think. Deven's gainfully employed outside, ministering to his flock, so we can indulge in Bristol Cream, instead of our home-made plonk.' Her eyes switched shrewdly between the young man and the two women, and she added, 'You can come too, Aiden. This is Emily, by the way. Cheryl's friend.'

Emily was aware of the way he was staring at Cheryl. She was deliberately cool towards him, though it was obvious that they had met before. Nothing had been going on between them, had it? Surely not. He was only a lad. Not much older than Tim, but she was very conscious of his lean hips under the blue jeans, the movement of toned muscle, the hazy glimpse of copper skin beneath his white string vest.

They wandered into Joanna's room, big, bare floored and rug scattered. It had an Eastern ambience, with round brass tables and little minarets, incense burners and drapes set with tiny mirrors and embroidery. She opened the filigree-cut-work door of a cupboard and produced a bottle of sherry and four glasses.

'I never thought I'd ask you this, sceptic that I am, but I need you to do a protective ritual,' Cheryl said, sinking down on a divan.

Emily, listening to this exchange, thought she was joking, but Joanna answered seriously, 'No problem. What's happened?'

'There's a man who wants to close St Jude's and buy the property himself.'

'It's my husband, I'm afraid,' Emily blurted, twirling the small wineglass round and round in her fingers.

'Don't be afraid.' Joanna smiled, resting back among the cushions, legs tucked under her. 'It's the guy who was with you at the party, isn't it? I wasn't impressed; could read him like a book. You dislike him, don't you?'

'I do, but I feel responsible for him because we're married.'

'He's not your responsibility. His behaviour is his concern, not yours.'

'I'll do anything to help you, Cheryl. You've been so kind to me,' Emily burst out, wanting to cry.

It was disturbing to have Aiden seated on a stool opposite, bare forearms resting on his denim-covered knees, watching her, and watching Cheryl. He was so blond, so brown, and had so many piercings. She had never been so close to someone who was brave enough to have this done, not once either, but several times. I'd do it too, she vowed. I never had the chance in my restrictive adolescence, and it was out of the question once I was married. Cheryl's daughter was pierced, but then, she was in the fashion industry and expected to be eccentric.

There's nothing to stop me. The rebellious thought was like a bomb exploding. All I have to do is find a shop that specialises in piercing and tattooing, and there are several in Westcombe. Something not too outlandish to start with – a rose tattoo perhaps, and I'd have my ears pierced. Then, gradually, I'd have another skin illustration and further holes punched in my ears, and possibly my nose. I admire those Indian-style nose-studs. And then – and then – here her imagination faltered. She wasn't sure where else the adventurous had rings through themselves but had read somewhere that the genitals were sometimes done – and the nipples.

She caught the glint of gold through Aiden's vest. He was the one to advise her. Unless her eyes deceived her, *he* had his nipples pierced. She wanted to jump up and grab him and demand to see, and was overjoyed yet frightened when Joanna, as if reading her mind, said suddenly, 'Aiden, take Emily to see the horses. Show her around. Cheryl and I need to talk.'

As if hypnotised, Emily followed Aiden where he led. Out through the patio doors, across a paved terrace, round the side of the house to a stable yard and in through wide-open double doors to a shady, dung-and-straw-smelling interior.

'Oh, aren't they lovely!' she exclaimed, going over to the stalls where two horses nodded their handsome heads, their hooves rustling the straw, their eyes rolling warily.

She patted their long, elegant noses and whispered to them in horse-speak, wishing she hadn't given up riding. Ruth and Eva did it, of course, entering local gymkhanas, but she had been relegated to driver, sandwich-maker and general factotum, while they collected the rosettes. She was so absorbed in the animals that she wasn't aware for a moment of Aiden standing right behind her.

'You've very gentle,' he said, and trailed his fingers over the nape of her neck. 'But I can tell by your aura that someone has hurt you, and this isn't right. You should be cherished and loved.'

'Is this how you feel about Cheryl?' she asked, floored by her own boldness.

'Cheryl is strong. She doesn't need me. She doesn't need anyone. She hurt me too, but I realise that it wasn't deliberate. My fault. I read too much into our encounter. Now, there's you, Emily.'

Not second best then, she thought, and felt chipper. But Aiden's fingers caressing her neck took some getting used to. No man had touched her there but John. Correction. No man had touched her anywhere except him. It's a mistake to be a virgin when you get married, she thought. I hope the girls experiment, and soon. I should talk to them, not that stupid sex-education they get at school, half-hearted and wishy-washy, but in-depth information about their clitorises. I've a theory that if girls were taught how to masturbate, it would cut teen-age pregnancies by half, probably more. They don't need to get embroiled with spotty oiks who are only out for a quick shag.

She continued to fondle the horses' muzzles, but her attention was elsewhere – on Aiden's cock, to be precise. He was taller than her and she could feel him pressing himself down the length of her body. His chest was against her shoulder-blades, his belly waist level, his prick managing to lie along the crack of her buttocks, his thighs following the line of her bare ones.

I could tell him to shove off, she thought, while still able to string a sentence together. I could threaten to tell Joanna. I could cry sexual harassment. But she knew she wouldn't do any of these things. Aiden gave her no time, turning her and holding her head steady with his hand, and her lips felt fuller and flushed with desire. His mouth closed over hers in a kiss that made her melt. She moved her lips under his, and then he sucked the lower one. In the rush of endorphins released by his closeness, she opened for him and his tongue slipped inside, playing with hers. He was in no hurry and his exploration of her mouth went on and on, till she was wobbly at the knees, wet at the crotch and more than ready for him to go further.

Still kissing her, he reached down and touched her breasts through the open jacket. Her nipples were hard under his fingers, lifting her bra and T-shirt. He pinched them into sharper points. With an exciting impetuosity, he propelled her back against the wooden stall. She could feel his hipbones and the upward-slanting ridge of his cock. He was erect and it was for her – all for her. She was flattered, aroused, filled with guilty feelings.

She freed her mouth and said, 'I'm married.'

'I know, but not happily or you wouldn't be here with me. Let me make you happy. I have nothing but praise for mature women. They're so much more interesting than girls. Their bodies are ripe, luscious, hungry for pleasure.'

Every word he uttered obscured those images of matrimonial life that grew fainter and fainter and then faded altogether. She opened her eyes and couldn't believe it was really happening. She shaped the muscles of his upper arms with her hands, loving the feel of him, then ran her fingers across his chest. It was firmly sculpted, the twin peaks springing up under her touch. And she had been right – he was ringed there, with a little chain linking the two. Emboldened, she drifted her hand across his belly, before closing it on his bulge. He brought his fist down over hers, pressing it closer, and she felt his cock jump under her palm.

Somehow – afterwards she was never quite sure what had happened – she found herself lying on a prickly bed of hay at the back of the stable. Aiden was half on top of her, his lips fastening on the long expanse of her throat. 'You smell delicious,' he said.

Emily laughed, and it didn't sound like her at all – it was a rich, throaty, alluring chuckle that had come from God only knew where. 'And you aren't so bad yourself,' she murmured, inhaling the odour of clean cotton, a recently showered body, deodorant and a hint of sweat. It was intoxicating.

He lifted her top, pushed up her bra, and feasted on her bare breasts, not only looking, but sucking. Emily's nipples tingled and an ache shot straight down to her womb. 'I want you,' she said, and could hardly credit that it was herself speaking.

'You shall have me,' he promised, and unzipped her shorts and pulled down her panties and had them both off in a trice. All she had on below were her trainers.

He leaned over her, placed a hand on each of her knees and prised them apart. Emily let her legs go slack, her private self open to him. He ran his hand over the fair fluff of her mons, then he dipped his head and nibbled at her navel. He made her wait, slowly coasting over her belly and parting the hair-fringed cleft, and finding the acme of her pleasure. She clung to him, hiding her face, ashamed that he should see her spread out so shamelessly. But she wanted that touch to go on, unable to help herself as he took her slowly and with great deliberation, up and up till she could feel the force gathering, tingling down her spine as heat poured though her. She came in a sudden, merciless rush, and Aiden held her close, letting her relish every spasm, then descend in her own time.

When she had stopped moaning and shaking, he laid her back and, kneeling up, unbuttoned his jeans. They gaped, and Emily saw the navel ring that pierced him, and the thick thatch of brownish curls that coated his lower belly. He reached inside and took out his erect cock, and she couldn't restrain a gasp. It wasn't only the size, though that was awe-inspiring; it was the black onyx ring that passed through his helm. It glistened with pre-come, contrasting with the redness of the tip. He cradled the shaft and rubbed it, sliding the foreskin up and down, watching it, then glanced at her, his tool bobbing with excitement.

When he let it go, it stood to attention all by itself, and he took off his shoes and removed his jeans, his long legs, firm thighs and hollowed flanks perfect in Emily's sight. John? Forget him. It was as if Aiden and he were from different planets. Had John been slim like him once? If he had, she couldn't remember, only seeing him as he was today – thickset – hairy – his large penis and heavy balls dangling grotesquely, convincing her that male genitals were Dame Nature's afterthought. *How shall we reproduce the species? I know, let's tack the equipment on outside the body. It's not neat, like the female's, but no matter. It'll do the job, even if it does look ridiculous.*

Aiden's privates were a different kettle of fish, and she reached out and cupped his testicles, enjoying the spongy feel of them and the crisp hair forming a nest for his cock. She closed her palm round it and eased the skin in a back and forth motion. Aiden groaned and crouched on his heels between her legs, his hands resting on her breasts. In that position she had free access to him. She tweaked the black ring and slid it round. More jism seeped from his slit.

'Do you have a condom?' he asked huskily.

'No.' This lifestyle was so new to Emily that she was not in the habit of carrying them around, just in case.

He reached out for his discarded jeans and fumbled in the back pocket, and she watched, fascinated, as he covered his cock, onyx and all, in skin-tinted rubber. 'OK,' he said. 'Here I come, ready or not.'

'Oh, I'm ready . . . so, so ready,' she whispered.

He kneed her legs apart and positioned the tip of his cock against her moist entrance. Emily brought up her legs and scissored them round his neck, crying out as he thrust into her body, burying himself deep till his balls tapped her bottom cleft. He was bigger than John, and she smiled secretly. Her husband would be gutted if he knew he wasn't nearly as well blessed as a man half his age that he'd probably condemn as a no-hoper, a hippy dropout. She writhed around that totem pole of a cock, grinding against it, her body expanding to take it as Aiden's thrusts became more frenzied. She'd be sore later, probably walking bow-legged, but what the hell!

* * *

232

Business concluded, during which she had explained to her mother about John Dempsey, Cheryl had said good-bye and decided to look for Emily in the stable. She had admired the way in which Joanna had grasped the situation from the start, despatching Aiden to relax the up-tight Emily. Cheryl was not in the least jealous, rather relieved, if anything. It would have been a pity if he had continued to have a fixation on her. This let her off the hook nicely. He wouldn't be offended, and she was sure he'd be available if ever she wanted him.

My God! How I've changed! The thought struck her like a thunderbolt. For better? For worse? It had to be an improvement, didn't it? She'd shucked off Mark, and deliberately controlled her emotions concerning Felan. He walked in and out of her life as he pleased, and she hadn't seen hide nor hair of him since the incident in the teashop. She was determined that the next time he turned up like a bad penny she'd tell him exactly where he got off. Oh, yes, indeedy!

After that final burst of heat, the sun had deserted Westcombe. Winter was just round the corner, and Ursula was already planning a bumper Yuletide at St Jude's, once Halloween and Bonfire Night were over, while Thomas was working on a culinary extravaganza. Simon had been talking about it too, and he and Laura had their heads together, already drumming up custom by taking half-page advertisement space in leading magazines. They intended to offer short-break deals over the festive season, with entertainment thrown in. Bronwen and Luke had plans too, but these were rather different. *Come to St Jude's Exclusive Club for a Spanking Christmas* had other connotations than holly wreaths and fir trees and tinsel. Santa Claus, maybe, but with a whopping great todger and a sack full of floggers and manacles. Ho! Ho! Ho!

The t'ai chi students had gone in, or walking or whatever they did when not working out and Deven had vanished too. Probably ascended to heaven on a golden cloud, Cheryl thought ironically. Though it was more likely that he was giving in-depth instructions to a nubile nymphet somewhere secluded and out of Joanna's range.

There was no one about and the stable seemed deserted. Cheryl entered quietly, her footsteps muffled by straw. She passed the horses, avoiding contact because equine scurf brought her out in hives, and was about to corner the stall when noises arrested her. Instantly recognisable, they were associated with sex; rustlings, grunts and groans that might have originated in the farmyard, or the rainforests. Only the sighs were in any way human. Cheryl edged closer, peering through the slats that separated her from whoever it was copulating.

She saw the back of Aiden's head, and his wide shoulders and Emily's legs and her blue and white trainers locked round his neck. His bare bottom was in frantic movement, driving his cock in and out of her with a liquid sound, his balls flip-flopping, his thighs braced in a kneeling position. She couldn't see much of Emily, but she could hear her mewling as if in pain. Cheryl knew it was far from that.

'You're so wet,' Aiden muttered. 'Oh, Emily, I want to drown in you.'

Cheryl was getting wet too. Just watching them was doing it to her. Stealthily, she wrinkled up her skirt and touched herself. The thin line of black silk gusset was hot and damp. She dragged a finger up it and her clit quivered. Aiden was bucking and pumping; Emily was tossing her head from side to side and yelping and Cheryl was rubbing herself outside her knickers, but this was more than enough. Aiden was racing towards climax; Emily was struggling to achieve it, and Cheryl got there first, going with the flow. She forgot herself and cried out with the exquisite sharpness of her orgasm.

'Oh, my goodness! There's someone here!' Emily shouted, pushing off Aiden who had collapsed on her. She huddled there, arms folded around her part-naked body.

'It's only me,' Cheryl said, lowering her skirt after

234

wiping her fingers inside the hem. She stepped out of hiding.

'Oh dear, I'm sorry . . .' Emily started to apologise straight away.

'Why? Didn't you enjoy it?'

The question was irrelevant. Emily's skin, flushed from her breasts to her forehead, told the story of extreme arousal and a dramatic climax. Aiden sat up, and Cheryl stared at his cock, still half erect, stretching its rubber overcoat to the limit. He peeled this off and disposed of it in a rubbish bucket. He smiled, aware of her interest, and his penis began to thicken again and the black ring beckoned.

It was tempting. Cheryl lusted to have him inside her, onyx and all. She'd climaxed, but this was nothing more than an aperitif. She wanted Aiden as the main course. What was it they said? A man should give his cock half an hour before he could expect to get it up again? This rule didn't apply to Aiden. The smell of pussy wafting from both herself and Emily, the novel situation of having two women with the hots for him and the ample opportunity for exhibiting his prize specimen all combined to raise his prick to stonking proportions within minutes.

Emily was looking at it with drooling admiration, and he polished the helm and massaged the stem with narcissistic concentration. It grew bigger and bigger. Cheryl went down on her knees in the hay in front of him and took the head of it into her mouth. The second time around was often the most satisfying. His serpent had spat just recently and would be easier to control. She would give Emily a lesson in fellatio.

She released Aiden's dick for a minute, saying, 'Watch closely, Emily. This is the proper way to give a man head.'

He was very aroused now, his cock jutting from his belly and she pushed his thighs apart and kissed and caressed other parts of his body, his nipples, his chest, his buttock crease, teasing him by holding off from touching him where he most wanted it. He nudged her cheek with it, a streak of pre-come glistening on her skin. She laughed softly and took him into her mouth again, running her tongue up the sensitive underside of the stem, as if she were slurping on an ice-cream cone. Then she tickled her tongue lightly round the foreskin and inserted the very tip between the black ring and his helm, making it rotate. Aiden groaned and, after slipping him from her mouth, she licked his balls, her fingers pressing down hard at the root of his cock to prevent him coming too soon. She wanted this game to last. In a perfect world it would go on forever.

She hovered over the bulging purple tip, breathing on it, soft as a whisper, and he lay back against a hay bale, gripping her shoulders with his hands, holding her off, controlling himself. 'Your turn to be mouthed,' he said.

He lifted her skirt and she slid up and over his body, thighs wide, a knee each side of him, the straw rough on her bare flesh. She was wearing a button-through, and he undid this all the way down, her breasts showing as it opened, supported by a coffee-brown brassiere. Adien examined those high-lifted globes, pinching the nipples into points. Then he groped for them with his mouth, sucking strongly till she squealed with joy.

Sitting back, facing him, she could feel his erection prodding against her silk-covered crotch. Frustrated, she leaped to her feet and untangled herself from her panties, then took up position again. She noticed that he'd used her brief absence to find another johnny. The boy must spend a fortune on them, she thought, and be pretty sure he'd get lucky.

His cock prodded her arsehole, but she wasn't in the mood for anal penetration, so wriggled a bit and sat in such a way that the only entrance he could penetrate was her pussy. It felt wonderful, though jabbing at her so hard that it hurt. On top, she could control how far he went in, and also rub herself against his cock base, but this wasn't enough to give her a second orgasm. She noticed that Emily had crept closer and was gently tweaking Aiden's nipples. She wanted to join in, a far cry from the demure wife who had turned up on St Jude's doorstep not so very long ago.

The pressure on Cheryl's clit was dulling rather than adding to the sensation, so she shifted up, leaving his prick behind and positioning herself astride his face. She could feel Emily behind her, keeping him at full stand with vigorous rubbing. His tongue flashed over Cheryl's nubbin, tormenting and teasing, then settling down to a steady friction. She arched her back and lifted her hips a little, giving him room to breathe, lest he suffocate in the heat of her strongly scented, extremely wet snatch.

She moved her hips delicately, afraid to disturb his tongue licking her with firm, steady strokes. He sucked her clit, stretched and extended it, worried at it like a terrier and the stable spun as she came, oblivious to Emily, the horses, anything but her own completion. Aiden shifted her down and she clung to him as he worked his enormous dick into her. She lunged against it, her inner muscles clenching round that solid bar of flesh, riding him hard till he reached his noisy conclusion. It was only then, as they were coming down from that rollercoaster ride, that she became aware of Emily beside them, masturbating as if there was no tomorrow.

Several days later John came in early from work, and Emily handed him an envelope. 'What's this?' he growled, throwing his briefcase down on the hall table. 'More junk mail?'

'I don't know,' she lied, having gone into every last detail with Cheryl.

He ripped it open and drew out a card. 'Well, well,' he said, on a self-satisfied note. 'So, she's thought better of it, has she? It's a dinner invite, with a view to discussing the future of St Jude's. By the by, she asks if you'd be kind enough to play the piano for her guests.'

'I suppose you mean Cheryl Barden. I'd be honoured,' Emily replied. 'When is it?'

'Next Saturday evening.'

'I'll book Mrs Macdonald to baby-sit the girls,' Emily suggested brightly.

It was really too easy, like taking candy from a baby. John's conceit made him putty in their hands. Cheryl planned to teach him so sharp a lesson that he'd bother her no more and Laura was on the same track, whereas Emily intended to wreak such havoc on him that he'd never, ever forget it.

Vengeance is mine; I will repay, saith the Lord, but in this case it was a wronged lady engaged in reprisals.

'And he's coming?'

'Wild horses wouldn't keep him away,' Emily said, reporting in to Cheryl.

'Good. Bronwen and Luke have arrived, and I want you to meet them. They know all about you and what's going to happen. It's high time you went into the towers. I think you're ready for it.'

'I can't wait. Making love with Aiden was all very well, but it lacked something. I don't think I like men all that much. From what you've told me, I find the idea of dominating them very exciting.'

'You do?' Cheryl wasn't in the least surprised. Emily was coming on by leaps and bounds. John wouldn't know what hit him.

She took her to the West Tower, where Bronwen and Luke had their quarters when in residence. Their rooms were plain and functional but gave them space to themselves, and Bronwen liked it when Laura or Cheryl or Simon called in. She had the ability to make everyone feel at home, and when she'd played mother and poured the tea and passed round chocolate biscuits, she came out with her programme for the next sex fest.

'We're oversubscribed already,' she began, seated on the edge of the couch, her slim legs encased in tight black denims with boot flares, her ample bosom displayed by the deep cleavage of her red chiffon blouse. 'Success or what? I've got pole dancers for next weekend, and the

238

Maestro – he's a popular dominator – and Mistress Discipline, who will be handing out punishment.'

'Emily wants to learn,' Cheryl put in. 'Can you teach her? She needs lessons in handling the whip and the strap-on dildo.'

'My pleasure,' Bronwen said, smiling encouragingly at Emily. 'Shall we adjourn to the bedroom? We can start there and then go to the dungeon. Come along, Luke. We need you too.'

Chapter Twelve

'Will you come to my wedding?' Joanna rang to ask.
'Your what?' Cheryl thought there was something wrong with the phone and shook it. She had been dozing in a hot, deliciously scented bath. Was this part of a dream?

'Deven and I are having a hand-fasting, a pagan ceremony. A druid will bless us at the stone circle, you know the one, the Seven Maidens. It borders Fell Tor, so is absolutely right.'

'Whoopee shit,' Cheryl said gloomily, fearing for her mother's happiness. Was Deven really in love with her, or was this just a ploy to gain more control?

'Don't be like that. You were quick enough to seek my help when you needed protection,' Joanna rejoined sharply.

'I still need it. I'm sorry. Of course I'll be there. When is it?' Instantly contrite, Cheryl was now being over-enthusiastic.

'On the last day of October. The night of Samhain, the feast of summer's end and the start of winter, and –'

To avoid a lecture on Celtic festivals, Cheryl broke in, saying, 'Fine. What time? What am I expected to wear? Are you sending out a wedding present list?'

'Cheryl, *please*! Would I do that? This is a spiritual, as

well as a physical, joining. Forget any other wedding you've ever attended. This will blow your mind. You may ask Daisy along, and Tim.'

'I doubt he'll come,' Cheryl said, thoughtfully popping the bubbles that lay like plastic wrapping on the surface of the water. 'And Daisy's still in Italy, as far as I know, shacked up with a designer called Alessandro. Apparently, she's sleeping her way to the top.'

'That's my girl. She's destined to do well,' Joanna replied, and Cheryl detected a hint of pride in her voice.

When her mother had hung up, Cheryl replaced the cordless phone on a chair by the bathtub and resumed her prone position. But the restful atmosphere had been disrupted and she found herself wrestling with the implications of this sudden announcement.

So, her mother was marrying again, was she? And would this unusual way of doing it prove to be legal when the proverbial fan-assisted dung started to fly? If it ever did, of course. They might live happily ever after.

She climbed out of the bath and dressed, deliberately putting a stop to wedding scenarios, and honing in on Emily and the coming dinner engagement. She hurried, for Emily would be there soon. The grand piano, once abandoned as useless by St Jude's former occupants and left in the assembly hall like a car wrecked by joy-riders, had been fully restored at considerable cost. It had been moved into the drawing room, where guests with a modicum of know-how were encouraged to play it, and professionals sometimes called in to entertain them. Since knowing that she was to perform publicly, Emily had been pitchforked into practising.

She was highly talented, and Cheryl deplored this wicked waste. Someone touched by God's little finger should use this gift to uplift others. Emily had the means at home to polish up her arpeggios, but was put off by the likelihood of John interrupting her. It pleased Cheryl to hear Chopin, Mozart or Beethoven resounding through St Jude's.

Her spirits soared and she was confident that her plan

would come to fruition. Emily was a gem and had thrown herself into everything Bronwen and Luke suggested, forgetting to be bashful. It had been amazing to see her stripping off and donning the revealing clothes Bronwen had offered her. Inches taller in high heels, her character had altered when she wore black leather attire, and Bronwen had hardly needed to show her how to flourish a whip. It came as second nature. And a dildo that could be fastened to the body by a harness had particularly fascinated her, with its ability to turn a woman into a penile creature, able to invade cunts and arseholes at will.

Bronwen had demonstrated its use, with Luke on the receiving end. When she inserted the greased vibrator into his anus, Cheryl had wondered if they were going too far and that Emily might cry off. Far from it. She embraced everything with a delight that was reassuring and declared that she wanted to learn all there was to know, to meet the people involved in the towers and take part in the weekend activities.

Now she was waiting for Cheryl when she came downstairs, talking to Simon who had printed out leaflets and stuck them up all over the place in and around St Jude's. Those who appreciated the pianoforte were welcome to drop into the drawing room after dinner and enjoy a recital by Emily Dempsey.

'That's me,' Emily said proudly, pointing to the noticeboard in the lobby.

'Absolutely. We should have included a photo. You must have some taken,' Simon said, twinkling at her. 'This might become a regular event.'

'I wish Rupert could come along,' Emily sighed wistfully.

'Later, maybe,' Cheryl replied, knowing Emily wanted to keep her association with the towers under wraps. 'We'll be having all sorts of jollifications in the hotel proper around Christmas, and you and yours will be welcome, apart from John, and I don't think he'll be

242

giving you grief again, not after our meeting with him tomorrow night.'

'Hello there,' said a voice from the doorway. 'You rang for me, Simon?'

Felan covered the hall in seconds and Cheryl kept still as he reached her side, leaning an elbow against hers on the top of the desk. She shifted away, collected her wits that were disintegrating in a shower of emotional mush and sex juice, and said to Emily, 'Let's go.'

'There's a patch of damp showing on one of the attic ceilings,' Simon answered. 'It's about as big as the map of Africa. Not dripping, just spreading.'

Like that in my knickers, Cheryl thought.

'The wind has dislodged a tile, I expect. I'll go and take a look, and if I'm right, I'll send one of my roofers along to fix it.' Felan spoke directly to Simon, as if Cheryl did not exist.

This couldn't be allowed. It was damned rude. She'd make him acknowledge her.

'Good morning, Mr Boynton,' she said crisply, refusing to remember that she'd ever crouched under a table with his dick in her mouth.

'Good day to you, Mrs Barden,' he answered, but his quirky smile and raised left brow told her that he hadn't forgotten, not by a long chalk.

Her face went red and her body burned and she turned away, walking briskly and not looking back.

All morning she was aware of him. His presence seemed to overshadow the house. Even when he had gone, and she was acutely conscious of the moment that happened, he continued to loom large in her thoughts. Lord knows, I've my work cut out with the enemy darkening my doorstep soon, without being bedevilled by Felan, she thought with a kind of angry despair. Why did he have to turn up like that, just when I was sure that I had my urges under control? Now I'm as hot for him as I ever was. I'll jump in the car, get over to Fell Tor double quick, find Aiden and fuck him like there's no tomorrow.

'Ah, there you are, Cheryl,' carolled Laura, coming down the central staircase and preventing her from going anywhere. 'Could I have a word? There's a slight mix-up with Colonel Jackson's room, that's a double for him and his wife, and a German couple who also think it's theirs. It's to do with the view, or something.'

'Can't Ursula deal with it?' I must get away, Cheryl panicked inside. I *must* screw someone else to stop myself pursuing Felan, dragging his trousers down and ravishing him.

'The Colonel wants to see you, in person.'

Damning the Colonel, the whole British army, navy and airforce, Cheryl stomped off behind her to soothe ruffled military feathers and Teutonic angst.

Chopin's études were compositions intended to train the player's skill but, under this master's unique touch, they became dreamy, drifting, lyrical things, almost love songs. Lost in the beauty of the one she was playing, Emily allowed the rapture to take over, yet part of her was aware of how the notes should follow one after another, the chords, the crescendos dying into quiet passages.

If there's another life beyond the grave, then I hope it's like this for me, she thought, so enraptured that tears blinded her sight, making her glad she had memorised the piece. An eternity of producing wonderful harmonies from an instrument as fine as this one, an ageless, timeless universe in which I'm surrounded by friends, and music, music, music . . .

John was in the audience, but she spared him hardly a glance. She was wearing a black velvet dress with a long-sleeved bolero, very plain and demure, but excitement gnawed at the pit of her stomach. She was aware of the absence of knickers and bra, but no one would guess. It thrilled her to think that as she sat on the piano stool her bottom was bare under her skirt and her crotch wet with anticipation of events to come. Every time her low-heeled shoes contacted the pedals, she could feel her legs parting, then closing, and catch a whiff of her personal musk mixed with that of talc and perfume. She finished the piece and the applause went to her head like mulled wine. She gave an encore, then Cheryl stood up, and announced,

'Perhaps Emily will be kind enough to play for us again some time. I've enjoyed this tremendously, and so, I believe, have you. Thank you, Emily.'

More applause, a few cheers and John came up to lean on the piano and lay claim to her. 'That was very nice, my dear,' he said, then half turned to speak to others who wanted to congratulate her. 'She's my wife, you know. I've always encouraged her. Recognised her remarkable talent. Isn't that so, Emily?'

She rose and excused herself. Now the game was afoot, and she knew Bronwen was waiting for her. Just before she left the room, she heard Cheryl say, 'I believe we have some unfinished business, John.'

He was still preening himself, basking in reflected glory as he replied, 'That's true. I hope you're going to see sense and accept my proposition.'

'Shall we go somewhere quiet and discuss it? My partner will join us,' Cheryl said, and led him towards the rear of the house.

At first John expected Cheryl to take him to her office. He was prepared to magnanimously accept her capitulation, offer her the bounty of his advice and succeed in wresting the property from her. Instead, he found himself entering a world within the West Tower that surpassed his wildest dreams. He could not believe his luck. Not only had he been right about Cheryl's business concerns being shady, but he found himself in a room decorated in the height of decadent luxury. His prick quivered as he saw the bold and desirable women who were draped over couches, or grouped together by the velvet-hung walls.

'I knew it!' he exclaimed, rounding on Cheryl gleefully.

'The hotel's nothing but a front. You're running a brothel.'

'No, John. This isn't a brothel. It's a club,' she replied calmly, that bitch who had turned him down, now a beautiful, competent and confident person. He wanted to touch her nipples displayed under the silk top. No brassiere obviously, her breasts moving freely. No panties either, he suspected, the sleek line of her skirt clinging to her thighs.

She snapped her fingers and John was surrounded. Hands touched him, fingers probed everywhere. Now he could see that the women were tall, leather clad – black leather with studs – some masked, all smiling. These were nothing like the compliant Peggy. Their smiles were cold, filled with malice and lust. He did not know whether to feel fear or desire. Their perfume filled his nostrils, mingled with incense that made his head spin.

He tried to laugh it off. Jesus Christ! It was the man who made the first move, wasn't it? 'Come on, girls,' he spluttered, half joking, half serious. 'Take it easy. I know you find me irresistible, but steady on. Line up or something.'

His eyes met Cheryl's, and she was smiling too, then female bodies overwhelmed him. Hands stripped off his dinner jacket, his tie and shirt. His vest was removed. Sharp talons, or fingertips in leather gloves, tormented his nipples. His cock was on fire, but he could not get hold of his rapists. That was it. The thought struck him like a thunderbolt. He was being violated! He almost ejaculated with excitement.

They were not careful with his expensive trousers. The top button pinged and came off; the zip was yanked down. Those strong women lifted him and both trousers and boxer shorts were hauled off. Now he was naked and feeling foolish in his black silk socks and lace-up shoes. But the hands were everywhere – playing with his engorged cock – toying with his balls – harsh fingers poking into his arsehole. He hovered on the edge of orgasm, roused to an unbearable pitch, but given no satisfaction.

246

Mocking laughter filled his ears. Wiry arms held him tight, and he was gazing at Cheryl who stood over him, masturbating shamelessly. She coated her fingers with pussy juice and touched it to his lips. 'Are you convinced, John?' she asked. 'Is this a whorehouse or a club?'

'Whatever you say,' he groaned. 'Have mercy and let me come.'

Using a back entrance, Emily and Laura arrived in the dressing room of the West Tower. There Bronwen helped them out of their evening gowns. Emily could not wait to get into a black calfskin skirt, the side seams held together with lacing. Suspenders ran down from the bottom of her corset and were clipped to the tops of smoke-grey stockings, and her thigh boots had stacked heels that made her look even taller and thinner.

'Will he know it's me?' she asked nervously.

'Not at the start,' Laura replied. 'We'll choose the moment to introduce him to his nemesis.'

She smiled widely, already changed into a scarlet bra with open tips, and skin-tight satin shorts with an open crotch. Her denuded sex lips protruded, pink and inviting, her clit as lustrous as a pearl.

Bronwen wore a catsuit, a single zipper running from the throat, down between her legs and up the crack in her bottom. The heels of her court shoes made her calves bunch, lengthened her thighs and emphasised her hips. 'Now for the important part,' she said, and Emily glanced down at the large latex phallus in her hand. 'You remember what I told you? Can you manage it?'

'Oh, yes,' Emily answered eagerly.

Soon she was admiring herself in the mirror. She lifted the skirt and was met by the shocking and exciting sight of the life-like godemiche sticking out from her pubis. The harness fitted perfectly, adjusted by buckles, cupping her mound and keeping the false dick in place, ready for vigorous action. Emily switched it on and yelped as its bristly inner side rubbed against her clit, bringing on orgasmic sensations. She had watched Bronwen penetrating

Luke with it, and seen how it affected both of them. He had come within seconds, and Bronwen had continued to fuck his arse until she rode out her passion.

'Ready?' Bronwen asked.

Emily nodded, lowering her skirt, but the outline of the vibrator showed, and she was aware of it with every move she made. It got in the way as she walked, and she guessed that this was how a randy male must feel.

The tower rooms were busy. It was like an outrageous fancy-dress party, with the emphasis on exposed genitalia. Naked men were led around on leads by their mistresses; pony girls in harness with tails thrust into their fundaments were meekly accepting chastisement from masters flourishing riding crops. Emily was aroused by the smell of leather, and the sight of the posturing dancers on the small stage. They cavorted lewdly round poles, their bodies gleaming with sweat, while punters stuffed paper money into their G-strings. There was an overall and one-pointed concentration on sex.

Bronwen took her into the dungeon. She had been there once before when Cheryl let her into St Jude's secrets, but then it had been empty. Now there were spectators watching while others punished and pleasured their partners. There was the sound of tawse on bare flesh, the swish of canes and slap-slap of paddles and a few moans, but no real cries of anguish.

Then Emily saw John. Surprise rooted her to the spot. Stripped and on his knees, his head was bowed and his hands manacled behind his back. He was wearing a blindfold and his shoes and socks. Luke was on guard and Cheryl stood near by, lightly flexing a slender whip. She glanced across at Emily and brought the lash down on John's hindquarters.

'Ouch! Unchain me, damn you!' he bellowed.

'Calm down. My word, you have been a naughty boy, haven't you?' she drawled. 'Bullying people around. It's time you were made to suffer.'

His head jerked up. 'I thought we were going to talk business. I never dreamed . . . didn't expect . . .'

'I got you here under false pretences. Dear me, I think you're rather enjoying yourself,' she said, and tapped his erect cock with the tip of her whip. 'Like being tied up and dominated, do you? I wonder what the snobs at the sailing club would make of it?'

'You won't tell them ... you daren't...' John blustered.

'Daren't? To me? Don't tempt me.'

She nodded to Emily who stepped forward, flanked by Laura and Bronwen. For the first time ever she was not afraid of John. He looked puny, weak and lily-livered and she savoured the moment. Each in turn slashed at his naked rump and the whip Emily held felt like the flail of an Egyptian god meting out just punishment. John jerked and squirmed but was kept in place by Luke's firm hand. Despite his noisy protests, John's cock told a different story. It pulsed, red-capped, and a trickle of juice seeped from its eye.

Bronwen dribbled oil on to his blotched rump and massaged it in, then slipped a hand under his body and pinched his nipples. He cried out and his cock swelled larger. She palmed it, rubbed it, and he strained forward, moaning, 'Oh, yes. Do it some more.' She took her hand away.

Emily stood behind him, raised her skirt and scooped oil into her hand. She anointed the dildo then, after a moment's hesitation, worked her slippery fingers into John's anus. It felt odd to be doing this to her husband, a very personal act that she had never expected to perform. He grunted but did not try to withdraw, his sphincter relaxing. Emily positioned herself, guided the dildo to his nether hole and pushed.

'Bloody hell!' he shouted, but she felt him hunching his arse towards the invasive object, and wondered if he had ever had a penis in him, or perhaps secretly longed to be sodomised.

She switched on the vibrator, closed her eyes and went with it, aping a man's movements when he mounted a woman. Thrusting into John's rectum was incredibly

249

satisfying. She was in charge, and the buzzing bristles at the vibrator's base chafed her pussy and stimulated her clit. John groaned and heaved his rump higher, swinging his hips as she part withdrew then thrust in again. It was a harsh, violent encounter, and she used all her strength to bugger him, the intensity of the vibrations almost too much. But she couldn't stop, forgetting John, flung into a vortex that whirled her higher and ever closer to orgasm. She came with a cry, just as John spurted on to the stone floor.

She withdrew and went round to stand in front of him, alongside Laura and Cheryl. The blindfold and manacles were removed, and he looked up into their faces.

His eyes widened as he saw Emily, who was still wearing the godemiche. 'You! It was you fucking my arse?'

'Yes, and it's the very first time in all those long years of marriage that I'd ever come when I was with you,' she answered steadily. 'Things are going to change from now on. I shall do what I want, when I want – and you can like it or lump it. I'm not afraid of you any more and shall leave you when the girls are older. And you'll stop bullying Rupert!'

He goggled at her, rendered speechless. 'You'll make no further attempts to cheat us out of St Jude's,' Cheryl said. 'You've been seen here, taking part in our naughty games. Photographs have been taken and I've even got it on video. If it leaked out, it wouldn't bode well for a prospective mayor, would it?'

'That's blackmail,' he spluttered, but there was a gleam of respect in his eyes as he stared at Emily, and accorded grudging admiration to Cheryl and Laura. He understood ruthless tactics.

'You could call it that. I prefer to look on it as self-preservation. Don't even think of taking it out on Emily, or you'll be for it,' Cheryl warned. She fastened a collar round his neck and handed the leash to Bronwen. 'He's still arrogant and he needs further punishment. Take him to Mistress Discipline.'

Emily watched him being led away, naked and chained, and felt nothing but relief. He would never dare humiliate her again. She unfastened the dildo and laid it aside, then linked her arm with Laura's and went back to watch the pole-dancers.

Cheryl made her way to the buffet table, fortifying herself with duck paté and a glass of white wine. She had not been all that surprised when John meekly accepted his role as a submissive. Men of his ilk often did, according to that oracle, Bronwen.

Now the rest of the evening was hers to do with as she liked and she stood by a pillar and eyed the talent, wondering if Karl might be there. She did not find him, but instead a tall figure appeared out of nowhere, covered from head to foot in a black cloak.

'I'm Death,' it said in a hollow, ghostly voice. 'The Grim Reaper come to collect you. Are you free from sin, Cheryl Barden?'

She squinted up into the blank darkness of the hood, a superstitious chill touching her spine. Then, 'Come off it, Felan,' she said, on a rising tide of anger. 'How did you get in?'

He threw back the cowl and his swarthy, handsome face materialised. 'Bronwen,' he replied. 'She's given me membership for free.'

'Why?' Can't I trust anyone around here? she stormed inwardly.

'I'm selling her one of my cottages. It's a snip; just needs a bit of cosmetic surgery and updating, that's all. She wants to bring her son down here sometimes and didn't think the atmosphere of the towers would be on.'

'Cottages? You're a property tycoon?'

'Hardly. I dabble a little. But I didn't go to all that trouble in order to stand here exchanging pleasantries. We've never been to bed together, not properly, not a night-long, pillow-talk-in-the-dark, fuck-every-half-an-hour, learn-to-know-each-other session from dusk till dawn. What d'you say?'

251

'I say, get off my case.'

He put out an arm and pulled her in close to his body under the folds of the cloak. 'You don't really mean that, Cheryl,' he whispered, and stuck his tongue in her ear, then lipped the lobe teasingly. 'If you do, then you're a stubborn little bitch who needs spanking again.'

'You're into this, aren't you? What goes on here is nothing new to you, is it?' she muttered, trying to free herself, though every bodily instinct was for staying there.

In fact, she wanted to move closer to that hard lump of cock pressing into her pathetically thin excuse for a dress. See-through silk chiffon cut like a nightie, no bra, and an apology for knickers. Even her shoes were insubstantial, though fashion statements, strappy, spool heeled, and not at all suitable for walking more than short distances.

'Does it matter? Suffice to say, I'm here. God, Cheryl, how much longer are you going to keep this up?'

'I don't know,' she answered obstinately. 'Maybe for ever.'

His attitude changed. He shook her roughly, fingers digging into her upper arms, growling, 'Stop it. I'm going to have you tonight, and in my bed, too.'

'Whoops! Get you!' she mocked. 'What a beast! I'm so scared!'

He swore at her and swung her over his shoulder and carried her at a run up the stairs, along the corridor and through a door that connected with the courtyard. He bundled her into his truck.

'I'm cold,' she complained.

He took off the cloak and flung it round her, then occupied the driver's seat and started the engine. She sneaked a glance at him. In the overhead spots, he looked darker, bigger, more menacing than ever, a cream wool Aran sweater broadening his shoulders, his lean hips tightly encased in blue jeans. He kept his eye on the winding road leading from St Jude's to the main drag, and his profile fascinated her, with the hawk nose and determined jaw. She knew a moment's fear.

'Where are you taking me?' she demanded, wondering if she could wrench open the door and jump out, but the vehicle was gaining speed.

'To my place,' he answered evenly.

'And where's that?' She wished she had grabbed up her bag and her mobile, but had absolutely nothing to aid her, should things go pear-shaped.

'You'll see,' was his noncommittal reply.

'Damn you, Felan. Why d'you always have to be so bloody difficult?' she exclaimed.

'Me? I'm the most reasonable person alive,' he said, with an air of injured innocence.

'Stuff off.' She slumped back in her seat and added, 'Have you any cigarettes?'

He trawled a packet from the dash and lit two, then handed her one. They drove in silence and the signposts indicated that they were approaching the coast. The way dipped, became narrower, winding lanes with sharp corners and stunted trees bent almost horizontal by winds gusting from the ocean. She could smell it now, that salty, distinctive odour of sea-wrack and bladder-wort, wet sand and limestone cliffs. They turned a bend and passed through a tiny hamlet, then drove a little further to an isolated spot where a single dwelling stood. He wheeled into the parking area, stopped the truck and helped her out. She could hear the sea breaking over the shingle on the beach not far away. They walked up a path bordered with cockleshells and he opened the low-framed front door, ducking his tall head and entering after she had gone through.

She found herself in a living room, dark beamed and with whitewashed walls covered in paintings, sketches, masks, ancient weapons and brassware. 'You're a collector?' she asked.

'I do house-clearances,' he admitted. 'A bit of a magpie, me. Can't resist memorabilia.' He kneeled on the rag-rug in front of the large, stone-surrounded hearth, took away

253

the guard, and put further logs on the already glowing fire. Wood smoke scented the air.

'And this is one of your cottages?' She took off the cloak and laid it over a chair. Her skin came out in goose bumps. The room was warm, but her dress was exceedingly thin.

Why am I here? she thought, but knew that just for tonight, she wanted to be nowhere else.

'That's right. I shall stay as long as global warming and coastal erosion doesn't proceed at too rapid a rate. Then I'll have to seek higher ground.'

'It's beautiful,' she said, admiring the deep settee and antique pieces black with age.

'A fisherman lived here once, with his wife and twenty children. In the summer, the older ones were sent out on to the common to sleep. No room, you see.'

They were talking, yet it meant nothing. Suddenly they stopped. He looked at her, then lurched to his feet and fell with her into the depths of the sagging, comfortable couch. His arm was round her shoulders, and his lips found hers. There was no escaping it, or her own rampant feelings. As his tongue pillaged her mouth, extracting a response from hers, so he pushed up her skirt and found the scrap of silk that had cost so much and covered so little. She let him do it, even encouraged him by parting her legs and heaving up her buttocks so that the briefs could be removed and tossed to one side.

His hand was between her folds, spreading her open, locating her clit. She rolled up his sweater, her fingers finding smooth, hard flesh, and he helped her to pull it off. The firelight glowed, making him as red as a demon, and she traced the dark hair that circled his pecs and wanted to follow it down past his navel to where it disappeared into the waistband of his jeans. He lowered his head and covered her neck with sharp, nibbling kisses, and she wanted more . . . unbuttoning his trousers and releasing his cock, dark-skinned and firm and ready.

They undressed by the fire and lay on the hearthrug. He heaved cushions off the couch and placed them under

254

her head. The fire scorched her on one side and his body heated her on the other. His lips brushed her nipples and then sucked them strongly. His beard was soft, scarcely a beard at all, adding to the delicious sensations. She wanted him to go lower, longed to have him mouth her clit, and he stroked her lightly, travelling the length of her body, and his tongue followed suit. He licked her folds and lapped at her entrance, then sucked her clit, teasing it, making her draw in sharp breaths.

'Go on! Please, go on!' she whimpered, and tried to hold his head against her.

He stopped what he was doing, sat up and held her arms over her head, then secured them with his belt. 'Be quiet,' he commanded. 'I shall decide how and when it will be done.'

He had changed, harsh-voiced and grim-faced. She felt fear again, and that shaking sense of extreme arousal. He had bound her before, had paddled her mercilessly, made her submit entirely, and it had been the most satisfying sex she had ever experienced.

Now he dragged her to her feet and said, 'Put on your shoes.' She fumbled for them and then Felan took her to the far side of the settee, stretched out her bound hands and pushed against the small of her back, forcing her to bend over it.

Her face was warmed by the fire, her breasts were hot too, pressed against the buttoned, chintzy material. It was an old couch, but sturdy, and her high heels lifted her bottom to just the right height for him. His cock could penetrate her easily, quim or anus, each orifice presented for his enjoyment. You're a slut, she thought, and her pussy quivered.

He was quiet, and she waited in tingling dread and lubricious lust. When she felt the touch, she wasn't quite sure that it was anything at all, till he repeated it. What was it? A switch? A branch? A thin cane? He tickled her with it, all down her spine and into her crack, nudging her feet apart and running it along the pursed lips of her pussy. He didn't spare her, pressing it into her folds, drawing it along her throbbing clit. Cheryl couldn't help wriggling her hips, letting him know that she wanted more.

He tapped her slit lightly, then harder, and she yelped. He started to whack the whippy cane against her bucking rear, and she couldn't restrain the tears. They ran down her cheeks and dripped off her chin. He stopped and leaned over to undo her hands. 'Stay like that,' he ordered, and she looked round to see his cock surging with arousal. 'I think you enjoy being beaten as much as I like doing it.'

'I'm not your slave,' she whispered.

'Who can say which is which? When I enslave you, then don't you control me? By your very submission, you make me want to beat you. Your tears, your sighs, your pain, drive me on.'

He was behind her, parting her buttocks, inserting his cock-head in her. Not an arse-fuck, but the real thing, and she pushed down on it, loving that feeling of being thoroughly filled. His chest hair tickled her back and his solid thighs worked his hips, in and out, till she thought he wouldn't be able to stop, worried because they weren't protected. She was surprised when he did, withdrawing, his tool coated with her juices.

She turned and put her arms round his neck, breasts chafing his chest, her eager loins grinding into his cock, her stinging bottom contacting the couch. He stared down into her eyes, a look of steel mixed with the blue. She wanted him so much that she nearly begged for it. Only pride kept her quiet.

He took her upstairs to his bed, lit by candlelight, the diamond-paned windows at floor level, the floors sloping, the ceiling too low for Felan to stand upright. He took condoms from the nightstand and swept the puffy duvet over them with his arm, and she cuddled up to him inside its warm, downy comfort. He soothed her sore backside until she didn't feel pain any more, then parted her legs and brought her to orgasm in a magical way, tender, loving, sensitive to her needs. When she had come, he kneeled between her thighs and her cunt opened, welcoming the stab of his cock in her depths. His lips and hands roved over her face and hair, and she clenched round his erection and heard him groan and chase the end and jerk in release.

The candle flame was as steady as eternal love, rising straight as if on a wire. She lay lazily in Felan's arms, and he kissed her ear and moved his mouth around her neck and suckled at her breast. They didn't soul-search or speak of intimate things or discuss the future or even suggest that they had one: just for now they could enjoy each other's bodies.

'Will you come to my mother's wedding?' she said at last, when he came back from downstairs, bringing a tray of tea. 'It's to be held at the standing stones.'

'Maybe. I don't know her, do I? D'you want a scone? I made them. I told you I could cook. You must let me make you dinner some time.'

'Thank you, but surely everyone around here knows my mother and Fell Tor.'

'Ah, yes . . . the hippy colony.' He was busy spreading strawberry jam and clotted cream on a fruit scone. He handed it to her.

'It isn't,' she said defensively, licking jam from her fingers and suddenly realising how much she loved Joanna.

'No matter. Yes, I'll come.'

This pleased her. She fancied him as her escort. 'And Laura and Simon are going on holiday to Argentina after Christmas,' she went on, sitting up, duvet tucked round her, sipping tea from a Desperate Dan mug. 'It wouldn't surprise me if they came back married.'

'What about you, Mrs Barden?' he asked, and gave her a penetrating stare. 'Don't you feel the need of a permanent man about the place? All this talk of weddings is making me want to get out my morning suit, or brides-maid dress or whatever.'

'Not for me, really. I value my independence. Once

bitten, twice shy, and all that,' she answered, wondering if her nose was about to grow as long as Pinocchio's.

'No?' he said, smiling at her, disbelief in his eyes. 'Are you sure you're not clinging to something you've grown out of?'

'I'll let you know,' she said, put down her mug and shifted over, coiling her arms round him. 'Meanwhile, what about another session? Top or bottom? What d'you fancy?'

LOOK OUT FOR THE ALL-NEW BLACK LACE BOOKS – AVAILABLE NOW!

All books priced £7.99 in the UK. Please note publication dates apply to the UK only. For other territories please contact your retailer.

Also to be published in October 2009

THE THINGS THAT MAKE ME GIVE IN
Charlotte Stein
ISBN 978 0352 34542 4

Girls who go after what they want no matter what the cost, boys who like to flash their dark sides, voyeurism for beginners and cheating lovers . . . Charlotte Stein takes you on a journey through all the facets of female desire in this contemporary collection of explicit and ever intriguing short stories. Be seduced by obsessions that go one step too far and dark desires that remove all inhibitions. Each story takes you on a journey into all the things that make a girl give in.

THE GALLERY
Fredrica Alleyn
ISBN 978 0352 34533 2

Police office Cressida Farleigh is called in to investigate a mysterious art fraud at a gallery specializing in modern erotic works. The gallery's owner is under suspicion, but is also charming and powerfully attractive man who throws the young woman's powers of detection into confusion. Her long time detective boyfriend is soon getting jealous, but Cressida is also in the process of seducing a young artist of erotic images. As she finds herself drawn into a mesh of power games and personal discovery, the crimes continue and her chances of cracking the case become ever more complex.

To be published in November 2009

THE AFFAIR
Various
ISBN 978 0352 34517 2

Indulgent and sensual, outrageous and taboo, but always highly erotic, this new collection of Black Lace stories takes the illicit and daring rendezvous with a lover (or lovers) as its theme. Popular Black Lace authors and new voices contribute a broad and thrilling range of women's sexual fantasy.

FIRE AND ICE
Laura Hamilton
ISBN 978 0352 34534 9

At work Nina is known as the Ice Queen, as her frosty demeanour makes her colleagues think she's equally cold in bed. But what they don't know is that she spends her free time acting out sleazy scenarios with her boyfriend, Andrew, in which she's a prostitute and he's a punter. But when Andrew starts inviting his less-than-respectable friends to join in their games, things begin to get strange and Nina finds herself being drawn deeper into London's seedy underworld, where everything is for sale and nothing is what it seems.

SHADOWPLAY
Portia Da Costa
ISBN 978 0352 34535 6

Photographer Christabel is drawn to psychic phenomena and dark liaisons. When she is persuaded by her husband to take a holiday at a mysterious mansion house in the country, she foresees only long days of pastoral boredom. But Nicholas, her deviously sensual husband, has a hand in the unexpected events that begin to unravel. She is soon drawn into a web of transgressive eroticism with Nicholas's young male PA. Within this unusual and kinky threesome, Christabel learns some lessons the jaded city could never teach her.

Black Lace Booklist

Information is correct at time of printing. To avoid disappointment, check availability before ordering. Go to www.blacklace.com.
All books are priced £7.99 unless another price is given.

BLACK LACE BOOKS WITH A CONTEMPORARY SETTING

❏ ALL THE TRIMMINGS Tesni Morgan	ISBN 978 0 352 34532 5	
❏ AMANDA'S YOUNG MEN Madeline Moore	ISBN 978 0 352 34191 4	
❏ THE ANGELS'S SHARE Maya Hess	ISBN 978 0 352 34043 6	
❏ THE APPRENTICE Carrie Williams	ISBN 978 0 352 34514 1	
❏ ASKING FOR TROUBLE Kristina Lloyd	ISBN 978 0 352 33362 9	
❏ BLACK ORCHID Roxanne Carr	ISBN 978 0 352 34188 4	
❏ THE BLUE GUIDE Carrie Williams	ISBN 978 0 352 34132 7	
❏ THE BOSS Monica Belle	ISBN 978 0 352 34088 7	
❏ BOUND IN BLUE Monica Belle	ISBN 978 0 352 34012 2	
❏ CAMPAIGN HEAT Gabrielle Marcola	ISBN 978 0 352 33941 6	
❏ CAPTIVE FLESH Cleo Cordell	ISBN 978 0 352 34529 5	
❏ CASSANDRA'S CONFLICT Fredrica Alleyn	ISBN 978 0 352 34186 0	
❏ CASSANDRA'S CHATEAU Fredrica Alleyn	ISBN 978 0 352 34523 3	
❏ CAT SCRATCH FEVER Sophie Mouette	ISBN 978 0 352 34021 4	
❏ CHILLI HEAT Carrie Williams	ISBN 978 0 352 34178 5	
❏ THE CHOICE Monica Belle	ISBN 978 0 352 34512 7	
❏ CIRCUS EXCITE Nikki Magennis	ISBN 978 0 352 34033 7	
❏ CLUB CRÈME Primula Bond	ISBN 978 0 352 33907 2	£6.99
❏ CONTINUUM Portia Da Costa	ISBN 978 0 352 33120 5	
❏ COOKING UP A STORM Emma Holly	ISBN 978 0 352 34114 3	
❏ DANGEROUS CONSEQUENCES Pamela Rochford	ISBN 978 0 352 33185 4	
❏ DARK DESIGNS Madelynne Ellis	ISBN 978 0 352 34075 7	
❏ DARK OBSESSIONS Fredrica Alleyn	ISBN 978 0 352 34524 0	
❏ THE DEVIL AND THE DEEP BLUE SEA Cheryl Mildenhall	ISBN 978 0 352 34200 3	
❏ DOCTOR'S ORDERS Deanna Ashford	ISBN 978 0 352 34525 7	
❏ EDEN'S FLESH Robyn Russell	ISBN 978 0 352 32923 3	
❏ EQUAL OPPORTUNITIES Mathilde Madden	ISBN 978 0 352 34070 2	
❏ FIRE AND ICE Laura Hamilton	ISBN 978 0 352 34534 9	

BLACK LACE BOOKS WITH AN HISTORICAL
SETTING

BLACK LACE BOOKS WITH A PARANORMAL THEME

BLACK LACE ANTHOLOGIES

❏ WICKED WORDS 8 Various	ISBN 978 0 352 33787 0	£6.99
❏ WICKED WORDS 9 Various	ISBN 978 0 352 33860 0	
❏ WICKED WORDS 10 Various	ISBN 978 0 352 33893 8	
❏ THE BEST OF BLACK LACE 2 Various	ISBN 978 0 352 33718 4	
❏ WICKED WORDS: SEX IN THE OFFICE Various	ISBN 978 0 352 33944 7	
❏ WICKED WORDS: SEX AT THE SPORTS CLUB Various	ISBN 978 0 352 33991 1	
❏ WICKED WORDS: SEX ON HOLIDAY Various	ISBN 978 0 352 33961 4	
❏ WICKED WORDS: SEX IN UNIFORM Various	ISBN 978 0 352 34002 3	
❏ WICKED WORDS: SEX IN THE KITCHEN Various	ISBN 978 0 352 34018 4	
❏ WICKED WORDS: SEX ON THE MOVE Various	ISBN 978 0 352 34034 4	
❏ WICKED WORDS: SEX AND MUSIC Various	ISBN 978 0 352 34061 0	
❏ WICKED WORDS: SEX AND SHOPPING Various	ISBN 978 0 352 34076 4	
❏ SEX IN PUBLIC Various	ISBN 978 0 352 34089 4	
❏ SEX WITH STRANGERS Various	ISBN 978 0 352 34105 1	
❏ LOVE ON THE DARK SIDE Various	ISBN 978 0 352 34132 7	
❏ LUST BITES Various	ISBN 978 0 352 34153 2	
❏ MAGIC AND DESIRE Various	ISBN 978 0 352 34183 9	
❏ POSSESSION Various	ISBN 978 0 352 34164 8	
❏ ENCHANTED Various	ISBN 978 0 352 34195 2	

BLACK LACE NON-FICTION

❏ THE BLACK LACE BOOK OF WOMEN'S SEXUAL FANTASIES	ISBN 978 0 352 33793 1	£6.99
Edited by Kerri Sharp		
❏ THE NEW BLACK LACE BOOK OF WOMEN'S SEXUAL		
FANTASIES	ISBN 978 0 352 34172 3	
Edited by Mitzi Szereto		

To find out the latest information about Black Lace titles, check out the website: www.blacklace.co.uk or send for a booklist with complete synopses by writing to:

Black Lace Booklist, Virgin Books Ltd
Random House
20 Vauxhall Bridge Road
London SW1V 2SA

Please include an SAE of decent size. Please note only British stamps are valid.

Our privacy policy
We will not disclose information you supply us to any other parties. We will not disclose any information which identifies you personally to any person without your express consent.

From time to time we may send out information about Black Lace books and special offers. Please tick here if you do not wish to receive Black Lace information. ❏

Please send me the books I have ticked above.

Name ....

Address ....

....

....

....

Post Code ....

Send to: Virgin Books Cash Sales, Black Lace,
Random House, 20 Vauxhall Bridge Road, London SW1V 2SA.

US customers: for prices and details of how to order
books for delivery by mail, call 888-330-8477.

Please enclose a cheque or postal order, made payable
to Virgin Books Ltd, to the value of the books you have
ordered plus postage and packing costs as follows:

UK and BFPO – £1.00 for the first book, 50p for each
subsequent book.

Overseas (including Republic of Ireland) – £2.00 for
the first book, £1.00 for each subsequent book.

If you would prefer to pay by VISA, ACCESS/MASTERCARD,
DINERS CLUB, AMEX or MAESTRO, please write your card
number and expiry date here: ....

....

Signature ....

Please allow up to 28 days for delivery.